A scuffle of running footsteps sounded some ways behind her, back at the corner where the lane met the Rue Verte.

"There she is!" came a boyish, crowing shout.

Oh, no! Not again!

She'd hoped the first time—near on a sevenday ago—would be the *only* time. And now! To be caught here like this, by those horrible, gloating boys.

Dropping her honeysuckle in the dust, she glanced over her shoulder, took a better grip on her lesson books, and strode away from the ragged bunch pelting after her.

There was no use running. She'd tried that last time, and they'd kept up with her effortlessly, leaving her only after they'd dumped her in the dirt with a stick jabbed between her flying ankles, laughter jeering on their lips. But Lealle was *shunned*—oh, Mamere wouldn't like that word, even if only in her thoughts—if she would just stand and take it.

The fastest of the boys dashed past her and then spun, dancing backward while taunting her. His greenish cap was tattered, his faded black trousers bore patched knees, and his scruffy gray jacket swung open on a stained cream shirt, one button missing, no waistcoat.

"Thinks she's too good for us, hoity-toity!" he yelled. "But she ain't so good she don't know honey when she tastes it!" His laughter held an ugly tone, echoed by the rest of the boys, now surging up around her.

Also by J.M. Ney-Grimm

NORTH-LANDS STORIES
Troll-magic

Perilous Chance

The Troll's Belt

Hunting Wild

LODESTONE TALES
Skies of Navarys

The Tally Master

Resonant Bronze

Rainbow's Lodestone

Star-drake

KAUNIS CLAN SAGA
Sarvet's Wanderyar

Crossing the Naiad

Livli's Gift

Winter Glory

MYTHIC TALES
Blood Silver

Caught in Amber

Devouring Light

Fate's Door

Serpent's Foe

The Hunt of the Unicorn

A TALISMAN ARCANE

THE PRINCE'S DJINN

BOOK ONE

by J.M. Ney-Grimm

Wild
Unicorn

ISBN-13: 978-1796928167
ISBN-10: 179692816X

Interior design by JMNG
Cover design by Deranged Doctor Design

Map on page 269 by JMNG

For Amy,
patron of the artist

A Note About Days

A Talisman Arcane takes place in Pavelle, a small country on the northern coast of the great continent occupied by the Giralliyan Empire. Pavelle's calendar has 7-day weeks (like ours), but the days have different names.

Because the characters in the story refer fairly often to the days of the week, I provide a key here.

Saidy (Sunday) *The Sabbath*
Lundy (Monday) *"Luna's Day"*
Maitredy (Tuesday) *"Master's Day"*
Ju-errant (Wednesday) *"Wanderer's Day"*
Fordaine (Thursday) *"Strong Day"*
Reindy (Friday) *"Queen's Day"*
Beldaine (Saturday) *"Gift Day"*

Table of Contents

The Seventh Day

LUNDY—LUNA'S DAY

Last Secrets

The First Day

Encounters

Chapter One

LEALLE SWUNG into the dirt lane running between the back gardens of the houses on Rue Verte with something like relief.

Not that the streets of Claireau weren't pretty enough, with their neat cobbles and slate-roofed brick houses, window boxes brimming with bright blooms. But, this lane . . . oh, this narrow lane of packed earth, dry in the summer warmth, was a *bower*.

Tall hollyhocks swayed above the high brick wall at her right shoulder, the pink fans of their flowers nodding in the light breeze. She loved the hollyhocks and wished Mamere would consent when the gardener suggested them for the border of the fountain court. But Mamere said they were vulgar, meant for cottages, not mansions.

Lealle sighed.

No matter. She was here now, the hollyhocks were beautiful, and the garden on her left was even better than the one on her right, because its white picket fence with the peeling paint was low enough to reveal the whole of the lovely confusion to her eyes. Fountaining rose bushes filled the corners, daisies and primroses and poppies dotted the rest, while a tangle of sweet peas threaded any gaps. It was glorious!

But best of all was the honeysuckle banked over most of the fence.

Lealle closed her eyes and snuffed the scent in, reveling in its sweetness. Then, allowing her eyes to open again, she shifted her books to her left arm and moved to pull one of the small creamy blooms off the vine. Plucking the tiny green knob from the narrow end, she raised the floret to her lips. A clear droplet of nectar formed and fell onto her waiting tongue. Sweet! It was piercingly sweet!

And how Mamere would hate to see her daughter sticking her tongue out and then placing the honeysuckle to her lips for the rest of the nectar.

"Ladies restrain themselves," Mamere would say.

And Lealle did restrain herself. Most of the time.

But no one would ever see her here, between these back gardens. Did she have to behave like a lady all the time? Even when no one else was present? Did Mamere never taste honeysuckle—not that there was any in the mansion garden—or . . . or smell the heavy scent of the roses and the light one of mint? Ever? Even when she was private?

But Lealle knew it wasn't that. It was Lealle sticking out her tongue and the enthusiasm of her enjoyment. A lady could enjoy things. Mamere enjoyed things. But she did it decorously.

Lealle sighed again, and defiantly plucked another honeysuckle.

At least her sticking-out tongue meant that the drop of nectar was unlikely to stray and spot the lace fichu that covered her shoulders and crossed in front to tuck into the blue sash of her blue frock. Mamere couldn't see her daughter here and now, but she'd notice any blemish to Lealle's garb fast enough once Lealle arrived home.

The sweetness of the nectar hit her tongue and spread.

A scuffle of running footsteps sounded some ways behind her, back at the corner where the lane met the Rue Verte.

"There she is!" came a boyish, crowing shout.

Oh, no! Not again!

She'd hoped the first time—near on a sevenday ago—would be the *only* time. And now! To be caught here like this, by those horrible, gloating boys.

Dropping her honeysuckle in the dust, she glanced over her shoulder, took a better grip on her lesson books, and strode away from the ragged bunch pelting after her.

There was no use running. She'd tried that last time, and they'd kept up with her effortlessly, leaving her only after they'd dumped her in the dirt with a stick jabbed between her flying ankles, laughter jeering on their lips. But Lealle was *shunned*—oh, Mamere wouldn't like that word, even if only in her thoughts—if she would just stand and take it.

The fastest of the boys dashed past her and then spun, dancing backward while taunting her. His greenish cap was tattered, his faded black trousers bore patched knees, and his scruffy gray jacket swung open on a stained cream shirt, one button missing, no waistcoat.

"Thinks she's too good for us, hoity-toity!" he yelled. "But she ain't so good she don't know honey when she tastes it!" His laughter held an ugly tone, echoed by the rest of the boys, now surging up around her.

She kept walking, but said nothing, glaring scornfully at her tormenters. She'd tried answering back last time, too, and it had worked no better than running had.

"Cat got yer tongue?" jeered a red-haired boy at her shoulder. "Or did that honey glue it down?" He sniggered, delighted with his clumsy wit.

"Nah!" yelled a blond boy at her other side. "Thinks her dad'll keep her safe, like all th' other Empire scum, but he's not *here*! Hah!" And he shoved her, hard.

Lealle stumbled into the red-haired boy, one foot catching on her other ankle. Red-hair shoved her back the other way, and now she was in trouble.

Papere was indeed not here. She was all alone, the gardens around her empty, Rue Verte too far behind her, and Rue Étroit much, much farther up ahead.

The ragged-capped boy ahead of her closed in.

"Daddy's girl, daddy's girl," he chanted. "That'll teach him to dock me own dad, the boot!"

Then he shoved her, too, backward into the crowd behind her.

Now she had to run, no matter how badly that had ended before. If she could. If she could get around Ragged-cap in front of her.

Lealle took a tighter grip on her books as rough hands from behind gripped her arms. She put her head down as those same rough hands propelled her forward. She ducked when Ragged-cap reached for her, slammed the heel of her half-boot down on the worn leather covering his toes, and wriggled under his arm, sprinting.

She'd taken them by surprise.

There were shouts behind her—"Clumsy oaf!" "Ow!" "Gerroff!"— before they sorted themselves out enough to give chase. She didn't have much of a lead. Their pounding steps were closing in. Someone's fingers gripped the ribbon holding her hair in a ponytail, jerked, and her hair fell loose, one curling chestnut tendril falling forward across her cheek.

She scanned her surroundings desperately, her feet racing as fast as she could make them.

The picket-fenced garden had given way to one walled by stone. Could she vault it?

Maybe, but the boys would simply vault after her.

The tall brick wall on her right continued all the way to Rue Étroit, so far ahead, but a peeling white-painted door interrupted it midway. Surely locked.

The hand that had taken her hair ribbon plucked at her lace fichu. Another got close enough to push.

Lealle kept her feet this time, using the momentum to draw ahead, just a bit. And then a bit more. Just enough that . . . when that white-painted door was *there*, she grabbed its knob, twisted, and—

—fell through.

∞

Ohtavie clutched the lump that was the pendant beneath her blouse and peered through the lace of the curtain, squinting to make out the afternoon scene beyond it. The pattern of the lace was very fine, very sheer.

She should have been able to see through it.

She *would* have been able to see through it, if it hadn't collected so much dust.

Her nose itched with the scent of it, dry and irritating. Even her eyes felt itchy. She'd not entered this small front parlor for over a year. Or was it two?

The curtains were not the only appointments to suffer from her neglect. Dust clogged . . . everything.

She should have at least thrown holland covers over the furniture, as the servants had done in the larger rooms when they were abandoned. She might even have taken the hangings down and rolled them in muslin. That wouldn't have been beyond her abilities the way stowing the carpeting must have been. She remembered the rug in the grand parlor had taken six manservants to wrestle it from under the furnishings, roll it, and then shove the massive log against the wall.

She should have allowed the servants to take care of . . . much more than she had, before she dismissed them. But she'd thought she would continue to inhabit more of the mansion than she had.

It was her home, after all.

She pressed a forefinger under her nose, stifling a sneeze. The knuckle was slightly swollen, her finger slightly crooked. She would not think about the changing shape of her nose, elongated and fiercely upcurving. It had once been dainty and short, with only a slight retroussé curve that her mother had insisted was charming. Now . . .

Ohtavie shuddered and hesitated there at the window—a *front* window—fighting terror.

If she peeked through the gap between the curtain and the molding, she should be able to see out, and no one would be able to see *her* in return.

But . . . looking out the front was unwise.

She should confine herself to the back windows. It was safer. She could be *sure* no one saw her. It was important that no one saw her.

Most of the townspeople assumed she was dead. It was better that way.

No. She would not look out this front window. Not today.

Moving slowly, she retraced her steps through the parlor and into a dim hallway beyond. The wide floorboards of the hall were dull and splintered, the white plaster of the walls cracking, but Ohtavie paid these signs of deterioration no heed.

Her shoulders, slightly stooped as they were, held no discomfort in them today. Which was lovely. And her knees ached only a very little bit. But with each step, pain stabbed the ball of her right foot. She suspected the hollow worn in the sole of her laced black servant's shoe made it worse.

She wondered if she should try a pair of her mother's shoes again. The fragile kid of the ball slippers had long since crumbled to unwearability, but surely a pair or two of the jean half-boots might survive. She should check her mother's wardrobes again.

She'd abandoned her mother's shoes when she ceased to wear her mother's dresses.

The pretty gauzes of the old evening gowns and the satins of the ball gowns looked absurd on an old woman. Not that she was so old, but she might as well have been. Even the muslins for day wear, with their high waists and low necklines, were nothing she cared to wrap herself in.

One of the dismissed parlor maids had been about her size, of medium height and a slight build, and the girl's old clothing had fit. So Ohtavie had adopted it for her own use: long, dark blue skirt; long-sleeved, white blouse; snug, light blue bodice with elbow-length sleeves; and a white apron.

She'd kept her own undergarments though. The fine lawn of her own pantalettes, her petticoat, and her chemise was so much softer against her skin than the coarse linen of the maid's.

But the maid's shoes might be why her foot was hurting more.

The dim passageway to the back corner of the mansion seemed

very long. How many more steps must she endure until she reached the refuge of the old housekeeper's rooms?

Oh! She'd reached them.

She put her hand on the tarnished knob of the closed door, then pulled it back.

She hadn't mustered the courage to look out the window of the front parlor, but . . . she refused to give in to her fears completely. She wouldn't crawl back into her shell in the housekeeper's sitting room.

She *would* look out. She would go to the morning room at the back of the house and look out onto the lilacs in the back garden. She was determined.

∞

Lealle slammed the garden door behind her.

She didn't have time for surprise, and yet she was surprised.

The high brick wall around this garden had spoken of wealth and ease and careful tending, but the space within it gave witness only to neglect. Knee-high grasses sprouted from the gravel walk. Rampant rose bushes narrowed that walk. And strangling morning glory vines twisted everywhere.

Lealle caught her balance and swung left along the path just inside of the wall, ignoring the tumbled disorder, ignoring the heavy scent of the rose blooms, intent only on getting away from the boys who would surely burst through the door behind her in mere moments.

Thorns from the overgrown bushes scratched her right elbow as she ran.

A tendril of morning glory ensnared her left ankle, but she tore loose, still running.

She dashed through an arch cut in a tall yew hedge, and stumbled down some shallow steps onto a flagged terrace around a dry rectangular fountain. Lichens besmirched the statue of a cherub at its center.

Behind her came the boys' voices, but not their pounding footsteps. Not yet.

"The witch might get us," whined one bully. "Let's not."

"Nah, she's dead," came a more assured voice. "C'mon! Hoity-toity'll get away!"

"Let the witch get *her*! Not us," insisted yet another.

Idiots, thought Lealle, as she raced for the steps and the yew arch on the other side of the fountain court. Witches—*troll*-witches—were a thing of the past, now that troll-disease could be treated. But the boys' ignorant hesitation had given her a chance. If she could find a good hiding place before they came in sight of her again—and this untidiness of reaching fronds and foliage must be rife with hiding places—she could stay hidden until the boys grew bored and left.

The yew arch led into an oval of tall grass with a sundial. No hiding places here.

Lealle dashed across the grassy oval and between a pair of huge lilacs on the far side, emerging onto what must once have been a lawn adjacent to the terrace at the back of the grandly columned house. *Still no hiding places!*

Except . . . except . . . what if she ran right up onto that broad, broad terrace and crouched behind the square marble base of one of the round white marble columns?

She was running before she finished the thought, and crouching even as she heard the rush and crunch of gravel heralding the boys' approach.

Was she fully hidden? Would they find her? Would they dare come right up to the house? She held her breath.

∞

Hanging onto her determination, jaw tight, Ohtavie slipped out from a servant passage into one of the nicer spaces of the mansion—one for family.

A flood of sunlight through its three double doors—glass-paned from threshold to lintel—shone on the white marble of the floor, warming the graceful loggia and its arched marble alcoves, warming *Ohtavie*.

She paused, tipping her face up and closing her eyes, letting the sun's embrace hold her. It had been a long time since any *person* had embraced her.

Ignoring all the doors onto the outside terrace, she angled toward her right.

There, double doors to the morning room stood open. If they'd been closed, if their handles had required her grip, if she'd had to *choose* to open them—or to not open them—she might have quailed. She might have stopped and not entered.

I can do this, she admonished herself.

Her hand wandered again to the bump that her pendant—worn next to her skin—made beneath her blouse. Did she hear something? Something outside the house? Voices, maybe?

She stood listening.

No. No, it was nothing. Or nothing nearby enough to concern her. When had she grown so fearful?

Except it wasn't really fear, or not just fear. Her life had grown smaller, and smaller, and smaller still, over the years. It had grown smaller so steadily that contraction felt familiar, felt right, felt inevitable. Moving to enlarge her ambit felt impossible, wrong almost. And even moving merely to preserve her scope—as she was now—felt questionable.

How small would she become, if she allowed her contraction to progress unchecked? *Could* it be checked?

Ohtavie shivered there in the sunlight, despite its warmth . . . and didn't step into the morning room.

She couldn't do it.

Her fingers pinched harder on the pendant—her talisman—beneath her blouse.

She wanted to retreat. She wanted *badly* to retreat. The dim corridor back to the housekeeper's sitting room—now her own—*called* her.

She could spin and run—well, no, she couldn't. The pain in the ball of her right foot stabbed her, and the ache in her knees strengthened. But she could turn and walk.

How she longed to sit down, to have someone fix a hot water bottle for her knees and a pan of ice water for her foot. She longed to hear a kind word spoken to her. To know that everything was all right. She longed to feel safe. And it felt like her sitting room would offer all that.

But . . . she knew it wouldn't. Couldn't. Not truly.

She might enter it, walk across the bare floor boards, and sit in one of the wing chairs. But she could not escape knowing that nothing had been right for a very long time. She would know that she was not safe and could not be. Her sitting room could offer nothing at all that any other room in the mansion might not offer. Except, well, it *was* cleaner.

One lonely woman might keep two rooms fresh, where an entire mansion was impossible.

Ohtavie swallowed.

She'd failed to look out the window in the front parlor. But now, here, bathed in the loggia's sunlight and envisioning retreat—imagining confinement in the two small rooms she'd made hers—she refused to fail again.

She took one step forward, and another. Her shoe soles against the loggia's marble floor tapped softly.

The house behind her lay very quiet in its emptiness. But outside, beyond the doors onto the terrace . . . what was that she heard? Birds? It wasn't the fluting calls of the usual songbirds. But it did sound vaguely birdlike. Gulls? They didn't often fly so far inland, but it could be gulls.

Ohtavie wanted to pause to figure out what she was hearing. But if she paused, she would fail. No more stopping, no more hesitating, no more waiting, no more doubting. Each step would be followed by another, until she achieved her goal.

The gull cries outside strengthened, and she realized it wasn't gulls.

It was children shouting. Playing in the lane on the other side of the garden wall, perhaps?

She passed through the open doors into the morning room.

It was a generous space, but all the furnishings were swathed in holland covers. Even the chandelier was swathed in muslin, and the paintings and mirrors on the white walls draped. The rug lay in a large roll to one side, and a vast rumpled canvas covered the entire floor.

She was glad. It had been such a pretty room, with its rose damask and rose brocade, its gilded white woodwork, and its vases of flowers. She much preferred to remember it in its glory—now shrouded and hidden from her sight—than to see it trammeled by her own miserable neglect, as it would have been if unprotected.

She picked her way across the canvas-covered floor to one of the tall windows and looked out into the back garden. Her breath caught in her throat.

A horde of boys poured through the gap between two of the largest lilacs, shouting.

"Where is she?"

"Where'd she go?"

"We'll find you Empire-toady, don't think you're safe!"

Ohtavie gasped. Her innards felt like ice, her breast, like stiff parchment, ready to rip. Had they come for her at last? Was her end upon her? For an instant, she stood frozen. Then she whirled to flee.

Her right foot caught in a fold of the canvas protecting the floor. A small, hideous crack sounded within the outer bone of the foot, along with intense pain, and she fell headlong.

✷

Lealle wrapped her arms around her knees, crushing her school books against her ribs as she crouched in the cramped space behind the square marble base of the column.

Out in the garden, she heard the skitter of rolling gravel pebbles give way to earth-muffled thumps. "Where is she? Where'd she go?" came the boys' yelling voices. "We'll find you Empire-toady!"

Were the boys crossing the grassy sundial oval? Next came a violent swishing sound—the lilac branches? More shouting.

"What a nasty ole hovel!" complained a voice, much nearer than Lealle liked. "A troll-witch would keep it nicer."

It was true the marble columns were dirty and the cream plaster on the wall cracked. Lealle had noticed that much even in her headlong flight. But the house was hardly a hovel, with its grandeur and its many large windows.

Lealle tried to make herself even smaller. Would the boy come up onto the terrace?

"Witches *like* hovels," asserted another voice, also too close. "Dirty crones deserve dirty digs." Was the boy on the terrace steps?

"Did hoity-toity even come this way?" demanded a more distant boy. "She'd be more scared of a witch than we would. Bet you she'd run away from the house, not toward it."

Murmurs of agreement drifted up.

Lealle crossed her fingers. Just *go*, she thought, *please* go!

Another violent swishing sounded, despite the lack of any breeze. The lilac branches again? Were they going? Had the whole lot of them shoved all together through the narrow gap between the lilacs?

Lealle stayed very still, listening.

There was nothing. Nothing. And then the faint scritch of footsteps on gravel—walking, not running—as bored boys scuffed their boots in disappointment.

Lealle's crouching got very uncomfortable. She wriggled her toes inside her half-boots, trying to ease the cramping sensation in her calves. She let her back relax and straighten a bit, easing the crush of her ribs and books against her thighs, wanting more than just shallow breaths. She inched her face toward the corner of the column base, trying to peer around the stone without revealing herself.

The terrace was empty.

The weedy, overgrown lawn was empty.

Lealle scrutinized the corners of the lawn, as well as the shadowed spots between the lilac bushes where the branches formed low nooks. No one. The boys were gone.

She waited a little longer, just to be sure, and then stood.

Her right leg went all pins-and-needles. She shifted her weight onto it, which helped, and stepped out from behind the column. Her boot heel clicked on the stone of the terrace, and the skirt of her frock rustled slightly in the silence.

As she approached the nearest steps down to the ragged lawn, a tattered cap atop a boy's head rose above the edge of the terrace. Ragged-cap himself straightened from his own crouch to grin cheekily up at her.

"Hah!" he said. "Thought you were safe, din't ya?" He bunched his fists purposefully. "Well, you're not!"

Lealle stopped, stone cold. He had her trapped. He'd reach her easily before she could cross to one of the other stairways down from the terrace.

He started up the steps, not hurrying. He didn't need to hurry.

Lealle whirled and dashed for the nearest of the glass-paned doors into the house.

The knob turned under her hand. It was unlocked!

Chapter Two

LEALLE SLIPPED inside, quick as a darting swift, noticing the thumb latch for a bolt as she closed the door. She turned it, relieved beyond hope at the feel of it snicking home. Now she was safe.

Ragged-cap strode up, reaching for the outside knob. It turned under his grip, but the door remained closed. He rattled it with no luck, anger in his face.

Lealle took a step back. Would he break one of the many glass panes? If he broke the glass, he could reach the latch for the bolt and open it. He could get in.

Instead he released the knob to shake his fist.

"You'll have to come out sometime," he threatened, his voice attenuated by the glass between them.

Yes, she would. But . . . now she had options. Surely there were other doors she could use. Or a servant who might be sent for help. She need not emerge right into Ragged-cap's threatened punch.

She took another step back, and lifted her chin, staring measuringly through the glass panes of the door. Take that, you bully, she thought.

He glared, rattled the door one last time, tried the others—two more pairs, and each locked—then turned angrily away.

Only when he passed between the lilacs on the far side of the untidy lawn did she turn away herself. The loggia she stood in showed none of the signs of neglect displayed by the gardens. Its polished white marble—floor, urn-filled niches, and high arching ceiling—gleamed in the light flooding through the doors and through the tall windows above them.

Lealle took a brief survey of her own person. She didn't want to look like a beggar child when she found that servant.

Her buttoned half-boots were dusty, so she set her books on the floor and fetched out her handkerchief from her sash to give the dulled black leather a wipe. Her white stockings were *not* dusty, thank goodness, nor falling down, but wrinkles at the ankles indicated they could use some pulling up.

She glanced around the loggia to make sure she was still alone. Mamere would hit the thatch if she ever learned of this, but that wasn't really it. Lealle herself would blush to be caught showing her knees in public.

But there was no one, which seemed odd. Surely the servants must have heard the racket.

Quickly, she tugged at the top of each stocking, smoothed the garter above each knee, and let her white petticoat and the blue skirt of her frock fall back to her ankles. There.

Her lace fichu had come untucked on one side, and she restored that end under her sash. But there was nothing she could do about her hair. The boys had taken the ribbon that restrained it, and now her chestnut curls tumbled onto her shoulders. She combed her fingers through the locks. At least they could be tidy, even if they were loose.

And now she was presentable. She picked up her books.

But, where was everyone?

"Hello?" she called cautiously.

Her voice echoed a little, but no one answered her.

"Hello?" she called again, louder.

Still no one. She would have to go looking, despite her reluctance to penetrate more deeply into someone else's home.

The outside terrace lay behind her. Some double doors on her right stood firmly closed. An archway ahead of her led into the heart of the house.

Double doors on her left stood open.

She turned left, entering a room entirely swathed in holland covers: furniture draped, wall ornaments hidden, even the floor blanketed. She stopped, daunted. Had the family removed from Claireau for the summer? Surely they would have shuttered the windows, if that were so. Yet this room had been prepared for long absence.

Perhaps the house really was untenanted. That would explain why no one had come to investigate all the noise made by Ragged-cap.

Lealle stood still a moment, clutching her books and nibbling her lip.

If no one were home, she could simply find a door onto the Rue Étroit, or onto Balard Square around the corner, and slip out. Except . . . that felt wrong, somehow. There was something amiss here. And if she simply left it behind her, perhaps leaving the house open to thieves— for how would she lock the door upon her departure, lacking a key— she would be guilty of . . . something. *She* would be wrong.

Lealle took another step forward.

With the changed angle, the black tip of a servant's laced shoe, peeking from behind a sofa, came into view.

Lealle stopped again. She was beginning to wish she'd never entered this house. Wishing she could just leave. Wishing she didn't have to confront . . . whatever she was about to confront.

She swallowed and moved forward again.

In a huddle of blue and white garments, a silver-haired servant woman sprawled on her side on the canvas-covered floor, one arm under her, her back to Lealle. The woman's legs, hidden by a long skirt, made awkward angles beneath the fabric. Broken? One foot—the right—lay caught in a fold of the floor covering.

The servant lay very still. Was she dead?

Lealle gasped, wanting to whirl about and run. But she *knew* that was wrong. Papere would say she must summon an armiger. In fact, that was exactly right. She was the daughter of Claireau's High Justice.

She *must* summon the armigers to take charge and to investigate.

Under the light blue bodice, the servant woman's ribs rose in a breath. She was *not* dead.

Lealle set her books down on the holland-draped sofa and hurried forward. Kneeling beside the injured woman, she suffered another shock. She'd thought the woman old, because of her silver hair, coiled in a graceful bun.

But it was not age that colored this woman's hair silver.

Studying the woman's face, Lealle saw the downward tilt of the closed eyes, the elongation of the upward curving nose, and the sallow skin that indicated untreated troll-disease.

Lealle checked the woman's ears to be sure. And, yes, though partially hidden under the strands of silver hair drawn back along the side of her head, the ears were enlarged, slightly cupped, and with drooping lobes. The woman *was* a troll. A witch, as the bullies had speculated.

But how could that be possible?

When Lealle was little—three years old? four years old?—troll-disease was a death sentence. But all that had changed when Lord Gabris of the Empire engineered a treatment for it. Now every retreat center in every town possessed at least one healer trained in the curative procedure. How could this woman suffer the malady absolutely untreated in this modern day and age? It was impossible. And yet . . . here she lay, untreated.

Lealle bit her lower lip.

This . . . troll-witch . . . could be dangerous. Untreated troll-disease led to insanity before it ended in death. And a troll-witch's magery was powerful. Perhaps Lealle *should* be running for the armigers. Should she? Would she? And yet, the woman's frail body—too thin under her clothes—made Lealle want to help her, not harm her.

She reached forward, noticing that her fingers trembled as she did so.

She touched the woman's upper arm gently, and the troll-witch's eyes opened: faded gray-blue and bewildered.

⁂

Ohtavie's head swam and her vision was black. What had happened to her? Was she ill? She felt ill.

Someone's hand touched her gently on the shoulder. A kind voice murmured.

Ohtavie worked to make her throat utter sound. "Mamere?" she asked.

She still couldn't see. Was she in bed? The mattress lacked any softness, pressing woodenly against her right hip. And where was the quilt? She gave an inarticulate protest, wanting warmth, wanting softness. Mamere was always so caring and loving when Ohtavie was sick. Mamere would make everything all right in a moment now. She always had, she always would. Mamere would keep her safe.

The kind voice spoke again. "Maitresse?"

Why would Mamere call Ohtavie that? 'Maitresse' was for grown women who possessed special skills and deserved respect. Ohtavie was 'Demoiselle' and would be 'Lady' when she was grown.

"Maitresse," came the voice again, a hint of uncertainty in its kindness. It wasn't Mamere; that was certain. But, oh, Ohtavie wished it were.

Whenever something was wrong, Mamere made it right. Or she had until . . . until what? Something had happened. Something dreadful. And Mamere had not made it right. Could not make it right. Even though Ohtavie was sick unto death. Mamere had failed.

Ohtavie stifled a sob.

Mamere had failed, but Ohtavie had not died. Instead, she'd— Ohtavie gasped—she'd become a troll, which was almost worse than dying. And Mamere had hidden her, because the townspeople would have killed her if they'd known. She would have died indeed.

Ohtavie's sight cleared abruptly to see a girl's sweet face hovering close above her. Bright brown curls fell over the girl's lace-covered shoulders, and her deep blue eyes were filled with worry, even fear.

Ohtavie started, wanting to push the girl away. But her arm did not obey her impulse. "Go away!" she croaked.

The girl's eyes widened. "But you're hurt, Maitresse. You need help." What a soft, pretty voice she had.

And she was right, oh, yes, Ohtavie needed help. She'd needed help for years, but there was no help to be had. And this girl could not help her. Any help she summoned would be death.

"Go away," commanded Ohtavie. "Pretend you've never seen me."

The girl's forehead wrinkled in puzzlement. "I think your foot may be broken," she said. "A physician should see you, or better yet an antiphoner skilled in the healing disciplines—"

"No!" Ohtavie interrupted her. "Physicians and healers have naught to do with the likes of me!"

The girl's puzzlement deepened. "You especially deserve their care. You . . ." The girl hesitated, then continued. "You suffer from troll-disease, do you not?"

"I harm no one!" Ohtavie insisted. "I've never harmed anyone. I never will. I keep to myself. You need feel no guilt for keeping my secret!" She hated the frantic note she heard in her own voice.

"Of course not!" answered the girl. "But your foot is broken, and you may have hit your head as well. Those injuries must be healed before your troll-disease is . . . is treated."

"Before they kill me, you mean," said Ohtavie fiercely.

"No!" The girl looked horror-stricken. "No!"

Ohtavie forced herself to speak more calmly. "That is what they do to trolls, you know. Lest we harm many in our final madness."

"Not anymore," the girl said firmly.

Now it was Ohtavie's turn to feel taken aback. Troll-disease had afflicted humankind ever since the first mage attempted magery too strong for him, his effort ripping the energetic structures within his being that held his body in health. There had never been a cure, only prevention, and death when prevention failed. For millennia, mages-too-bold had fallen to their disease—troll-disease—and been executed. What could this girl mean? Was she so innocent, so ignorant as to not know this? Or did she aim to deceive Ohtavie and thus keep her quiescent?

"I must have your word that you will say nothing of me."

The girl hesitated.

Ohtavie made a convulsive effort, and her hand shot out, gripping the girl's wrist. "Your word!" she demanded.

"I . . . I promise," said the girl.

A sigh gusted from Ohtavie's lungs. She let her hand fall away. "Good. Good. Now you may leave me."

The girl's chin lifted. "I'll keep silent," she said. "But I didn't promise to leave you helpless. I . . . I couldn't!"

Ohtavie felt her brows draw down. "Then what will you do?" she asked. It seemed a bit of an impasse. She wanted the girl to go, to leave her in her familiar solitude. Having a stranger present felt . . . uncomfortable. Very uncomfortable.

The girl bit her lower lip. "I'm not sure. But . . . but I'll do something." She swallowed. "I've studied antiphony since I was eight. And I know how to do a few small healings with it."

Ohtavie scrutinized her: slight in stature, a child's face, straight of body. She couldn't be more than fourteen, if that. And most children gave no sign of their enigmatic powers until the age of thirteen. Although Ohtavie herself had been early. "How old are you?" she demanded.

"Fifteen," said the girl.

"Hmm."

"My mother says she didn't grow until sixteen," offered the girl.

"Help me to sit," said Ohtavie abruptly.

The girl nodded and carefully freed Ohtavie's right foot from the fold of floor canvas that still held it. Then she eased her arms around Ohtavie's shoulders, still careful to avoid jostling her, pulling Ohtavie toward her and up.

Ohtavie's head swam anew. Her innards felt queasy, and her right foot felt strangely large, the shoe very tight. But she was sitting.

She swallowed down her nausea, pinched the pendant beneath the linen of her blouse between her fingers, and waited for her head to clear.

The girl moved around to her back to hold her upright more easily. Ohtavie didn't like her so close, and at Ohtavie's back. She hitched herself along the floor toward the nearest sofa to lean against its low holland-swathed arm.

The girl crept along with her, clearly worried Ohtavie might topple. "You need help," she insisted again. And she was not wrong. But . . . Ohtavie wanted not to accept such help.

The skin around the girl's eyes tightened. She nibbled her lower lip again. The forefinger of her right hand pressed against its neighboring middle finger.

"I'll fetch you some water," she announced, cast one last perturbed glance at Ohtavie, and hurried toward the door.

Ohtavie felt some of the tension go out with her.

It was relief to be alone.

∞

Lealle probed the servant corridors of the mansion, expecting to find stairs down to the basements where the kitchens and pantries lay, but she soon realized that this house was arranged differently than home. Two low wings off each side of the residence held the practicalities that made the place work, although Lealle wondered how it *did* work. Dust lay thickly on all the surfaces, and the necessary equipment—dustpans, baskets, trays, kettles, and such—seemed entirely absent. Stored away in the cupboards, unused? Or missing altogether? Stolen?

And where were all the staff?

Glass-fronted cabinets in the butler's pantry displayed elegant serving vessels of all sorts, and Lealle easily found a bowl and ewer among them. Even protected behind glass, the china bore a thin film of grit. How long had it sat untouched on its shelf?

Off the vast kitchen, she found a scullery, rimmed by ridged porcelain counters draining into a multiplicity of deep porcelain sinks, all except one clearly unused. That one bore a cake of soap at its edge and a damp cleaning cloth draped over the faucet below the pump handle.

As Lealle worked the pump to rinse the ewer and bowl, she cudgeled her brain about what in the north she was going to do. The injured troll-woman had ordered her to leave, wanted Lealle to leave. Lealle herself wanted to leave, and she was accustomed to obeying her elders. That obedient part of her felt she *should* leave.

But . . . some other part of her knew that was wrong. The troll-woman needed help.

And Lealle couldn't bear the thought of leaving her alone and hurt. But Lealle had promised to tell no one about her. She supposed she could bring someone without a full explanation of why. But Papere spoke often of the spirit of the law being just as important as its letter. The spirit of her promise meant protecting the troll-woman's secrecy.

If she couldn't summon help—and she couldn't . . .

If she wouldn't simply depart—and she wouldn't—then she'd have to provide help herself. The troll-woman had been doubtful, when Lealle suggested antiphony. *Lealle* was doubtful. Her teachers said she was advanced for her age; they said she was good. But her antiphonic accomplishments went only so far as accelerating the healing of some bruises, a sprain, or relief for a headache. How in the north could she mend a broken foot? Or a broken head? The first thing she'd learned was that a healer must first do no harm. She suspected she could do quite a bit of harm in her ignorance.

Biting her lower lip, she checked the surface of the ewer and the bowl. Clean and cold. The water had been very chilly.

She filled the ewer and dug out a towel from a well-stocked drawer below the counter beside the sink. So . . . the house was not denuded of housekeeping tools. They were merely tidied away and largely unused. Which gave her an idea.

Drying the bowl and the outside of the ewer, she considered where she might find the supplies she would need. Mamere had arranged a few sessions for Lealle with their housekeeper, the beginning of her learning how to manage staff, as she would need to when she was grown and married. Lealle was largely unfamiliar with the details of housekeeping as yet, but still . . .

She was hopeful that amidst this wing of the offices—pantries, larders, laundry, napper, and so on—she might find a stillroom. Antiphony—magery—was not the only way to aid the injured.

∽

Ohtavie sank back against the holland-swathed arm of the sofa and wished she were sitting on its cushioned seat instead of on the canvas-covered floor beside it. The floor pressed hard against her sit bones, and the straightness of her knees hurt. The shoe on her injured right foot felt even tighter. No doubt the foot was swelling.

The light flooding through the tall windows onto the back garden made her head ache. It was too bright. If she were sitting on the sofa, the light would be behind her, but her wrists felt weak, almost too weak to permit her to touch the pendant hidden beneath her blouse. She needed to recuperate a little before she could move. And she needed to think what she would do about the intruder, the girl who wanted to help her.

Why did the girl want to help her? No one helped trolls. And Ohtavie was indeed a troll. She remembered all too well the dreadful ripping sensation within her that accompanied the sundering of her radices, the energetic anchorages for her being. She'd fainted then. But that had not been the worst of it. The worst had come when she awoke.

And after she awoke.

She'd lost her humanity when the troll-disease claimed her, but she'd lost everything else after.

For the longest time, she'd blamed her great grandmother for her losses. Were it not for Grandmere, she would not have wanted to prove herself adept at magery. Were it not for Grandmere, she would not have been practicing in the cellars. Were it not for Grandmere, she would never have found . . . what she did find. Were it not for Grandmere, her parents would never have hidden her away.

But Grandmere had possessed her own burdens. Ohtavie knew that now.

And yet . . . the old memories still stung.

She could see Grandmere in her mind's eye now: Grandmere sniffing and looking down her thin, aristocratic nose with disdain; Grandmere smoothing her old-fashioned gown with its wide, wide skirts of dark purple brocade, so dark as to be almost black, and its stiff bodice cut low across Grandmere's scraggy bosom and compressing Grandmere's torso with its whalebone stays.

She could smell Grandmere's perfume, almost as though Grandmere stood beside her now: an unpleasant musk mixed with a more pleasant citrus.

Grandmere had never been an easy person to be around, and she'd disapproved of Ohtavie amazingly.

"Stand up straight, missy!" she'd used to say, multiple times every day. "Your mother should make more use of the backboard." That was a horrid contraption that Grandmere had suffered in her own girlhood, a plank of maple strapped to her shoulders and upper back with leather, forcing her to hold herself very much up.

And then when Ohtavie came into her magery young, Grandmere had urged Mamere to withhold the necessary lessons in enigmology. "She'll not catch a husband, if she's trained as a mage," she'd insisted.

But Mamere had stood fast in the face of Grandmere's arguments.

"Every child with the gift deserves lessons in its use," she'd said. "That's hardly training her as a mage. And, really, Grandmere, you should not use that term. You know you shouldn't."

"I'll speak as I see fit," had retorted Grandmere. "Pish on your modern enigmologists! They're naught but troll-mages awaiting an accident."

"Training will help her avoid accidents. Indeed, they are necessary for her safety," had answered Mamere.

And yet, Grandmere had proved correct in this instance. Ohtavie had suffered exactly the accident Grandmere had foretold. Nor had she ever married.

But all that lay in the past. This was the present. Ohtavie was a troll, and she had an intruder to deal with, an intruder who threatened the secrecy that kept Ohtavie safe. What would—what could—Ohtavie do about the kind-faced girl who wanted to help her?

She couldn't make the girl leave. And even if she did . . . that did nothing for Ohtavie's safety. She needed for the girl never to have arrived in the first place. Although the girl *had* said she would say nothing. Really . . . the shortest route to the girl's departure would be to accept her help.

And the sooner the girl went, the sooner she might start forgetting all about this odd little detour of hers. (What was she doing here, anyway?) The sooner she forgot, the less chance she might let something slip. And then Ohtavie could have her blessed solitude again.

Yes. She would stop protesting. She would accept whatever help the girl offered graciously. And she would rejoice to see the girl's back.

Immediately in the wake of this decision, footsteps sounded in the loggia, and the girl entered the morning room, well-laden with provisions: basin and ewer, vinaigrette for faintness, and all the paraphernalia of first aid.

"My name is Lealle Mcridar," said the girl, bending to set down her burdens and offer Ohtavie a glass of cool water. "May I know yours?"

The water tasted divine, clearing Ohtavie's head enough to make patent that it had been very far from clear before. "I am Ohtavie de Bellay," she answered. "Thank you."

The girl's eyes—Lealle's eyes—widened. "You're Lady de Bellay?" she questioned. "I thought—" she broke off.

"You thought the family De Bellay had died out," Ohtavie finished for her. "We will. Presently." She suppressed the bleak smile that wanted to quirk her lips. "I am the last." The distant cousin who would inherit the house bore another name.

Lealle's right forefinger pressed against her right middle finger. Was that the girl's usual nervous foible? "I'm—I'm just learning antiphony. I'm worried I'd hurt you. I'm not that good."

Ohtavie studied the girl again, not that she could really tell much about a person's inner self from the look of her outer self. But Lealle's eyes possessed a directness of gaze more in character with an older girl than that of the child Ohtavie had first taken her to be. And her mouth, delicately formed, held some firmness in its disposition. She had the feeling that Lealle could be quite capable.

"I suspect you're very good," Ohtavie corrected her, "but that you lack experience."

Lealle's cheek dimpled. "Yes! But I really *am* good at ordinary first aid. Wrapping your foot in plaster bandages would be a lot safer than working on it with antiphony, don't you think?"

Ohtavie felt the tension in her shoulders ease. First aid. Why hadn't it occurred to her? A *physical* bridge from injury to healing, rather than a magical one.

She nodded.

Lealle proved to be very capable, as Ohtavie had guessed. Who had drilled the girl so well?

She removed the shoe from Ohtavie's foot by cutting its laces with scissors, and the stocking, the same. Separating the shoe from the foot was a little trickier, but Lealle bent the leather tongue all the way back, away from the bridge of Ohtavie's foot, and spread the side flaps very wide, and the shoe practically fell away.

Her foot looked very puffy indeed, with the start of a bruise already coloring its outer edge.

Lealle insisted on soaking the foot in cool water for quite an interval before she gently dried the pale skin and went in search of the wool stockings once worn by the footmen of the house. These she doubled, placing one inside the other, and then snipped the toes off.

When she drew the doubled sock over Ohtavie's foot and lower leg, it was snug, but not tight.

As she set the plaster bandages soaking, Lealle's fingers did their pressing-one-another maneuver again, and she bit her lower lip. "I—I think I should check that the bone is straight," she said. "That will take antiphony."

Ohtavie's breath caught. She'd loved enigmatic magery. Once. Been proud of her own. But now . . . now she thought of enigmology—enigmology gone wrong—as the root of her troll-disease. It *was* the root of her troll-disease. Could she bear for Lealle to enigmatically examine her foot?

"You shall merely look, shall you not?" She fought to keep the sharpness from her voice. "You shall not . . . manipulate my flesh with it?"

Lealle's mouth firmed. "I will not."

"Very well." Ohtavie braced herself.

Lealle settled herself, sitting cross-legged and very tall, inhaling slowly, exhaling more slowly still. A comforting warmth stole into Ohtavie's bruised foot, and the unbruised portion looked slightly less white.

Lealle's controlled breathing went on for a bit, then ended in a gusting sigh, and she opened her eyes. "It's broken," she said, "but the bones are straight. I could *see* them!" What would she have done, if they had not been straight? Ohtavie had no idea. But the break *was* straight. It might heal straight, if all went well. And Lealle's enigmology—antiphony, Ohtavie corrected herself—hadn't hurt in the least.

Smoothing the plaster bandages onto the foot and lower leg proved a messy business, cloudy water dripping everywhere off the plaster-imbued muslin, which wanted to stick to itself even before Lealle got the first strip arranged. The girl kept having to remind Ohtavie to keep her foot positioned at a right angle to her shin. Ohtavie kept having to remind *herself* of that necessity. Her foot kept wanting to droop down.

And then they had to wait for the plaster to set.

Lealle tidied up the mess, while they waited. Ohtavie leaned back against the sofa arm—she was still on the floor—and closed her eyes, exhausted from the ordeal. Did she even doze a bit? Perhaps.

Lealle turned both ends of the double socks over the plaster, forming thick cuffs, one revealing Ohtavie's toes, the other just beneath her knee.

"You—you won't want to stay here, will you?" Lealle looked around the holland-covered room, large and white and unready for use.

"My bedchamber lies on this floor," answered Ohtavie. "It is not far."

But it was too far for her, with but one foot to set to the floor.

She tried hopping, with her right arm shored up by Lealle's shoulders, and Lealle's left arm wrapped around Ohtavie's waist. But Lealle was just too slight to give steady support, despite her unexpected strength. And Ohtavie was too weakened to hop far with only the aid of balance.

She sank down to the dull planks of the servants' passageway, having barely made it out of the morning room.

Lealle stood over her, biting her lip and tapping her forefinger against its fellow. Ohtavie ignored her, concentrating on regaining her equanimity in the wake of this failure. She *would* get to her bedchamber. She *would*. Or at least to her parlor. Why did that sound so familiar? Of course, she'd been vowing something similar just a few hours ago: that she would look out at least one window. And see where that had brought her!

One try at scooting along with her hands just behind her derriere, her good foot out ahead, and her broken foot held up, ended immediately. The plaster cast was so heavy, and Ohtavie was so tired.

"Did none of your footmen ever break a limb?" asked Lealle. "A foot or a leg?"

"Oh!" Ohtavie sagged in relief. "Thomas—no, Pierre—broke his ankle. And used two crutches once he was able to get out of bed." Ohtavie closed her eyes, trying to think where those crutches must have gotten to. "Not the attics. Nor the cellars." None of the many closets in the kitchen wing, or even those in this wing—the housekeeper's wing. "The front door!" she exclaimed. "There's a water closet that never drained properly. The one under the stairs, not the one across the vestibule."

She was beginning to be glad Lealle had not obeyed her, when she'd ordered the girl to leave. How in the north would she have managed . . . anything . . . alone?

The crutches, which Lealle succeeded in finding, were very uncomfortable, the wooden cradles under Ohtavie's arms too high (Pierre had been taller than she) and bruising in their hardness, the crosspieces for her hands likewise unpadded and barely within reach of her grasp. The wooden tips showed a tendency to slip on the wooden floor. Ohtavie was glad the planks lay so dully, unpolished. The boards would have been much slipperier, if well-maintained.

"They're so old-fashioned," murmured Lealle. "I'm so sorry," she added, for all the world as though it were her fault. "Was it very long ago that Pierre's ankle broke?"

Ohtavie thought a moment. Had it truly been so long? "Seventeen years," she said.

But, with all their discomforts and dangers, the crutches permitted her to travel to her small parlor, with its comfortable wingchairs and cozy, although bare, hearth, and then through the room into her bedchamber.

Chapter Three

FOLLOWING OHTAVIE along the dim servant's hallway, Lealle winced each time Ohtavie's crutches scraped and slipped. They were so primitive; no horsehair-stuffed cushioning softened the cradles under the arms, no quilted leather wrapped the handholds, and no rubber tips capped the ends.

She didn't want to think about what might happen if the troll-woman fell again. Lealle might need to break her promise not to tell anyone about her. Maybe she should have broken her promise as it was. This whole situation felt impossible. She wished she could ask Mamere what to do. Mamere would know, with all her experience running the chapel soup kitchen and her position on the boards for the almoner's hospital, the orphanage, and all the other charities she favored.

But Mamere was not here, and Lealle was. Lealle would just have to do the best she could.

Ohtavie had come to a halt before a closed door.

Lealle squeezed ahead of her to open it, and then stepped through to be out of Ohtavie's path. Cool northern light from two windows illuminated the space, a small sitting room that seemed very austere to Lealle's eyes. No pictures graced the plain white walls, no carpeting softened the bare boards of the floor, and the furnishings were sparse: a dark secretary desk against the door wall, a small glass-fronted bookcase, two wingchairs upholstered in a dull gold brocade before a small, empty hearth. Matching brocade curtains framed the windows.

It must have been the housekeeper's sitting room, but . . . even a housekeeper usually possessed more comforts than this. Mamere's housekeeper inhabited *two* parlors, not one, each crammed full of knick-knacks and superfluous decorative tables. Had Ohtavie . . . deliberately removed most of the original appointments here?

Lealle bit her lower lip and moved to the open door across the room. It led into a bedroom, somewhat larger than the sitting room, but nearly as barren.

A spare four-poster stood out from the door wall, draped only with a plain quilt of cream muslin, no canopy, no bed curtains. The narrow console of black oak across from the door must be Ohtavie's dressing table—it bore a brush, a comb, and a hand mirror—but no lacy flounces softened its dark wood. A washstand with basin and ewer occupied the other side of the door, and a wardrobe filled the wall beyond. Heavy silk curtains—nubby ecru spattered with pale pink cabbage roses—flanked three windows. Remnants of the housekeeper's choices? They seemed . . . sumptuous, more luxurious than all the rest.

Ohtavie was tapping her way across the sitting room.

"I—I think you should lie down," Lealle said.

Ohtavie nodded. "I think so, too."

Lealle turned down the muslin quilt and was relieved to find a beautifully light blanket of white cashmere, with soft linen sheets below that, exuding a faint floral scent. Three pillows, too, were cased in linen. The bed was comfortable, even if understated.

Its mattress was quite high, and while Ohtavie managed to sit, she could not swing her right leg, with its heavy plaster cast, up enough. Lealle bent to lift it, placing one of the pillows beneath Ohtavie's knees and removing her left shoe, before she spread the top sheet and the blanket over Ohtavie's legs. The troll-woman looked very small and frail.

"Shall I—shall I bring you anything else?" Lealle asked.

"Sleep will be my best medicine," answered Ohtavie. She smiled, her faded blue eyes holding Lealle's gaze. "Thank you, child."

"I—I wish I could do more," stammered Lealle.

"Which door did you come in?" asked Ohtavie, her smile fading.

Lealle felt herself blushing. "Some schoolboys caught me in the lane between the gardens," she explained, "and . . . and started pushing me. Taunting me. I ran away and hid, but . . . they found me after all. And your terrace door was open."

"Ah." Ohtavie shifted on her pillows. "I saw the boys. They were in a nasty humor, I thought."

Lealle swallowed, still feeling obscurely guilty, even in the face of Ohtavie's understanding.

"I'm not blaming you, child. Merely giving thought to how you might depart. I'd rather you didn't pass through the front door."

"Oh!" Lealle felt marginally less guilty. She *had* trespassed. "I—I'd rather not go back through the gardens. The boys might still be waiting for me." Although that seemed unlikely. It must be early evening by now. Surely they would have gotten bored, even if they had lurked for some while.

"There's a side door out of the kitchens. And a key on the hook beside it. Will you lock the door behind you, please?"

"Of course!" Lealle hesitated. "The terrace doors are all locked. I made sure, when one of the boys tried to get inside." Had Ohtavie blanched? She looked suddenly strained to Lealle. "Are there any other doors you'd like me to check?"

Ohtavie shook her head. "No, I know . . . how that one door came to be unbolted." Did the unbolting of the door come with some unpleasant memory? Lealle wondered.

"You should go," said Ohtavie.

Lealle knew she should. And yet . . . she felt reluctant. How would Ohtavie make supper, later? How would she empty the basin from her washstand after she'd cleaned her face and hands? How would she get back in bed after visiting the water closet? There were no servants present—or anyone—to help her with anything.

"I'll manage, child," chided Ohtavie, acerbic. "Best foot forward, now."

Lealle went, secretly resolving to visit Ohtavie on the morrow. Ohtavie wouldn't like it, but Lealle would do so anyway. Because it was the right thing to do. Even Mamere would agree to that, although Mamere must know nothing about it.

∽

Lealle had envisioned herself thinking over all that had happened as she walked home, but it didn't turn out that way at all.

She found she couldn't think.

Instead she scanned the numerous passersby, as though looking for someone specific. She jumped a little when a street urchin shouted to his friend across the way. And she looked nervously over her shoulder at intervals.

The evening was perfectly ordinary.

Its golden light gave a pleasant mellowness to the slate flagways, the cobbled streets, and the brick buildings as all of Claireau headed toward home. Housewives hurried briskly from the shops with the fixings for supper in their baskets. Businessmen locked their offices, hefted satchels of papers, and strode out purposefully. Children who'd had a late music lesson, or gone to a friend's house after school, carried their instrument cases and books.

Lealle fit right in. Why was she so uneasy?

Only when she reached the river and the Valendras Bridge, passing onto the span under the arch of the massive square tower guarding its western end, did she realize the source of her disquiet. She'd been expecting Ragged-cap and his gang to find her again, to do . . . something . . . to her, even with all the people on the streets as witnesses.

That made no sense, but she felt safe on the bridge, as though all her concerns had been scraped off in the passageway under its western tower and left behind. Was it because she was nearing home?

She paused by the stone parapet at the bridge edge to look upriver.

The water was very smooth, reflecting the deep turquoise of the evening sky overhead and the yellow-gray stone walls of the many townhouses lining the banks. Farther along the far bank—the east bank—a patch of brilliant green interrupted the stone walls: the gardens of Tour de Nileau. And rising from the gardens were the rounded towers of the medieval castle with its strange square keep: home.

It was the traditional seat of Claireau's High Justice, and Lealle had lived there all her life. She couldn't imagine living anywhere else. And right now . . . she was eager to be walking into its courtyard.

She shifted her books from her right arm to the left, and hurried her steps toward the Fortin de Garde at the bridge's eastern end. She'd be home in minutes, if she didn't linger along the way.

Forgetting all about Ragged-cap and his cohort, forgetting even about Ohtavie, she began to enjoy the gentle evening air, the soft bustle of the passersby, and the comforting scent of sun-warmed stone.

When she reached home, passing under the always-raised portcullis in the front curtain wall, the narrow courtyard of the castle stood entirely in shadow, the nighttime flambeaus as yet unlit. The luminous sky overhead prevented any sense of gloom in the space, but Lealle wished Mamere would countenance a few urns filled with flowers in the corners. Or something. The cobbles underfoot with the massive stone walls surrounding them were very severe. Mamere said it was historic, but Lealle thought preserving history at the cost of present comfort was silly.

As she passed the covered well at the center of the courtyard, her little brother bounced out from behind it, yelling, "Hou!"

For just an instant, she mistook him for Ragged-cap, and jumped.

He broke into delighted laughter, bending to clutch his stomach, and then she realized her mistake, taking in his short stature—he was small for his age, like she was—his tidy trousers and buttoned jacket, and his neat crop of short brown curls. Aside from his aggressive approach, he resembled Ragged-cap not at all.

"Remy!" she gasped.

"Ha!" he yelled, still gleeful. "I got you! I made you jump!"

Lealle swallowed, stifling a brief impulse to slap him. She loved her little brother . . . she did, but she wasn't liking him much right now.

"Well, you needn't kill yourself laughing about it," she said sourly.

That, of course, made him laugh more, dancing around her and chanting, "Made you jump, made you jump!"

She ignored him, aiming for the stair tower at the inmost corner of the courtyard, passing through its heavy, ironbound, wooden door—more history—and starting up around the spiraling stone treads. Remy tagged after her, his giggles subsiding in her wake.

"Where've you been all afternoon anyway?" he asked, his voice curious.

Oops. She hadn't really decided what she would say.

"Today's one of my antiphony lesson days," she answered. That was true, if incomplete.

"Aw, you never stay this late at the retreat center," insisted Remy, a touch of whine in his tone.

Lealle shrugged as she reached the landing outside the great hall and the chapel—yet more history—and crossed to the next flight of steps. "I got held up," she said indifferently.

That was true, too, although again misleading.

"I bet you went to Celeste's and got toffees and peppermint sticks and lemon drops," Remy speculated. "I bet they tasted good. And then I bet you went to the river and ate them all and skipped stones on the water." He sighed enviously.

No doubt that's what *he* would have done with a stolen afternoon, especially since Mamere limited sweets and forbade him the river.

Lealle paused on the landing to the small dining room, allowing him to catch up.

"You missed tea, you know," he said.

Yes, she knew. "Is Mamere still in the parlor?" she asked. Lealle *was* late. "Or is she dressing for dinner?"

"Dinner," mumbled Remy, scuffing his feet.

Lealle frowned, abruptly noticing the mud on his shoes. "You're the one who's been to the river," she accused him.

"W-e-l-l . . ." He scuffed his toes some more.

"Don't *do* that!" Lealle admonished. "Mamere will get just as mad at you for scratching the leather as she will for playing by the water. C'mon!"

"Where?" he asked, surprised.

"My room, of course."

Mamere had had a sink installed in Lealle's bedchamber, at the same time that she'd modernized the kitchens. Thank the saints! Many of Lealle's friends still used basin and ewer—like Ohtavie—which meant one was always running out of clean water. Maybe Mamere was not so wedded to history as Lealle thought. She'd replaced the old privies with comfortable water closets before Lealle was born, after all. But Remy did not have a sink in his room. Mamere knew quite well that Remy would play in it, and make a mess.

The doors on the next landing led to the castle's bedchambers, the first to the guest wing, the second to the family rooms.

Speeding her pace—if Mamere was dressing for dinner, it was later than late—Lealle dove through the second doorway and darted down the short hallway, Remy clattering at her heels. Bursting into her room, she went straight to the small pedestal sink beside her wardrobe, a tall cabinet fancifully painted with garlands of yellow roses. Setting her books on the floor, she dragged her handkerchief out of her sleeve. She'd already dirtied it dusting off her own half boots in Ohtavie's loggia; she might as well finish the job on Remy's.

She turned the spigot for cold water, moistened the fine lawn, then knelt and started scrubbing. Remy fidgeted, tapping his fingers against his leg.

"You won't tell, will you?" he asked as she finished. "That I went to Parc Monceau and played at the colonnade fountain with Felix?"

Lealle paused a moment, crouching there on the floor at his feet. Mamere would be relieved that he'd been in the park, not at the river, but she'd be angry that Felix was his companion. Felix . . . swore. Or so Mamere said. If Lealle told her that Remy had spent the afternoon with him, well . . .

"Of course I won't tell," she said, looking up into Remy's face. "Why would you think that I would?"

"I know I was naughty," he confessed.

Lealle grinned. "So your guilty conscience is making you think you *deserve* to be found out."

Remy grinned back at her. "Well, yeah," he said.

Lealle nodded. "I won't tell," she said again. "But Remy . . . ?"

His face went anxious.

"Watch your words. If you say 'merde' or 'shun it' or, especially, 'connard' at dinner, Mamere will know, even if I say nothing."

Remy sighed. "They're such good words," he complained. "When I'm mad or surprised or, or . . ."

"Or want to explain just how horrible someone is," said Lealle, thinking of Ragged-cap. Ragged-cap was definitely a *connard*, but she'd better not borrow her brother's swearing habit, even in her mind, or *she* would get in trouble. "I know. But if you must disobey Mamere and Papere, you should also learn to be smart about it."

Speaking of which . . . what was she going to tell Mamere and Papere, if *they* asked where she'd been that had caused her to miss tea, the way Remy had asked. Despite her advice to her brother, she preferred obeying over being smart about disobeying. And she didn't think she *could* lie. Which meant she'd better work out how she could tell the truth without telling all of it.

She had a promise to keep to Ohtavie.

Standing up, she crossed the room to her dressing table. It was a delicate piece of furniture, painted pale yellow, to match the roses on her wardrobe, and ornamented with gilt arabesques. But she paid no heed to that, focusing instead on her own appearance in the mirror. She needed to be tidy for dinner, and . . . she was not: chestnut curls blowsy and unconfined; lace fichu slightly askew and with a smudge; at least her sky blue frock seemed unsullied.

As she picked up her brush to attack her hair, Remy wandered over to her side.

"I won't tell on you either," he said. "About sneaking sweets. Or going to the river."

Lealle worked a little longer on the tangles in her hair, then set the brush down, and quickly plaited the locks into a neat braid, tied off with a ribbon from the shallow drawer of the dressing table. Only then did she answer.

"But you don't really know, do you," she pointed out.

"N-o-o," he replied uncertainly.

"And I'm not going to tell you." She smiled composedly, not really sure where her assurance came from. "And you're not going to ask."

He looked surprised. "Okay," he agreed.

She stripped off her smudged fichu and fetched another from the bureau beside her dressing table, along with a fresh handkerchief. Swiftly, she draped the fichu across her back, crisscrossed its ends over her front, and tucked them into her sash at the sides. She checked her stockings—clean and straight—and her half boots. She was tidy now, and ready to face Mamere and Papere. She even knew how she would answer their questions.

She would tell them about Ragged-cap and fleeing, first into the garden and then into the unlocked house. She wouldn't say one word about Ohtavie. Instead she would dwell on her reluctance to emerge too quickly from her place of refuge, lest the bullies be waiting. Which reluctance had been real, even though events had rapidly distracted her from it.

Nodding firmly to herself, she headed toward the spiral stairs. At the door from her room into the short connecting hallway, she noticed Remy wasn't following.

She paused, looking over her shoulder.

"Lealle?" he asked, hesitant.

She knit her brows. "What is it?"

"Thank you." A shy smile swept across his face. "You're the best sister. Ever."

Her return smile felt a little crooked. She wasn't sure what he was thinking, but she *was* sure that at least he wouldn't provoke Mamere and Papere into probing into Lealle's doings this afternoon more deeply than was natural to them.

"C'mon, let's go," she said.

∾

Entering the small dining room, Lealle thought she'd made a mistake.

Mamere and Papere wore the formal garb required for when they entertained guests.

Despite the gleam of candlelight on the bald spot atop his head, Papere looked very grand in a beautiful skirted coat of brown and silver brocade, with the snowy whiteness of his waistcoat, shirt, and neckcloth peeping from between its broad lapels. And yet, even when Papere was at his most imposing, as now when he wore evening dress, or in his judicial robes when presiding in court, Lealle could sense the kindness behind his formality.

Mamere seemed a bit . . . preoccupied, somehow. She wore a low-necked gown of rose and gold brocade with elbow sleeves and full skirt. Her honey-brown hair was up, held by diamond combs above her ears and a diamond-studded net over the elegant coil at her nape. She was definitely expecting guests. And Lealle should have turned Remy over to the nursery maid for a full change of clothes, as well as changing herself. Except . . .

Mamere was not frowning.

Instead, she swayed forward a graceful step, held out her arms, and said, "Dear ones! Your Papere and I must attend a dreadful squeeze given by Lady Mendirbin—on Balard Square, you know—but I thought we might have a comfortable family dinner before we left."

Lealle stifled a sigh of relief—noting privately the coincidence that her parents' party was so near where she had just been—and went to kiss the scented cheek Mamere offered her. Remy made his bow, very properly, and then both of them greeted their father. Papere ruffled Remy's hair and asked casually about Lealle's day, but she could tell he didn't really expect any detailed answer.

"Just as usual, Papere," she said.

His hazel eyes twinkled at her. "More dull and tedious than you'd like, eh?" he followed up.

She nodded. The school part had been boring enough—just end of term permissions—but its aftermath . . . she almost shook her head, which would have induced more questions. Luckily she caught herself. But she would have compounded for a boring afternoon, had it been possible. Except . . . the thought of Ohtavie lying on that canvas-covered floor, injured and alone, gave her pause.

"Your Mamere and I have come up with a scheme to relieve your boredom," said Papere, moving to his seat at the head of the table, while Mamere shooed Remy to his chair on one long side and took her own at the foot.

Lealle noticed that most of the extra leaves had been removed from the table, which could seat up to twelve. But the white cloth was immaculate as always, the tapers in the center epergne fresh, and the sparkling cutlery extensive. Mamere would say that informal dining need not be slovenly, Lealle felt sure.

A footman brought round damp finger napkins and took them away again once they were used. Another served from a platter of minced pork tartlets, while the first returned to offer cups of cheese soufflé, which Lealle declined. She didn't care much for cheese. Papere himself poured wine into his and Mamere's glasses, and orgeat in Remy's and Lealle's.

Remy's eyes lit; he loved the sweetness of orgeat. Lealle repressed a grimace; she didn't.

Mamere's gaze crossed Papere's. "Really, Bello," she protested, although her voice held an indulgent note. "Your mother will spoil them enough, while they're in the country. You needn't jump ahead a day with extra treats."

"Oh!" exclaimed Remy. "Are we going to stay with Bonne-mémé and Bon-papy? Is that the treat, Papere?"

The corners of Papere's eyes crinkled as he nodded. "That's it. And you'll go tomorrow. It won't hurt you to miss the last three days of the term. I've already cleared your absence with the headmaster."

Lealle's insides sank.

If she and Remy were sent to Fontenay, she wouldn't be able to check on Ohtavie. And she wanted to. Ohtavie had no real claim on her. Ohtavie herself would prefer that Lealle *not* check. But Lealle couldn't help remembering how small and frail Ohtavie had seemed under the blanket of her bed. Lealle knew she *should* let the troll-woman go, but she couldn't, somehow.

"Lealle! Lealle!" screeched Remy, almost as though he were two instead of ten. "Do you think Bon-papy will take us to the gypsy carnival again? Do you think Bonne-mémé will—"

"Use your courteous voice, darling," interrupted Mamere.

"Yes, Maman," said Remy, reverting even further in his use of his baby name for Mamere.

Lealle withdrew her attention from him, letting Papere and Mamere respond to his excited burbling. She needed to think, to come up with a really good reason why she must stay in town for another few weeks. There had to be something.

Papere didn't notice her silence until the footman had served the first course of a fricassée of fowl and mushrooms, filets of sole with a chervil sauce, and the remove of a chilled haricot of beans and lettuces.

"You're not pleased, Lélé?" he asked, reverting along with Remy to an infant name.

"I'm longing to see Bon-papy and Bonne-mémé," she answered. That was true. She loved visiting them at Fontenay, and Papere would think it strange if she didn't want to go. Besides, she did want to go. Just not tomorrow. "But Tiffanie Mercier requested that I take tea with her this Beldaine"—four days hence—"and I told her I would." That was true, too. Although Lealle would ordinarily be relieved that she need not go after all. But Mamere served on the board of the Sanguine Almoners' Hostel with Madame Mercier, who was always pressing a friendship between her daughter and Lealle.

Mamere straightened in her seat, saying quickly, "I wouldn't want the children traveling on the sabbath, of course"—the day after Beldaine—"but Lundy would do just as well, wouldn't it, Bello? And that would give the maids a little more time to pack as well."

Yes, Lealle had thought a mention of Tiffanie's invitation might catch Mamere's attention.

Papere's mouth straightened. "Six days from now, instead of tomorrow? No." Did his voice hold a hint of exasperation? Maybe not. But Lealle could tell that he was not going to bend to Mamere's schedule change.

"Mamere said I might help in the chapel soup kitchen this Reindy, in the afternoon." That was three days ahead. "I—I was really hoping I might," Lealle put in, before Papere could say more. Actually Mamere had requested that Lealle help, and Lealle had agreed, even though she hadn't really wanted to until right this instant. Right this instant, anything that kept her in town was something she wanted to do.

Papere's left eyebrow rose. He knew she didn't share Mamere's enthusiasm for charity work.

It wasn't that she didn't like helping those in need. It was more that the ladies who dispensed soup to the homeless and visited the sick and so on—including even Mamere—seemed as much interested in displaying their benevolence as acting on it. Plus, Lealle was attracted to less straight-forward problems, like . . . like the one Ohtavie posed.

It wasn't just that Ohtavie was injured and alone. She needed to be persuaded to accept treatment for her troll-disease, persuaded that it was safe for her to do so, persuaded that it was safe for her to emerge from her seclusion. And Lealle . . . was realizing that she wanted to attempt all that. Maybe she couldn't do it. But it was worth trying. And . . . Ohtavie had crossed Lealle's path, not someone else's. This was Lealle's task—gift?—to attempt.

Papere's glance moved from her to Mamere. "There will be plenty of time for Lealle to help in the soup kitchen when she returns from Fontenay." Papere's tone was firm, but his eyes kind. He set down his fork and stretched a hand toward Mamere. "Margaux, you know why this is important," he added, more gently.

The footmen entered to lay the next course and remove the first. Lealle realized she'd barely touched any of it. She eyed the dishes being arrayed on the table—breasts of roast duckling, minced lamb, and braised celeries. She needed to remember to eat.

Papere's attention returned to Lealle as the footmen retreated.

"The Court of Audire is hearing a—" he hesitated, apparently seeking the right word "—a controversial case this month, and there may be some disturbance among certain—" he paused again "—among the dissenters of Claireau." He meant the small minority of those who had not prospered since the Empire annexed Pavelle, and who blamed the annexation for their circumstances. "The man on trial, Robecheux Laurent, has a number of angry friends still at loose. I doubt their rhetoric will come to much, but . . ." Papere smiled. "I prefer you comfortably in the country for an interval."

Abruptly Lealle remembered Ragged-cap's name. The other boys had shouted to him, "She's a Bazin-berk like her papa, Laurent! A pivot-pute!" She'd thought Laurent his given name, but . . .

Papere's smile gave way to a worried frown. He was too good at reading faces. Her widening eyes must have given her away. "Lealle? Has someone troubled you already?"

She couldn't say no. But she had to say something.

"Will you and Mamere be safe?" she asked.

Papere sat back, relaxing. "Of course, Lélé." Her baby name again. "*You* would be safe enough in Claireau, but there may be unpleasantness, and there's no need for you to suffer it."

Unpleasantness? Was that what Ragged-cap and his friends had directed at her? It had felt like more than unpleasantness. She'd been scared. Not so much the first time, but this second time had been different. The first time, they'd been teasing her. It had been unpleasant. This second time . . . there'd been an ugly, hostile note in their shouts. And if she told her father about it—or let him send her to Fontenay—she could be sure it wouldn't happen again. But it would also mean she gave up on Ohtavie.

It was lucky she'd not needed to use her prepared excuse for her lateness getting home. If she'd already told Papere about the bullies, there would be no avoiding Fontenay.

She picked at her serving of minced lamb, almost surprised at its rich flavor, while she delved for another good excuse.

"Maitresse Aubry said I was ready to begin learning the Phoenix sequence of antiphony," said Lealle. "It's advanced work," she explained. "I—I'm afraid that if I take a break from my lessons at the retreat house, I'll be reviewing the Bellerophon sequence"—the most difficult of the intermediate work—"for weeks before I'm ready again for the more advanced stuff."

Papere, like most people, had no antiphonic abilities. Would he understand how important her antiphonic studies were to her? How she hoped to have antiphony as a tool in solving puzzles like . . . like Ohtavie? She'd never said as much to him. She'd never even really said it to herself. It was only now—in the aftermath of encountering Ohtavie—that some of her dreams for herself were coming clear.

Mamere re-entered the conversation. "Bello, she's progressed far beyond the basics that ensure she avoids dangerous mistakes. If she's completed the intermediate coursework, it's time she stopped altogether." Mamere did *not* approve of Lealle's antiphonic skills. She felt they were inappropriate for the well-mannered society damsel she wanted Lealle to be.

But Papere . . . Papere had always seemed sympathetic to Lealle's desire to do more than grow up and marry an affluent suitor of good family, and then occupy her time ever after with charity work like Mamere. He'd suggested she consider the law, perhaps training as an advocate, even aiming at a judgeship. There were two women serving as justices in Pavelle, and a few more in other cantons of the Empire. And . . . his vision for her had attracted her. It wasn't quite right. She'd not known what exactly would be right. She still didn't know precisely, but helping Ohtavie was the right kind of thing.

Would Papere support Mamere? Or would he support Lealle?

"That's a discussion for another day," said Papere, firmly. He nodded at Mamere, and then turned his focus back to Lealle. "Could you not practice the Bellerophon sequence while at Fontenay, to be sure of not losing ground? Maintain your readiness for the advanced work that way?"

Lealle felt some of the tension ebb from her neck and realized she'd been pressing her fingers against one another, a habit Mamere disliked. Luckily that hand was in her lap. Mamere couldn't have seen it. But

Papere was asking questions, not moving immediately to Mamere's position. There was hope.

"My teacher can see tiny inaccuracies in the angles of the energetic patterns I make and unevenness in my energetic current that I tend not to notice still," she explained. "Of course I must practice, but I'll lose ground if all I do is practice. I—I need Maitresse Aubry's correction." It felt a little odd to admit it. She was more accustomed to railing—mentally—against her teacher's unrelenting exactitude.

"I see," said Papere.

"Bello, we should discuss this before our daughter"—had Mamere placed a slight emphasis on 'our daughter'?—"takes up advanced antiphony!"

"Of course, my dear," said Papere. "But there's no harm done if she learns the preliminaries of this—this *Phoenix* sequence this summer."

Mamere's sigh was not audible. She would no doubt consider an audible sigh vulgar. But Lealle would bet that Mamere was doing more than sighing in the privacy of her thoughts.

"Very well," Mamere acquiesced. "Then Lealle is not starting for Fontenay in the morning?"

"I'll get Bon-Papy all to myself! Ha!" crowed Remy, emerging from his concentration on his braised celery. He must have been really hungry.

Papere's mouth quirked. "What? You've no wish to stay in town and work with your tutor?" he teased.

"Papere!" Remy protested.

Lealle couldn't help giggling. Remy hated school lessons.

Mamere's expression had softened, too. She wanted Remy to be well versed in the classics, as any gentleman should be, but she didn't want him to become a scholar either.

"I think," continued Papere, "that I'll assign Boucher"—one of the baillies who stood guard in his courtroom—"the job of escorting Lealle to and from lessons and visits and outings and such."

Lealle winced.

She could not check on Ohtavie with an escort at her heels.

∞

As the footmen carried away the remains of the second course, Lealle realized that she'd failed to eat much more of it than she'd managed of the first, a mere few mouthfuls.

Remy brightened at the sight of a strawberry jelly and the platter of almond custards arriving. He would! But Lealle needed something more substantial than that. Was the third course going to consist entirely of sweets?

A tray of fresh peach slices landed near her right elbow, and she slid several onto her plate. She liked peaches. But . . . she'd be hungry again within the hour.

When the last footman brought in a casserole of baked eggs, Lealle accepted three with relief and ate two before she spoke again.

"Papere, I'd rather not be accompanied everywhere I go, like . . . like a nursery baby." She tried to sound amused. Not whining. Or desperate.

Papere nodded, to indicate he'd heard her, but continued discussing the historical pageant of the ages that Mamere had brought forward. The pageant was to be performed later in the summer with the intent of soliciting contributions for a new wing on the Sisters of Rouge children's hospital.

Lealle ate her third egg, trying to come up with another way to avoid a continuous escort.

When she looked up, she saw Remy studying her across the epergne.

At the next break in the conversation, he weighed in on his sister's need for accompaniment. "*I* could stay in town, instead of going to visit Bon-papy and Bonne-mémé"—his tone revealed that giving up Fontenay for the summer would hurt—"and keep any bullies off Lealle. They wouldn't dare say anything mean then."

Lealle was touched. It was true he was better at bandying words with would-be tormenters. She'd seen him best one of her classmates—a girl five years older than he—in a verbal battle. But Ragged-cap and his friends had not confined themselves to words. Remy wouldn't fare so well in fisticuffs. He was too small. And Lealle doubted Papere was thinking about mere boys anyway. Would Robecheux Laurent's cronies—grown men—really even notice . . . her?

"If I keep to the main streets, where the armigers patrol, I doubt anyone will bother me," she offered.

"Perhaps not," agreed Papere. "But there was an ugly incident over in Bellefleur last month, when a dissident was sentenced for thievery. We'll be smart, not count on fortune." He nodded to Mamere. "You'll take a chair, my dear, when you go out."

Mamere smiled. "Naturally. But perhaps that might be best for Lealle as well. No need to discommode the baillie. I can't imagine that he'd enjoy tagging at Lealle's heels all day. And surely you can't really spare him. Indeed"—Mamere tilted her head—"I almost think Lealle will escape more notice, if she simply adheres to her usual ways. You know the children at school, and those who also have lessons at the retreat house, will observe Lealle arriving in a sedan chair, or accompanied by the baillie, and remark upon it. It wouldn't be pleasant for her."

Lealle swallowed. The image conjured by Mamere's words was all too accurate. But who would have thought Mamere would champion Lealle's cause. She usually advocated less freedom for her daughter, not more.

"But you mustn't frequent the back lanes you seem to prefer," continued Mamere. "Will you agree to that?"

Lealle nodded. She had every intention of avoiding the back lanes. That was where Ragged-cap had caught her both times.

"Make a spoken response, dear," chided Mamere. "Gestures are for those who do not mind misunderstandings."

"I'll avoid the back lanes," said Lealle.

"Bello?" Mamere raised her left brow. "Will that suffice?"

Papere looked bemused. It was rare that Mamere went against his direction.

"Remy to Fontenay until the month of Labresse, Lealle to join him then, and an effort made for her to walk with friends," he temporized.

He turned to Lealle. "Will you do that?" he asked.

She started to nod, but then remembered Mamere's stricture. "Yes, Papere," she answered aloud.

Papere did nod. "Very well," he agreed.

The Second Day

Complications

Chapter Four

OHTAVIE AWOKE in the night, heart pounding from a dream of falling, falling endlessly. A monster had broken through the lilacs in the garden, and she'd turned to run, but a fold of canvas entrapped her foot, and she fell. And fell. A pit opening beneath her into endless darkness swallowed her whole.

Clutching at the pendant beneath her blouse, she reassured herself: it was just a dream.

Moonlight shone in through the windows across from her bed, making rectangles of silver on the floor boards and catching the edges of her dressing table. The night was very quiet. She lay alone in her bedroom, alone and unthreatened.

She should draw the curtains across the windows—why hadn't she done so when she lay down to sleep? Why was she lying on her back, when she preferred her side? And why was her right foot throbbing so uncomfortably?

Abruptly it all came back to her: the boys in the garden, her flight, Lealle.

There *had* been an intruder. She *had* fallen. Her foot was broken. And her long secrecy . . . was broken also.

Would Lealle keep her promise to say nothing? The girl was . . . young, accustomed, no doubt, to obeying her elders. Lealle had promised in good faith. Ohtavie knew she had. But . . . there were ways to make a child speak. Ohtavie knew that also.

So she might not be safe, here, any longer.

If they came for her—the mob, to burn her, or the watch, to behead her—what would she do then? Would she fight with her troll-magery? That was the exact event that they feared, the mob and the troll watch: that a witch—or a warlock—would massacre hundreds in her madness and power.

In Ohtavie's case, their fear was groundless. She'd not continued her practice of enigmology—antiphony, as the Giralliyans called it—after the troll-disease claimed her.

Oh, she could still do little things: summon mage light, strengthen a fraying stitch in a worn glove, or keep a cooling cup of tea warm. But she'd not pursued the greater powers that troll-magery—*incantatio*—supposedly permitted.

No, if they came for her . . . she must surrender. Let them drag her from her house. Suffer the stoning, the fire, or the beheading.

Ohtavie shuddered.

Please all the saints that it would not come to that. Lealle would say nothing and eventually forget that she had something to say nothing about. And Ohtavie would return to her safe obscurity.

She started to turn onto her side, and her foot twinged.

She really should check it. Be sure the blood still reached to her toes, though the saints only knew what she would do if it didn't. Remove the immobilizing plaster? She needed that plaster in order for her foot to heal straight.

Still, she should check. If her toes were white—or worse—bluish, the flesh might grow gangrenous. She had to check.

The first step was to sit up, and then ease the sheet and blanket down. It was surprising how difficult these simple tasks became, when a bulky and heavy chunk of plaster weighed down one appendage.

But she managed it.

The cast and her toes looked very white in the moonlight that now reached the end of her bed.

She needed more than moonlight for examining her foot. She needed half a dozen candles, at the least, better a full dozen. And she had precisely none. Neither she nor Lealle had brought one with them in the afternoon.

Her crutches leaned against the wall right beside the head of the bed. She could go in search of candles. But the thought of crutching her way to the cupboard that held them—trivial with a sound foot, a labor with an injured one—daunted her.

Very well.

She would summon mage light.

She shifted around in the bed. She needed a straight spine for this, and she wouldn't be sitting cross-legged, not with that plaster cast. She closed her eyes and let her sit bones settle, let her knees go soft, still supported by the pillow Lealle had placed under them. She slowed her breathing: gently in, even more gently out.

The curling traceries of silver light that formed her energetic arcs sprang to life in her mind's eye, scrolling through the core of her body, connecting the root radix at her base—glowing a muted silver—to her belly radix—a subdued, pearlescent white—and on up the rest of the radices of her torso to her crown.

None of her radices were in the right place. The root radix was a little high. The crown radix at her head was a little low. That was what it was to be a troll. The radices were no longer anchored as they were in a healthy person. Unanchored, the radices drifted, slowly deforming the arcs that connected them. And the energetic deformation eventually manifested in the flesh.

Ohtavie's hair was silver, because her crown radix was low. Ohtavie's nose was elongated and her ears enlarged, because her brow and throat radices were low. If she lived long enough, the demi-radices in her palms would drift, elongating and twisting her thumbs.

But now was not the moment to assess her troll-disease. There was nothing that could be done about it. There never had been.

Now she must summon *enigmatic* light—mage light.

She *reached*, in that way that only the enigmatical permitted, and in her mind's eye silver sparkles of light emerged from each of her seven major radices—root, belly, plexus, heart, throat, brow, and crown—to flow along her arcs to her heart and then down her arms to her palms. She cupped her hands, and the stream of sparks leapt from her palms to form a globe in the space above them.

She concentrated, still with her eyes closed, seeing the *enigmatic* flow with senses other than the sight of her body's eyes.

The silver blue natural to mage light would not work for her purpose. She needed the clear light of day to see if her toes were properly rosy.

She moved her hands slightly, bringing the thumbs closer to one another, transforming the open cup of her fingers into an enclosing sphere, all the while drawing enigmatically from her radices.

The darkness behind her eyelids became a warmer black, then warmer still, and finally a dark red.

She opened her eyes.

A glowing sphere of clear light hovered just above the loose enclosure of her hands. She lifted them, and the light lifted too. When it neared the ceiling, she initiated the inner constriction—difficult with her unpracticed enigmatic skills—that would transfer the sphere of light from the energy streaming out of her palms to a fountain rising from her crown.

There.

Now she could look at her toes.

She allowed her hands to fall to her sides and tipped her gaze down.

Her toes were pink, thank the saints. A little puffy, yes, but not so much that the pressure of the cast cut off their circulation. She would heal straight. Thanks to Lealle.

She glanced around her bedchamber. The dark wood of the dressing table was indeed bare of a candlestick. Just a brush, comb, and hand mirror lay on its surface. A fold of curtain from one of the flanking windows was caught between the back corner of the table and the wall. Ohtavie loved those curtains.

When Madame Garnier, the old housekeeper, had inhabited these rooms, she'd spread the bed with a coverlet of pink silk, the pink a little darker than the pale hue of the roses splattered across the nubby ecru of the curtains. Ohtavie had *not* cared for that coverlet. But she did love those curtains.

The curtains—

Dear Thiyaude on His throne. The curtains hung *beside* the windows, not across them, with her mage light shining like a small sun, illuminating the room, illuminating *Ohtavie,* for all to see through the unobstructed glass panes. If anyone stood in the lane or on Rue Étroit— or even Balard Square, at the right angle—that someone now knew the Maison de Bellay was inhabited. If they were paying attention, they now knew the inhabitant was a troll.

Horrified, Ohtavie doused her mage light.

Then she lay and shook.

Had anyone seen her? It was very late—or early—well past midnight. She knew that by the position of the moon, low in the west, moving toward moonset.

Were any of the families on Balard Square giving an entertainment, something that might send guests streaming away all through the small hours? If there were a party or a ball, someone might have seen her light, seen Ohtavie. If there were not . . . she might still be safe.

What was the use of Lealle staying silent, if Ohtavie herself announced her own presence. She had to be more careful.

No more light at night—of any kind, even candlelight. And no more toying with the idea of going out into the garden by starlight. That was how that terrace door had come to be unlocked. A little over a sennight ago, when the moon was new, she'd stood at that door, hesitating with the bolt drawn, trying to turn the knob and step out onto the terrace.

The first of the lilacs had just begun to bloom, and she'd longed to smell their fresh, sweet scent.

But she'd been no more able to turn that knob and step through that doorway than she'd been able to draw the lace curtain aside to look out on Balard Square this morning. Yesterday morning, she supposed, since midnight had passed.

She'd turned the knob of the terrace door a quarter turn, and then rushed away from the exit, rushed away from the starlight, to hide beneath her bedcovers like a scared child. Leaving the door unlocked.

She'd forgotten that the bolt no longer secured the entrance.

Until today, when Lealle had come through it.

∞

Ohtavie awoke next to daylight, the sky pale in the dawning outside her windows, the lane still in shadow. When the sunlight touched the trees, birdsong would fill the air, but this was the moment when all lay still and quiet.

She stirred, trying to ease the uncomfortable stiffness in her joints produced by lying on her back all through the night. Her sheets rustled, giving up the fragrance of lavender potpourri, and the bedstead creaked slightly. She swallowed, aware of how dry her mouth had grown. If only she could pull the bell cord that still hung by the bed she'd occupied as a daughter of the house and summon a maid who would bring her chocolate—or better, mint tea—to sluice away the sourness on her tongue.

But no servant would be coming to this room, or any room in the house. If she wished for tea or anything else, she must see to it. And she'd better.

Her clothes had that rumpled, coarse feeling that came from wearing them to sleep in. And a visit to the water closet was fast becoming a matter of urgency. At least her right foot no longer pained her. It would, later in the day, she knew.

Awkwardly, she hitched herself to sitting. The plaster cast on her foot wasn't quite as heavy as it had been—perhaps it had finished drying—but maneuvering it out from under the covers wasn't easy. When she swung her legs over the edge of the bed, her foot started aching abruptly, not liking the vertical position. So. Later was now.

Crutching her way to the water closet in the servants' hall and back was every bit as laborious as she might have expected. Getting herself dressed—wobbling on one foot in front of her wardrobe—was worse. And it all took about twice as long as it should. By the time she was ready to head for the kitchen wing, it felt like she ought to be done with all morning endeavors.

Pressing her lips straight, she set off.

In the main kitchen, she checked the pass-through beside the outer door. Nothing.

But there had been a delivery just a few days ago, several jars of strawberry preserves and just one of pickled greens. And the shelves of the cook's pantry were very full, overly full.

The deliveries from the Dubois farm had been arranged long ago for a household with a full family and a staff of over forty. Ohtavie had reduced the standing orders as she reduced her staff, but hadn't thought to pare them down yet more before she dismissed the last of the servants. She'd not risked a trip out to the farm. She'd already been pent within the house for years by that time.

So the foodstuffs remained calibrated for eight, not one—paid for all these years by standing instructions at the bank serving the De Bellay family.

Repressing a sigh, she reached for a small crock of duck confit and stopped. How would she carry it?

She looked at her apron, which did have a pocket, but one too narrow to take the crock. She'd have to improvise.

Leaning against one of the shelf posts, her crutches loose under her arms, she gathered the apron at its hem and lifted it to form a pouch, slipped the crock into that pouch, and tucked the hem firmly into the apron's waistband. There. Would it hold? She thought it would.

Gingerly, she moved back toward the massive table at the kitchen's center, the heavy crock knocking at her thighs, her crutches more stable on the flagstone floor than they had been on the wood in the hallways.

Then it all fell apart.

One corner of the apron hem came untucked, tipping the crock to the floor, where it smashed in a spray of ceramic fragments followed by the splat of the potted meats within. Her right crutch skidded on the mess, and she went down, hard, on her right side.

For a moment, she just lay there, horrified and with the wind knocked out of her. Had she broken her arm this time? How in the north would she manage with a broken foot *and* a broken arm? The thing was impossible.

Then she heard a key turning in the kitchen door onto the lane. *Another* intruder! Galvanized, she turned over and sat up, grabbing one of the fallen crutches.

The door opened to reveal Lealle, haloed by the rising sun and heralded by a cacophony of birdsong. The girl's dark curls were neatly braided this time, and she wore a pretty frock of mint green, with her fichu neatly tucked into its sash. Her eyes went very wide when she spotted Ohtavie on the floor, brandishing a crutch.

"Are you hurt?" she gasped.

"Shut the door!" Ohtavie snapped, habit trumping her relief. If her neighbors saw that door open . . .

It wasn't relief that made her snap, relief that help had arrived. Of course not. Of course she was relieved that the intruder was Lealle, not someone else.

"I'm not hurt," Ohtavie added. "Not *newly* hurt," she corrected herself. Then she checked, moving the arm slightly, noting the fresh bruise on her wrist, but realizing that her elbow and shoulder were fine. She'd been lucky.

"I knew those crutches were too wobbly," said Lealle, distress in her voice.

"They're better than no crutches at all," Ohtavie replied crisply.

Lealle nodded and bit her lower lip. "I think I should check to be sure you've not broken another bone," she said.

Ohtavie swallowed her instinctive protest. Lealle's intrusion might be uncomfortable—*was* uncomfortable—but the girl was no enemy. She meant to help. And Ohtavie needed help, however much she wished she didn't.

Like yesterday, Lealle's enigmatic scrutiny did not hurt. Indeed it soothed the bruise on her wrist. And when the girl extended her examination to Ohtavie's foot, it eased the ache there as well.

Lealle sat back on her heels with a sigh when she was done. "You're all right," she said, relief in her voice.

Ohtavie found herself wanting to snap irritably again. Was it just that she was so unaccustomed to receiving help? That she hated needing help? Or . . . that, down beneath her resistance and unease, she longed for a little human caring? She forced herself to quell her irritability.

"Thank you," she said instead.

"Shall I—shall I tidy up?" asked Lealle.

Ohtavie nodded. "I'd appreciate that," she answered. This time she managed her tone of voice better.

Lealle brightened and got to work.

Ohtavie could see that the girl was not practiced at such tasks. Small wonder. She was clearly a gently bred child, like Ohtavie had once been herself, with little experience of wiping up spills, sweeping up messes, or washing dirtied flagstones. But Ohtavie made suggestions, and Lealle applied them, along with some common sense, to get the job done, albeit with some awkwardness and false starts.

When the floor was clean, and Ohtavie wearing fresh clothes, Lealle asked if she'd broken her fast.

"Have you?" Ohtavie queried in return.

Lealle smiled shyly. "I snuck out before breakfast," she confessed.

"So I supposed," said Ohtavie. "Will you not join me, then?"

Lealle's smile grew less tentative. "I'd like that," she said.

Lealle proved no more experienced at serving a meal than she'd been at sweeping or washing, but spooning duck confit from a new crock onto plates, peach preserves into bowls, and filling two goblets with water was not beyond her, again despite some clumsiness.

As they sat side by side at the kitchen table, Ohtavie noted that Lealle ate gracefully and without having to pay much attention to what she was doing, able to converse easily while she ate. Decidedly, her skills were those of Claireau's elite.

Lealle glanced at Ohtavie, her eyes curious. "Do you never cook your meals?" she asked. "This is delicious cold, but I shouldn't think everything would be."

"I dare not risk smoke rising from the chimney," Ohtavie explained. "And most preserved fruits and vegetables and meats taste good, provided they were prepared properly."

"Then in winter, when it is cold, how do you stay warm?" Lealle asked.

"If the fogs have risen from the river, I'll light a small fire. Otherwise, I wear my papa's old wool overcoat and wrap up in blankets when I am sitting."

Lealle nodded.

"On your way home yesterday, were you able to avoid the bullies who had chased you into my garden?" Ohtavie asked in her turn.

"I didn't see them," Lealle answered. "And I'll stay to the more traveled streets going forward. I shouldn't think they will risk being *seen* at mischief."

Lealle looked down at her plate, suddenly and unexpectedly awkward. "I have something for you," she said. Then she thrust her hand into a pocket in the side of her frock, drew it out, and set two small cups made of a flexible red-brown substance on the table. "I didn't think I could carry the crutches our coachman used last year through the streets without causing remark, but these are the rubber caps from their tips. If they fit your crutches, you'd be a lot steadier, wouldn't you?"

"I would!" agreed Ohtavie, feeling a surge of real hope. "Let's try them!"

They were a tight fit, but they fit. Unfortunately they also added just enough height to the crutches that Ohtavie could no longer grip the hand pieces. She fought the discouragement that swept over her. There had to be some way to make this work.

Lealle was frowning, too, but not with discouragement. More as if she were parsing a difficult mathematical problem. "Our groundskeeper has a small croft near the kitchen gardens with all sorts of tools in it," she said. "I remember he fixed my little brother's wagon once. Remy told me all about it. How old M'sieur Lemoine used a—a *saw*"—Lealle was clearly unfamiliar with the name of the tool—"to cut off the shaft, which was broken, before he attached a new and longer one. Did—did your groundskeeper ever have a workroom like that?"

Ohtavie felt a chill pass through her. The Maison de Bellay did indeed possess such a craftsman's retreat, but not in the gardens— which were much less extensive than those of a country house. In the cellars. The idea of Lealle descending to the cellars . . . no. Ohtavie couldn't allow that.

∽

As a child, Ohtavie had loved the Maison de Bellay's cellars. Not the ordinary ones under the kitchen wing, where the roots and wines were stored, but the mysterious ones where no one ever seemed to go. They were so shadowy, with their tall vaulted ceilings, oddly shaped columns, and squashed crescent windows high up on their walls.

When she would sneak down the narrow spiral steps tucked behind and beneath the grand front stairway that connected the foyer there to the upper floors, she used to imagine that she'd find a treasure in a locked and forgotten chest, or a magical portal to an enchanted land in one of the abandoned rooms.

Or she dreamed that the mysterious spirit of the evening dwelt there, her shadowy beauty refreshed by the underground darkness during the day, and made ready for her emergence at dusk. Or perhaps a lovely queen from the days of old lingered in the shadows, working a magic of immortality from the darkness.

When Ohtavie began learning the mythology of ancient Ennecy and read the legend of the monster who lurked at the center of a buried labyrinth, discovered by the hero Tyge and helped by the princess Aranya, she rebuilt her imaginings from the foundations up.

No longer were the cellars a treasure vault or a secret refuge or a hidden palace. No, they were a stone maze, where a fearsome beast inhabited its inmost chamber. But the beast was both terrifying and wonderful, depending on the heart of the one who found him. Approached with courage and generosity, he would grant miracles. Sought in desperation or greed, he would bequeath fell dooms.

And one day, if Ohtavie searched cleverly and persistently enough, she would find him.

No one knew of her secret forays to the cellars, but still she'd been unable to explore as thoroughly as she wished, because all too many of the spaces had neither windows nor gas lamps nor even oil lanterns to push the darkness back. The shadows lured her, rather than scaring her, but even she needed to see where to place her feet.

All that changed on the day Grandmere invaded the schoolroom.

Ohtavie was eleven and had grown very proficient with her addition and subtraction, her ability to locate Pavelle and neighboring Auberon on the globe, and her skill on the pianoforte and the mandolin. But she was new to magic—enigmology, as it was called in those days, before Pavelle was annexed by the Empire.

Not only was she new to enigmology, but she was quite bad at it, and she didn't want to be. She wanted to be good at it, the way she was good at arithmetic and grammar and singing.

Her teacher had reminded her that she'd needed to practice all those things she was good at before she'd become skilled, and so she was practicing the simplest of the enigmatic formularies: mage light.

She was alone. She'd drawn the curtains over the windows and turned down the gas lights to the merest glimmer. They'd been lit, because the day was rainy and gray.

And just as she succeeded in conjuring the globe of soft blue radiance, very pleased with herself indeed, Grandmere thrust the schoolroom door open and stalked through it, her dark brocade skirts swishing imperiously and her black eyes snapping with anger.

"So!" Grandmere exclaimed. "I might have known it! Do I find you practicing sums on your slate? Or writing a list of all the principle cities in Pavelle? Or even enduring your hour of the backboard? Or anything worthwhile at all? No! Instead you dabble in magery the moment my attention spares you!"

If Mamere had been present, Ohtavie would have had to be circumspect in her response. Mamere hated it when Ohtavie argued with Grandmere. But Mamere was not present, and Ohtavie had chosen to defend her choice of activity.

"Maitresse Blanchet said I should practice. So there!" she'd insisted.

Grandmere stood even taller, and her eyes snapped even more fiercely. "Maitresse may have said you should practice, but I doubt she said you should disrespect your elders, missy!"

But Ohtavie had refused to back down. "But you disrespect me!" she'd accused.

Grandmere had seized her by the arm, her fingers very hard and bony, and jerked Ohtavie to the inner corner of the schoolroom and forcibly sat her down in a chair facing the walls.

"You will stay here all the afternoon," Grandmere had commanded. "I will fetch you when it is time for dinner, unless I can persuade your mother that bread and water in solitude is the proper treatment for such an impudent little hussy as you!"

And then Grandmere had swept out, closing the door behind her a touch too firmly for good manners.

Ohtavie had been too angry herself to do anything but sit and seethe for a few moments. How dare Grandmere bruise her arm! How dare Grandmere condemn her practice of enigmology! How dare Grandmere punish her at all?

And then it occurred to her that Grandmere did not, in fact, *have* the authority to punish her. Mamere always insisted that Ohtavie treat her great grandmother with respect, and would often require Ohtavie to apologize for rudeness. But Mamere had always been gentle and reasonable with the consequences she imposed. And she'd never allowed Grandmere to determine what those consequences would be.

Grinning, Ohtavie bounced up out of her chair, and then she had the most marvelous idea.

If she took her practice of mage light to the cellars, she could explore all those unexplored antechambers and galleries and niches hidden in darkness. What might she find? Her eagerness washed away her resentment as she scampered for the front stairs. They were rarely used, so it was unlikely anyone would intercept her before she reached the entirely unused cellar steps.

In the cellars, surrounded by shadows and the aroma of cold stone, she found the summoning of mage light to be easier than it had ever been above ground. Did enigmology flow more readily when you really needed its result, Ohtavie wondered for a moment, and then dismissed the question as she entered the darkness.

And it was all more interesting than she would have expected for the foundations of a house. Perhaps the labyrinth of her imaginings, haunted by—or hallowed by—its terrible beast really might be present. The stone pillars were sculpted to resemble fantastic creatures—tree women, leaping gryphons, and rearing pegasi. Bas relief murals depicted scenes out of myth, drowned lands rescued from the sea, a magical sword dispelling a whirlwind. Really, it was more like a temple than anything else. Had the Maison de Bellay been built atop ancient ruins from the past? Ohtavie didn't know—Mamere and Papa had never said anything of the sort—but a stone block carved all over with fruiting vines looked remarkably like an altar.

There were things that didn't fit in a temple, however. Wooden crates filled with crumbling scrolls. Or did priestesses keep records of their rites? But surely the smith's anvil possessed no sacred connection. Or did it? Hadn't the ancient forest tribes of the north worshipped a smith-god?

On her way back toward the stairs and the daylight, she discovered evidence of something hidden by deliberate artifice rather than by the happenstance of darkness. In a room with paired niches in each of its four walls, one niche was bricked up. But no mortar secured the bricks. They were merely neatly stacked.

What secret lay behind them?

If she really wanted to know, Ohtavie could dismantle the stack. Brick by brick.

Chapter Five

LEALLE DIDN'T understand Ohtavie's reluctance to permit access to the cellars. It was almost as though the troll-woman believed monsters or ghosts lurked down in the darkness. But that wasn't it. Even Remy knew better, and Ohtavie didn't say it was haunts. Or any specific danger.

Lealle had overborne her protests, determined to render Ohtavie's crutches safer. Only when Lealle started for the stairs in the hallway outside the kitchen did Ohtavie explain how to find the carpenter's workshop, insisting in the same breath that Lealle stay strictly away from the vast sprawl of the cellars adjacent to the carpenter's space.

"I'm not going *exploring*," Lealle had replied, a little exasperated by the argument.

Had Ohtavie blushed? Ever so slightly? Perhaps not. But Lealle suspected the troll-woman was growing more willing to accept help— even wishing it—and reluctant to let that help out of sight.

The carpenter's shop was exactly where Ohtavie said it would be, in the undercroft right next to where the stairs debouched. An array of half-moon windows at the top of the outer wall let in a flood of morning light. Shelves and pegs on the inner wall held a large collection of tools, very dusty, and most of them mysterious to Lealle in their functions.

But she understood the sturdy table in the middle of the space well enough, along with the big clamp fastened to its edge. Finding the cutting tool she needed—the saw—might have been difficult if Remy hadn't dragged her to old Lemoine's workshop to see the one the carpenter had used to fix his wagon. But he had, so she knew what she was looking for.

She pinched her thumb getting the first crutch secured in the clamp.

Brandishing the saw, she hesitated. She need only remove a finger's width of the crutch tip to make it short enough for the rubber caps. But if she removed a full hand's width from each crutch, they would actually be the proper height for Ohtavie. The rubber caps alone would make the crutches much safer. But they'd be safer still, if they were the proper height.

Lealle nodded firmly, and then set the saw blade to the wood.

It was much harder than she'd thought it would be.

At first the saw teeth slipped on the hard surface of the wood, not biting in or cutting at all. Then they stuck so firmly that she couldn't move the blade. Eventually she discovered that if she moved the saw in one direction only—pulling it toward her, then lifting it and placing it down afresh for another pull toward her—she could make a groove. And once she had that groove, she could saw back and forth very lightly.

The sawdust sifted down to the floor, catching the light as it fell. The scent of the sawn wood rose delicately on the cool air.

It felt like it took forever. No wonder Ohtavie hadn't wanted her to do this. Lealle really might disappear into—not the cellars—but the workshop, sawing and sawing until she missed the start of school and her lessons altogether.

When she got near the end of her cut, the handspan of wood at the end broke off, taking a great splinter of wood with it. But she'd done it! And she suspected it hadn't really taken as long as she'd felt it had. That was just her unfamiliarity with the tool and the task.

When she got the first crutch unclamped, and the second one clamped, she measured the shortened crutch against the still-long one, marking her cut with a piece of carpenter's chalk.

This time it went more smoothly, and she knew to go much more gently at the end, so that the piece came off cleanly, without making a jagged splinter. There was only one problem. The round stalks of the crutches were thicker at their new ends than they had been at their old tips. The rubber cap fit, with a little stretching, on the crutch with the splinter removed. She couldn't get either cap to fit the unsplintered crutch.

Lealle gritted her teeth in frustration. Shun it! She was going to make this work. (And without apologizing—even mentally—to Mamere for the swear word, either.)

She closed her eyes almost without thinking and began the focusing discipline for antiphony. Slow breath in. Slow breath out. And then the sparkling traceries of her energetic arcs bloomed in her mind's sight.

Drawing from deep within herself—from the glowing radices that fed those sparking arcs—she directed the antiphonic energies along the arcs of her arms, through the demi-radices of her palms, and out her fingertips onto the too-thick stem of the crutch. The wood appeared as a mass of soft, irregular ovals, glowing gently green to her inner vision. She *squeezed*, and the ovals shrunk.

Once should be enough. She didn't want the wood to become too small. Then the rubber cap would be too large and not stay attached.

She allowed the inner vision to fade.

It still took some wrestling to get the rubber cap over the wood, but it went. And it wouldn't be falling off.

She looked around for something she could stand on to check the length of the crutches against herself. She was a little shorter than Ohtavie. Surely there would be some scraps of wood that she could stack. This was a carpenter's shop, after all.

But it wasn't an active one. And she couldn't find any scraps. Or anything else that might do either.

Of course, she could always go back upstairs and measure the crutches against Ohtavie herself. But . . . Lealle wanted them to be exactly right when she presented them. And if they weren't right . . . Ohtavie might insist they were good enough. She'd not wanted Lealle going down in the cellars in the first place. She'd undoubtedly protest her descending anew to make minor adjustments.

I'll just look in the nearby spaces, she told herself. It won't take long.

The adjacent room was utterly empty: cracked slate floor, blank stone walls, dirty half-moon windows, and nothing else. The next two were the same. But the next possessed four pillars sculpted to resemble great, twining serpents. And the next—windowless—featured a bunch of bricks stacked below a partially bricked-in niche in the wall.

Lealle brought up her mage light without thinking—the room was dark, without windows—and retrieved two of the bricks. She noticed each wall had paired niches, but that seven of the eight recesses were open. And empty. Lealle shook her head. Why had one niche, but none of the others, been bricked up? And why did the snake room have such ornate and sinister columns? It was an odd find in an ordinary house. Perhaps Ohtavie had good reasons for her avoidance of the cellars.

But never mind. Lealle had things of her own to worry about.

Back in the workshop, she stood with one foot on each brick and arranged the crutches under her arms. The arm cradles touched near the top of her ribs, which was where they should. But the hand pieces were entirely out of reach from her grip.

Lealle bit her lip. Hard.

Shun it! Why hadn't she realized that merely making the crutches shorter wouldn't be enough? Old Lemoine would have known. But she had not.

∾

Ohtavie sat at the kitchen table, looking out at the brightening morning and thinking.

Lealle had tidied up before she descended to the cellars with the crutches, and there was nothing for Ohtavie to do. Which should have been a good thing. Even with crutches, she'd barely managed to dress and wash her hands and face. She'd not managed to serve herself breakfast. Carrying the dirty dishes to the scullery, washing them in the sink she favored, and setting them to dry on the drainboard would have been entirely beyond her. All that would have happened would have been another mess of broken crockery and food fragments. Even with crutches.

Without the crutches, taken into the cellars with Lealle . . . the remains of the meal would have had to stay on the table.

She *was* grateful that Lealle was here.

But she didn't want to be, because . . . there were so many reasons why. She was accustomed to being alone. She didn't trust that someone—anyone—knowing of her existence was safe. Oh, the last of the servants she'd dismissed a dozen years ago undoubtedly remembered her, but they had been almost like family in their loyalty. And surely their memories of her must be very faded after such a stretch of time. They would have no reason to think of her, or speak of her, now.

How many times could Lealle visit the Maison de Bellay without being discovered by someone? Her nurse? Her mother? A too-astute stranger? Once was a risk. Twice . . . even more of a risk. Too much of a risk.

The story spread by Ohtavie's old housekeeper—that the heir to the De Bellay estate had no interest in the Claireau mansion, and merely sent his agent at irregular intervals to assess the property and see to its maintenance—would explain the small anomalies that Ohtavie's presence might produce. But it wouldn't cover regular visits by a schoolgirl.

Those were the obvious reasons, the reasons Ohtavie felt comfortable admitting to herself.

But there were less palatable reasons. Ohtavie had enjoyed their conversation over breakfast, and she could not afford to long for human company. She was a troll, and trolls could not—should not—expect companionship. She *must* retain her contentment with solitude. And she *must* evolve ways to manage on her own.

Aside from loneliness and a desire for . . . a friend?—which she must *not* cultivate—she couldn't grow dependent on Lealle to solve the challenges of ordinary living for her. She needed to be able to fix her own meals, tidy up after them, and do all the other small chores required to get through the day.

She touched the pendant beneath her blouse and shifted in her chair, uncomfortable with her thoughts, and aware that her foot was throbbing again. Lealle's enigmatic examination had soothed the ache, but sitting with the limb down was causing it to swell a little.

She turned sideways and used her hands to help lift the leg onto the seat of Lealle's chair. The angle was awkward, producing an uncomfortable pull in the back of her thigh, but elevating the foot brought almost immediate relief to the throbbing tightness beneath the plaster cast.

She repressed a sigh.

There was little point in repining over what had happened. What had happened . . . had happened. She'd fallen and broken her foot. Lealle had helped her. So be it. She needed to look to the future, not the past. She must insist that Lealle promise not to visit her again. And she must learn to manage on her own. She could. She would. She'd managed to learn everything that needed doing after she'd dismissed the servants. It hadn't been easy, but she'd done it. She could do this too.

Where was the girl? Surely she'd been down in the cellar workshop long enough to shorten those too-tall crutches three times over. She couldn't truly have encountered danger. Could she?

Ohtavie's fear of the cellars came not from her knowledge of any positive threat, but from what had happened to her there, a peril of the past, long diffused. But if Lealle didn't emerge soon . . . Ohtavie was going after her. She could lower herself to the floor and scoot across it to the hallway where the nearest stair descended, and go down the steps sitting. She was not so helpless as she felt. There were ways to get around without standing or walking, and she would use them as she must.

A step sounded in the hallway.

Ohtavie looked up from contemplating her foot on the chair in front of her to see Lealle march through the kitchen doorway, crutches held triumphantly before her.

"I did it!" the girl announced, her voice jubilant. "I think they'll be perfect." She ducked her head slightly. Remembering modesty? Embarrassed at her boasting? "I *hope* they'll be perfect," she corrected herself.

"Let's see them," said Ohtavie, smiling and reaching out her hands.

Lealle placed the crutches in them.

The rubber caps had thinned at their rims, where they stretched tightly around the bottom stalk of each crutch. Ohtavie could see a gouge of lighter wood, where a large splinter had come away, with rough edges. She would need to be careful not to knock her legs with that part of the crutch, but she wouldn't, not using them properly.

The repair to the hand grips was much more interesting. It looked almost as though the wood had become clay or mud and then been sculpted into position, with rounded indentations for Ohtavie's fingers.

"How did you do this?" Ohtavie asked, curious. Surely the girl couldn't possess wood carving skills. Nor had she been absent long enough for such a project.

"It was hard sawing off the crutch tips," Lealle explained, gesturing. "I—I almost couldn't do it. At first."

Ohtavie nodded. She remembered how hard some of the domestic chores she'd had to learn had been, at first.

Lealle continued, describing how the hand grips had been too low. "I knew I could never saw them loose, not without ruining them. And even if I didn't ruin them, how would I reattach them? I'm sure Old

Lemoine could do it easily, but—but I hadn't the least idea. And even if I did, the knowing wouldn't mean the doing was something I could manage."

Ohtavie nodded again. She understood that, too, all too well.

"So what did you do?" she asked.

Lealle's chin came up. "I moved them antiphonically!"

Ohtavie swallowed. Enigmology—antiphony—would always make her uneasy, but she was well aware that most practitioners used it without harm. She repressed her urge to open her inner sight so that she could check that Lealle's radices remained anchored. Of course the girl was fine. She'd not tried something beyond her strength, clearly. There was no sense of strain in her. She'd not—

Ohtavie cut off that line of thought. Lealle was *fine*. "Shall I try them?" Ohtavie asked.

Lealle nodded eagerly. "I stood on two bricks to check their length, but . . ." The girl bit her lower lip.

Two bricks?

Ohtavie barely refrained from shaking her head. She wouldn't think about bricks.

Instead she leaned the crutches against the table, slid her casted foot off the chair seat, and stood up, balancing herself on her own chair back. Then she maneuvered the crutches beneath her arms, where their cradles touched her upper ribs, and gripped the hand pieces, which were exactly within reach. Every element was where it was supposed to be. The cradles weren't jammed into her armpits. The hand grips weren't nearly beyond the curl of her fingers. The crutches weren't on the verge of skating away from her under the least provocation. She felt steady and stable.

"They fit!" Lealle exclaimed joyfully, clapping her hands.

Ohtavie smiled. "They fit," she agreed. And she swung them forward, planted them, and then swung herself through. How secure she felt! It was marvelous. Again! Swing the crutches forward, plant them—those rubber caps were lovely and gripping on the flagstones—swing herself through.

She increased her speed. Swing, plant, swing. *Swing, plant, swing.* She was trundling along.

She turned and came back beside the table, stopping in front of Lealle, who'd stood watching her. The girl bounced on her toes in her excitement.

"I'm so glad!" Lealle said.

Ohtavie suspected she was beaming as brightly as was her young benefactor. She calmed herself before she spoke. Enthusiasm was one thing. Undignified enthusiasm felt . . . unseemly.

"Thank you, sweetheart," she finally said, sincere, but collected.

Lealle nodded and glanced out the window. The sun had risen above the roofline of the neighboring house, and Ohtavie could just see over the garden wall that a milkman was exchanging a few words with a kitchenmaid at the neighbor's door onto the lane.

"You should go," said Ohtavie.

"I'm almost late for school," Lealle admitted.

"Lealle . . ." Ohtavie hesitated. This conversation had to happen now. But she almost hated to spoil Lealle's pleasure by the request she was going to make. "Your help has been invaluable. Truly. Things would have been very difficult, perhaps even dangerous for me, without you."

Lealle's face flushed rosily, and her eyelids lowered.

"I appreciate all you've done for me. And I appreciate your silence to others about me," Ohtavie continued.

"I've kept my promise," Lealle reassured her.

"I know you have," said Ohtavie. "And now I need you to promise something else. Promise me that you won't return again."

Lealle's bright face dimmed.

"Every time you visit me, the risk that I shall be discovered increases," Ohtavie said. "And there's risk to you as well. An angry mob does not discern between the innocent and the guilty so reliably."

"But it's not like that anymore," insisted Lealle. "Things have changed!"

"Can you tell me that it was not a troll they hounded through the streets three years ago?" asked Ohtavie.

"Cassende Ridault," gasped Lealle. "Maitresse Ridault," she amended.

Ohtavie refrained from nodding. "Perhaps the law has changed, but people have not. And they are right to be afraid. Trolls are dangerous."

"But Maitresse Ridault escaped! And she came back! She—she lives in her cottage in Osier and—and visits her grandchildren every third day, when she comes into Claireau for her treatment."

That made no sense. There was no treatment for trolls.

"Lealle, you must not visit me again. I shall manage very well with these. Very well, indeed." She patted a crutch with one hand. "Promise me!"

Lealle's chin firmed. "I won't."

"When you lock the door behind you, place the key in the milk pass-through," said Ohtavie. "Then we'll be finished." She felt rueful. This was not the right ending note. "I'll always be grateful, you know," she added. "And I'll always remember you."

"I'll check on you this afternoon. After my antiphony lesson," said Lealle. Her eyes had reddened slightly.

"You mustn't," said Ohtavie.

Abruptly Lealle leaned forward, clutched Ohtavie around the shoulders in a quick embrace, and then whirled away to the side door. A moment later, she was through it. The lock turned under her key, and then she was gone.

Without placing the key in the pass-through.

∽

Ohtavie stood for a moment, steady on her crutches, staring at the closed side door. Its white paint was dingy, and the bronze knob and thumb latch, tarnished. At least it was locked. At least no one apart from Lealle could get in. Unfortunately, Lealle herself could not only get in, but intended to do so that very afternoon.

Ohtavie felt her lips press flat. She would merely have to try again to extract that promise. Nothing to be done about it now.

What could be done now . . . was tidying up her bedchamber.

The rubber tips on the crutches made all the difference to her stability. That and Lealle's adjustment to their length. She reveled in the ease with which she passed from the kitchen wing, through the loggia, and then into the housekeeping wing. It was marvelous to move quickly and without the persistent fear of falling.

When she arrived in her bedchamber, it was a simple matter to bend while steadying herself on one crutch and swoop yesterday's crumpled garments off the floor.

She'd not truly realized just how much independence good crutches could confer. Was it because any shrinking of her ambit had felt so natural? She'd long ago accepted losing all that lay beyond the Maison de Bellay. And within the house she'd ordered the public rooms shrouded as she'd reduced the staff, then ceased to use the upper floor when she dismissed the last of the servants. Her world had grown inexorably smaller. Perhaps reducing it down to the bed in her bedchamber had seemed the next unavoidable contraction.

It was ironic that now, with a broken foot, she had the illusion that she could go anywhere, anywhere at all, merely because a pair of crutches freed her from bedrest.

She made the bed, carefully straightening the sheets, plumping the pillows and stacking them tidily, drawing the white blanket and the cream-colored quilt neatly over all. She completed a few more chores, dusting and even a bit of sweeping. She had lunch.

And then she was abruptly exhausted.

Her knees felt weak, her foot was throbbing again, and her eyes threatened to close even as she surveyed all the good work she had done.

Maybe . . . maybe, she would have to confine herself to bed after all.

She resisted the idea for a moment, wobbling on her wonderful crutches for the first time since Lealle had refurbished them. Then practicality rescued her from the melancholy narrative she'd been telling herself. It was true that her world had shrunk and shrunk again over the years, but climbing into bed because she had an injury that would heal better with sufficient rest didn't mean she was foregoing the freedom she'd felt.

She'd take a nap, which was sensible, and try on freedom again when she awoke.

The Third Day

Resisting Epiphany

Chapter Six

UNFORTUNATELY that sense of possibility—that she was free, that she could go anywhere, anywhere at all—was notably absent when Ohtavie awoke to the cool light of the next day's pre-dawn hour.

Her mouth was uncomfortably dry; her joints ached from her forced position on her back; and her skin felt chafed from sleeping in her clothes. She'd envisioned a short nap, not sleeping all the way through till next morning.

If she'd known, she'd have changed into a nightgown and pulled the curtains closed. If she'd known—no, she'd needed the rest. She could feel it in the absence of fatigue. She felt *better* for all those hours of sleep. But she wished she hadn't needed them. It made her feel like one of those sad old women with no friends save their cats, and no one to care or be inconvenienced by their odd hours.

Ohtavie winced. She didn't even have cats.

Although . . . where was Lealle? Unwilling and resisting though she was, she did have Lealle. Where was the girl?

The quiet of the house lay softly in this time just before sunrise. Had Lealle come and gone the previous afternoon or evening while Ohtavie slept? The idea made her skin crawl. It had been uncomfortable enough to suffer an intruder—even a benevolent one like Lealle—while Ohtavie was awake and aware. Sleeping through such . . . no, she didn't like that at all.

Might Lealle have heeded Ohtavie's prohibition on returning?

Ohtavie liked that possibility much more, but it seemed unlikely.

She flipped the bedclothes off her legs and checked her foot. The toes were pink enough and seemed less puffy. That was good. And there was no pain.

She swung her legs off the bed and to the floor. Still no pain.

Changing clothes, clinging to a chair back, she felt better. It was so nice to get out of her rumpled garments. Her trips to the water closet and then to the kitchen wing were entirely uneventful. Good crutches were wonderful.

The sense of freedom she'd discovered earlier began to creep into her soul again.

She unearthed one of the voluminous aprons once used by the cook, with a pinafore front that swathed her to the shoulders, and a vast three-part pocket in the skirt. The pocket was perfect for transporting crocks of preserved foodstuffs. She wouldn't be spilling this breakfast on the floor as she had yesterday's, which was fortunate since yesterday's rescuer remained absent.

Finding competence—even with a broken foot—reassured her. She was managing. She *could* manage.

But, really, where *was* Lealle?

There were no signs that she had come and gone yesterday afternoon, nor was she present this morning as Ohtavie kept half expecting. Surely the girl would not truly have changed her mind. She had been most stubborn about returning.

Which meant Lealle must have been prevented.

Ohtavie wondered if she should worry. Could there have been an accident and Lealle injured? Had those angry boys accosted her? Was Ohtavie actually wishing Lealle were present?

Ohtavie shook her head.

Most likely, Lealle had simply been required to conform to the schedule and wishes of those in authority over her: a teacher, a nurse, her mother, or her father. Ohtavie hadn't had to bend to anyone's will save her own for decades, but she remembered well enough what it was like to be a child.

As she washed the dishes, she remembered to be relieved. Better that Lealle should *not* come. That was what Ohtavie had wanted. Why was she now wishing for the girl's company? That was foolish. And unwise.

Alone was good. Alone was safe. Alone was what she was accustomed to.

It was absurd that she'd felt the impulse to sit down to a cup of tea with a good friend and converse. Trolls didn't have friends. And she had work to do. Without servants to help, if she wanted clean clothes and at least a few clean spaces, she was the one who had to do the household tasks.

Which meant that . . .

What day was it? She'd lost track during the turmoil of her injury and its aftermath.

She did a quick reckoning on her fingers. It was Fordaine, which meant she should be taking her clean clothes and linens down from the lines in the drying room, folding them, and putting them away.

She felt her mouth press flat again.

The linens were awaiting her attention, whether she wanted to attend to them or not. Grimly, she set to work, making adjustments as needed for her crutches, managing, but feeling as though she'd taken a wrong turn somewhere, feeling as though she should be working toward something she truly wanted rather than what was merely necessary.

What *did* she want?

There was a dangerous line of thought. Anything she could want would be impossible for her to receive. And the chores still needed to be done. Shirking the possible just because she couldn't have the impossible wouldn't help anything.

She kept folding.

The light and warmth flooding through the south-facing windows of the drying room and the clean scent of the laundered linens soothed her, as did the calm and repetitive motions of her task.

But . . . did all of this need to be done? At this time?

Couldn't a lot of this wait until her foot had healed and could bear her weight.

Standing there on her crutches, surveying her stacks of now-tidy laundry, dissatisfaction swept through her.

When had she become little more than a scullery maid?

Her mental weariness supplied the answer readily: when she dismissed the last of the servants.

She'd deemed it to be necessary. Her troll-disease had advanced, and she was growing to look too much like what she was—a troll. Her hair and skin and eyes were fading, though she was a young woman, then. (No longer young. Not now.) The curve of her retroussé nose was becoming more pronounced, its tip more elongated. Her ears were slightly enlarged.

If they did not already suspect it, the servants would soon have realized what she was. And let it slip, sooner or later, provoking the angry mob that would come for her. Or—if they were not as loyal as she believed them—one might summon the Incantors' Watch and the executioner to provide her lawful end. By the axe.

No, she'd had to dismiss the servants. And she'd told herself that the housework required by one lone troll—herself—would be much less than that necessary for six servants and herself. It wouldn't be so bad. She could do it. She would learn how.

And she had learned. She had done the work.

But unlike a scullery maid, she had no hope of advancing through the dirty cleaning chores to the lighter dusting and tidying and, eventually, to a position of authority and ease, such as cook or housekeeper or even lady's maid. There would be no escape or respite for Ohtavie.

She had saved herself from exposure and death, but at a cost.

Restless and discontented, she turned away from the further chores beckoning her.

She would do them later. Or not at all. She would do something else. Something . . . enjoyable? And what might that be?

Crutching along the hallway of the kitchen wing, she pondered. What did she usually do, when she wasn't cleaning or laundering or tidying or fixing a meal? What *did* she do?

Ohtavie turned through one of the interior arches to the grand entrance hall where the great double staircase rose in easy flights to the upper floor, and where clerestory windows above allowed bright sunlight to shine down, illuminating dust motes on the air and a coating of grimier dirt on the marble floors and balustrades.

This was a space she neglected, just as she neglected all the holland-swathed public rooms, indeed all the rooms save the few she herself used.

She stopped and stood still, right in the beam of the sunlight.

Why was she thinking again about housework? She'd just decided she was going to do something that was *not* housework. Why was she allowing her thoughts to pull her back to it? Was it because she'd been unable to think of anything enjoyable to do?

Fine.

If there was nothing enjoyable in her life to do, she'd do something unenjoyable, something unpleasant, something that scared her.

She would look out one of the front windows.

The slow pound of her heart seemed to intensify at this decision, not speeding, but pushing more blood with each heavy, pulsing beat.

❧

Ohtavie had failed in this exact goal—looking out a window at the front of the house—on the afternoon when she'd broken her foot. Trying and failing to look out the window of the small parlor was why she'd been looking out a back window instead.

This time . . . this time, she would succeed.

She stood there a moment longer, heart thumping almost painfully. Her mouth felt dry, and an uncomfortable fluttering disturbed her stomach.

She didn't have to do this. She could change her mind. What did it matter anyway?

She tried to tell herself that, in fact, it *didn't* matter. But it did. She knew it did. It mattered the world.

The fluttering in her stomach grew wilder, and each beat of her heart felt like it might rock her off her balance. She took a crutch swing forward, and another. The clerestory windows far above her seemed to grow yet more distant, as though the house were gaining increased height, or as though she were shrinking.

Her head began to spin, but she kept moving, passing through the hall and under the arch into the foyer.

Three shallow steps descended toward the front vestibule.

She almost hesitated, wanting to grab the pendant beneath her blouse, but then moved forward without that comforting touch. She would look through the inner glass-paned doors of the vestibule, and then on through the windows gracing the upper halves of the double outer doors onto Balard Square.

She would. But first, the steps.

Placing her crutches on the first step down was simple, but felt terrifying. Swinging herself down to it, for a moment suspended in the air before she touched down, was scarier still.

She alit safely. She did not fall. And did not fall again, when she moved to the next step, and the next, and then the floor.

Now the slow, powerful beat of her heart did speed, as though Lealle's 'Old Lemoine' swung a hammer again and again.

Ohtavie leaned toward the vestibule doors. She felt sick.

She lifted her gaze.

And there it was, through two sets of windowed doors: Balard Square.

Tall oaks surrounded a central fountain, casting a pleasant shade along the edges of the space, allowing cheerful sunlight nearer the water feature. She saw that the nursery maids were out, pausing with their perambulators to talk with other nursery maids, or supervising tots who wanted to float toy sailboats in the fountain.

Ohtavie's heart slowed again, but each beat felt strong enough to knock her to the floor.

She was looking out. She'd done it. She was doing it.

Triumph swelled within her. If she could do this—and she was doing it—might she turn other defeats into victory? Maybe, just maybe, she could.

Her throbbing heart calmed, her stomach settled.

She let go a breath of relief.

No school children ran races or rolled hoops or tossed rings in the square. Did school children still play such games? Or had they invented new ones? Ohtavie didn't know, but she need not confront the ghosts of herself and her friends as they used to frolic in this very square.

Then she was confronting them anyway, remembering the bright air, the freedom of movement, the laughter, the scent of the spraying water, the sheer wonder of being alive and the goodness of it all.

She'd not felt that wonder for a long, long time.

She was alive, but she was not living.

Swallowing down . . . something, she looked down. She crutched her way into the adjacent front parlor, the one where she'd failed to look out onto Balard Square the day before yesterday.

Now she knew why she'd failed.

That had been no failure. That had been success. Success at avoiding this bitter truth: that she'd saved herself from the angry mob—or the executioner—only to serve an endless prison term, imposed by herself. And, like a prisoner, what she *did* was pace. From the back of the house to the front. From the front of the house to one side. From its west side to its east.

Even on Saidy—the sabbath—she'd not run through the service for lone worshippers, nor prayed, nor read the holy book of the Divine Mother's Prince for . . . years.

She cleaned and she paced. And she flirted with happy memories, approaching them because they *were* happy, fleeing them because their contrast with her present made her despair.

For this, she had saved herself? Why had she bothered?

∞

Ohtavie's mood worsened as the hours passed.

Determined not to spend the day pacing, and equally determined against housework, she tried sitting with her foot propped on a stool. She found herself reciting multiplication tables.

It was a relief when she realized that she was hungry and that it was past the luncheon hour.

The flavors of the food she chose—cinnamon-spiced pork, pickled cucumber slices, and sweet strawberry preserves—beguiled her palate, luring her thoughts away from the wretchedness of her self-imposed imprisonment, and focusing her on the sensory. The pork was wonderfully savory, the pickles fresh and sharp, the strawberries lusciously all that berries should be.

When she finished her meal, tidying up after felt both natural and reasonable, even though she'd set herself against housework. Compulsively filling her time with such might be the wrong choice, but some chores did need doing.

Then she was left confronting herself and her empty hours again.

What had she normally done after she finished all the folding on Fordaine, her folding day?

She could have read from her father's library. It was extensive. She might have played her mandolin. It rested safely in its case. She could have tuned it and then enjoyed a musical interlude. She might have sketched the view from one of the windows, tatted some lace, or embroidered a decorative hanging.

But she hadn't done any of those things.

She'd been content to rest, because Fordaine was one of her easy days. She was usually tired after a laundry day for linens, a second laundry day for her clothes, and then the day of sweeping and scrubbing floors, all of which preceded her folding day.

But now . . . now she understood that even though those chores needed to be done, she'd done them as much to have something to do as because they were necessary. She'd told herself that she didn't want to do them, but that she had to. Which was true. She'd told herself that she was lucky she'd even figured out how to do them, which was also true.

Because she'd not realized how much skill they took, and hadn't bothered to ask the servants for lessons or tips before she dismissed the last of them. She'd thought the chores were just work, and fairly straight-forward work at that. It had been a most unwelcome surprise when the sheets came out of their first laundering as dirty as they'd gone in.

That had been one of the few fragments of enigmology she'd permitted herself: enchanting the soap flakes so they would actually clean. It was only much later that she'd discovered a book of household hints that explained that hot water was necessary in order to fully dissolve the soap and then fully rinse it out again.

But beneath the truth that cleaning was both hard work and took some skill, and beneath the truth that cleaning neglected over time led to living in squalor, was the harder truth that Ohtavie needed the cleaning both to occupy her time and to tire her out so that she could welcome rest. More pleasant occupations—reading poetry, playing music, doing fancywork—left her too unwearied, left her thoughts too free to dwell on her loneliness and boredom.

She almost cursed herself when she came away from putting away the dishes only to find herself pacing again. It was almost as though her house were a maze, and she were exploring dead end after dead end, wild to escape.

But she could not bear to sit doing nothing—or reciting multiplication tables. Nor could she develop any enthusiasm for the pursuits of a fine lady, the one she had been trained up to become. She wanted nothing of the entertainments that existed in this house—her home, her prison.

She wanted . . . to walk by the river or in the square or even along the streets, anywhere outside.

She wanted to pay a morning call on a friend. Or an acquaintance. Or even an enemy.

She wanted to attend a card party or a ball.

She wanted—longed for—a wider world than the one confined by the walls of the Maison de Bellay.

Stopping once more to look out at Balard Square, this time from the small and grubby front parlor, she fought the nausea that arose— would merely looking outside always be this hard?—and considered an option she had never allowed herself to consider before.

What if she *went* out of doors?

What if she left her refuge?

What then?

The mob might catch her in the end. It would catch her. Or deliver her to the executioner. But she would have felt the sun on her hair and the breeze in her face. She would have heard children laughing, townspeople talking. She would have had a few lovely hours surrounded by life. It would be worth . . . almost any risk, any price.

And what if Lealle were right?

Perhaps things had changed. Perhaps there was a cure for trolls. Perhaps she now trammeled herself within her prison for nothing!

She would go out. She would go right now! Immediately. This instant.

And yet . . . she was not going. She'd dropped the dusty lace curtain, as though to turn and move, but she was not moving. She wanted to move. She intended to move. And yet . . . she did not do so. She *could* not do so. She could not make herself.

Am I so frightened, she asked herself.

And she was. Indeed she was. But that was not the ultimate truth. The ultimate truth was that she feared the sense of freedom that would come with leaving her home even more than she feared the mob or the executioner. Oh, she feared her death, yes. And she feared pain. But the vision of going anywhere she pleased, of venturing beyond the familiar into the unfamiliar, perhaps into the utterly unknown and unexpected, terrified her. She did long for it, yes. *Longed* for it. But shunned it more strongly still.

The truth tasted bitter in her mouth.

Even were she free to leave the house, even were Lealle completely right about her safety outside, she was not free where it mattered most. Her habit of seclusion had transformed into a compulsion.

The memory of her inability to look out past the very lace curtain confronting her now came back to her, vividly. She'd wanted to look, but hadn't been able to do so.

But I looked just now, she told herself.

And she had. But could she do it again?

The scent of the dust rose strongly to her nose. She pressed her mouth straight and forced her fingers to touch the dirty lace, to take it and pull it aside. Slowly, she bent forward and peered out. The dappled shade under the tall oaks in the square looked very inviting. The dancing fountain sparkled in the strong afternoon sun. A group of children raced around the water's low parapet holding up pinwheels to spin in the breeze of their passage.

Ohtavie let the curtain fall, shaken.

She'd done it. She'd done it twice now. She *could* do it. But would she be able to do it tomorrow?

Looking outside was *hard*.

But it had not been the angry boys from whom she had run when she fled the window overlooking the lilacs. It had been the knowledge that those boys trespassed where she could not. The knowledge that her cage—formed by her own . . . experience, her own . . . mind?—was iron.

She'd not been able to go out onto the terrace a fortnight ago, just as now she'd not been able to pass her own front doors. No, she'd not even been able to approach her front doors.

And that was even more terrifying than her terror of the freedom she longed for.

Dear. Saints.

She was as warped in mind as she was becoming in body.

∾

Ohtavie forced herself to enter her father's library.

She *must* not keep pacing. She would go mad, if she did. She would do no more chores either. The occupations of fine ladyhood might not appeal to her, but she must occupy herself somehow.

And, really, she had faced this challenge before. Perhaps not so honestly as now, but this was not truly new. When she'd dismissed the last of the servants and found herself utterly alone, day after day, she'd nearly died of the loneliness. And she'd forced herself into the discipline of housekeeping. Her lie was that it was necessary, to prevent herself from living in squalor. But discipline had not come easily, for all its supposed necessity.

Now she must learn a new discipline.

She would read, and not merely the poetry that had been her favored choice in the past. She would read history and philosophy and mythology and more. The more challenging the text, the more it would hold her awareness, if she could muster the focus.

Standing just inside the doorway of the library, she surveyed the room.

It was shrouded in holland covers, just like the morning room at the back of the house. Thank goodness she had managed that much for most of the public rooms. It shamed her that she'd failed in that for the small front parlor. But where the morning room was pale and light-filled, the library was dimmer and cozy, although no less spacious. The dark maroon leather of the armchairs lay hidden beneath protective swathings, as did the carpet with its somber gold and rust pattern on rich brown. But the coffered walnut ceiling and the matching book shelves—glass-fronted—overshadowed the pallor of the holland covers, and the light sifting in through the generous windows on the north wall illuminated the space without bleaching its warm tones.

The room held a peaceful quiet as inviting as its warmth, and the scent of the books threaded its atmosphere. It felt like refuge in more ways than one. This had been her father's sanctum. Was that why she'd avoided it? Not wanting to be reminded of her loss of him?

Perhaps so.

He'd been a quiet man, and she'd never known him well. But she'd always felt . . . safe in his presence, as though some inner serenity lapped out from him to enfold those around him. She hadn't let herself remember how much she missed that. She mustn't let herself do so now.

She found herself moving instinctively toward the cabinet with all the poets—Brauneau, Coumisal, Tennisoie—and corrected her course. Poetry would just remind her of the past, her own past. She needed material that was less personal. The long dead past of the ancients—old Ennecy, Eirdry, and Istria, the birthplace of the Giralliyan empire—would be appropriate.

Fetching up before the cabinets of history, shelves and shelves of weighty tomes, she opened the glass doors protecting the nearest. A study of the war against the troll-lord Gohgohl held little appeal, nor did a biography of the saintly Exemplar Alcea. In fact, none of the thick volumes confronting her appealed to her much.

Resolutely, she continued perusing their spines. She would find *something*. She refused to return to pacing and useless rumination. She would exert control over herself. She must.

She almost missed the slim booklet covered in pale green and concealed between two hulking tomes about the rise of the Exemplars of Gebed. *A Legend of Ancient Navarys* read the text on its meager spine.

The idea of reading about the mythic city-state that had once flourished on an island far off the continental coast did appeal. What could be farther from her person and her present than that?

Ohtavie tucked the book into her sash, made her way over to one of the armchairs beside a window, pulled the holland cover off it, and sank down onto the comfortable leather. She propped her crutches against the adjacent window sill. Opening the book, she flipped past the preface to where the legend started.

She straightened a little when she read the first lines.

"The tale is usually told with the great Palujon Clisto as rogue and thief, and the legendary Zandro Mytris as hero and savior. But one mother of ancient Navarys knows the truth."

So! This was not so much a history as it was a story told as though by a woman who lived through the events. Abruptly, Ohtavie was no longer forcing her attention. Was the city-state of Navarys real? Had it once existed? Had its citizens truly come to the continent, long, long ago?

She was deep in the tale about this "mother of Navarys" when she heard Lealle's voice calling faintly from somewhere inside the house.

"Ohtavie? Ohtavie? I'm so sorry I did not come yesterday! Are you all right?"

⁓

Looking up from her book, Ohtavie noticed that the light outside in the square had taken on the deep golden tinge of evening, and that the square itself was largely deserted, the nurses and their charges gone inside for an early supper.

She'd been so absorbed in the story of the wave approaching Navarys—a crest so colossal that the island's geomancers forecasted it would top even the high peak of the mountain at the center of the island—that she'd not realized the afternoon had passed.

Her throat was dry, and she found herself longing for a swallow of cool mint tea, liquid and thirst-quenching. But—but!—her foot did not hurt. And truly, it should have, resting down on the holland-covered carpet like that. She should have dragged a footstool near so that she could put it up. She'd meant to, but she hadn't, distracted by the Navarean legend she was reading and intrigued by the *"energea-stones"* the Navareans used to focus their energetic powers, which powers seemed to be some version of the enigmology that she had learned as a child.

Lealle's clear voice called again, and then the girl herself skipped through the doorway, bringing a breath of fresher air into the slightly stale atmosphere of the library. She wore a frock of pale yellow with a cream sash at the waist and a fichu of cream lace wrapped around her shoulders. Her curling brown hair was pulled back in a braid confined by a matching yellow ribbon. She made a charming picture.

Ohtavie felt her lips turning up ever so slightly. The gowns of today were so much prettier than the ones from Ohtavie's girlhood, following the natural curves of the waist, instead of billowing out from a short yoke just below the bust. She wished she had one of the modern gowns in one of the wardrobes in the house.

But it wasn't Lealle's prettiness that made Ohtavie glad to see the girl. Reluctant as she might be to admit it, it was Lealle's kindness and her company that were so welcome.

"I *thought* you might have thought of books as a way to pass the time!" Lealle exclaimed, coming to a halt beside Ohtavie. "Did you find something good?"

Ohtavie chuckled softly and held up her book.

"*A Legend of Navarys,*" Lealle read aloud, wrinkling her nose. "History?"

"Really ancient history," answered Ohtavie. "But it's more a tall tale than a scholarly work, I think."

"Don't you have any novels?" asked Lealle. "That's what I like best. And some of the new ones are really good! I like the ones by Jeanne Auguste especially."

Ohtavie frowned. She was not familiar with the term, 'novel.' "Do you mean the old chansons de geste? From medieval times. The . . . the romances of knightly deeds and courtly love?"

"No-o," said Lealle uncertainly. "Those are poetry, aren't they?"

"I like poetry," Ohtavie admitted. Her Grandmere had disapproved of that taste. Truly Grandmere had disapproved of most things. "But this library has received no new books for more than twenty years, you know."

"Ooh!" Lealle almost sighed. "Then you haven't read *Nolworth Abbey* or *Ariane*. Or *Deliberation and Delight*. That's my favorite, about two sisters whose brother breaks a deathbed promise."

Ohtavie was beginning to be amused. Just so would she once have spoken of *Sir Launfael and the Faeries* or *The Song of Huon,* her favorite epic poems when she was about Lealle's age.

"Was your papere a scholar?" Lealle asked, somewhat abashed. "Are there only histories and lectures and sermons here?" Her tone was disappointed as she gestured to the glass-fronted cabinets lining the walls.

"My mamere collected quite a few works of entertainment and amusement," Ohtavie replied. "Enough to fill an entire cabinet." The one Ohtavie had avoided in her determination to read something other than poetry.

"Where?" demanded Lealle.

Ohtavie pointed.

Lealle returned the *Legend* to Ohtavie's hands and scampered over to the indicated pair of glass fronts. Opening them, she canted her head sideways to read the titles on the spines. "*The Bride of Bethpaarean, The Pirate King,*" she murmured. Then, skipping down, "*An Inquiry into Comedy. Beneath the Green.*"

She bent to her knees suddenly, pulling a volume from the very lowest shelf. "*Pascalina!*" she exclaimed. "Satourdi Riquefils doesn't make me laugh the way Jeanne Auguste does, but he tells a good story. And . . ."—Lealle lowered her face to peruse the rest of the books on the shelf more carefully—"it looks like there are several others like *Pascalina*." She looked up. "A story told in letters, you know."

Ohtavie shook her head. She didn't know, but the concept intrigued her. And she was ready to try something new. *Legend* had been engrossing. Perhaps Lealle's recommendations would be equally so.

The girl piled a short stack of books in her arms and rose to bring them over to Ohtavie. Setting the stack on the deep sill of the windows, she nibbled her lower lip.

"I'm so sorry I wasn't here yesterday," she said, real regret in her voice. "Mamere sent me to school in a hansom cab, and this morning, too. And she met me yesterday afternoon in the headmaster's office to escort me home. She said it was to take me to the florist shop to choose flowers for the wreath I'm to wear for the Fête d'Esprit Sanctus. And we did choose flowers, starflowers and sweet peas,"—Lealle looked briefly pleased—"but that wasn't why. I know it wasn't."

"Did you tell her about the bullies?" Ohtavie asked gently.

"I didn't!" Lealle protested. "For exactly that reason!"

"It's natural that she guard your safety," said Ohtavie.

"But I didn't tell her," Lealle repeated.

Ohtavie frowned. "There is another reason for her concern?" she asked.

Lealle nibbled her lip again, with greater intensity.

"Lealle?" The girl's reluctance to speak bothered Ohtavie.

"My papere is Justice to the Court of Audire," Lealle admitted.

Ohtavie's breath caught and her hand flew to the knob of the pendant hidden by her blouse. A justice, and not to one of the lower courts either. She'd been worrying about the mob and their reactions to trolls, when a much greater danger stood right beside her. It was Lealle's father who would call out the Incantors' Watch—the Troll Watch—to drag Ohtavie from her home and incarcerate her in an enigmatic cell. It was Lealle's father who would hear the Incantor's Witness and then order the executioner to behead her. Dear Saints. She felt barren of thought, reason submerged by her realization.

If anyone discovered Lealle had been here, Ohtavie would not be devising ways to avoid a riled mob. She would be confronting certain doom.

She'd been about to grant Lealle permission to visit, as the girl had wished from the start of their accidental acquaintance. But now . . . Ohtavie couldn't, mustn't.

"Papere said he's hearing a controversial case," Lealle explained further. "That there might be trouble, partisans who would be angry, who might visit their anger on Papere's family."

Ohtavie couldn't believe she'd considered accepting Lealle's assurance that things had changed, that civil disorder was unlikely to sweep Claireau again. Clearly . . . violence always lurked beneath any surface peace. She *knew* this. Why had she wavered?

"What's wrong?" faltered Lealle.

"Just the day before yesterday, you urged me to believe that I was safe amongst Claireau's citizenry," Ohtavie said, working to keep her tone even. Lealle did not deserve her disappointed anger. She was a child. Ohtavie was and must be the adult here. "What you describe now does not sound particularly safe for anyone."

"I didn't know then," cried Lealle. "I found out that evening."

"Do you realize that it would be your father who would condemn me?" she asked, gently.

Now Lealle looked as blank as Ohtavie had felt a moment ago. "Papere?" she exclaimed. "Never!"

"It is the Audire Justice who summons the Incantors' Watch and passes sentence on the trolls they find," she said.

"But that hardly ever happens anymore!" Lealle burst out. "Only when a troll avoids treatment. Like *you* avoid it! And then only if they become dangerous."

"There's a treatment," Ohtavie questioned, her voice still level, not inquiring. She'd meant to ask about this very thing, yesterday, if Lealle had come then. The girl had mentioned it in the course of casting Ohtavie's foot, and however dubious Ohtavie might be, she had to follow up on the possibility.

Lealle nodded earnestly. "When I was little, just starting school, Lord Gabris in Bazinthiad, the capital"—Lealle's emphasis showed her to be impressed by that location—"and Lord Panos, the Arch-antiphoner for all of Giralliya, devised a perilous experiment. And they succeeded!"

"You know this," said Ohtavie, testing.

Lealle nodded. "They teach it even to the very littlest students now. And keep teaching it all the way up. My civics and government lessons always include it, every year, and my physical culture studies as well."

Ohtavie swallowed, with difficulty, reminded by the discomfort of her thirst. She could accept intellectually that Lealle might not be mistaken about this development of history. Probably she was correct. But the change felt too momentous for Ohtavie to take in. A treatment for trolls. A treatment for *her*. What did that really mean? How might it change . . . everything? She couldn't really imagine it.

"I must think on this," she murmured.

Lealle nodded and looked earnestly into her face. "I can't believe . . . I can hardly believe that you didn't know. I—" she shook her head "—you've lived entirely isolate since . . ." She shook her head again.

"I've been alone in this house for twelve years," said Ohtavie. Had it really been twelve? It felt like fewer, but also more, as though time had been both stretched and compressed.

Lealle's lips parted. "Will you at least grant me leave to visit you? I know I've come in against your wishes, but I'd—I'd rather have your permission." She looked almost confused by her own words. No doubt she'd intended to simply carry on without Ohtavie's leave. She'd not intended to ask.

Ohtavie's lips curved slightly up. She felt a little churlish to be glad that she were not the only one to be so disconcerted.

"Are you certain no one has seen you enter this house?" she asked.

Lealle nodded decisively. "I'm really careful," she said. "I make sure no one is coming along the lane before I go through the gate. And I check the windows across the way, too."

Ohtavie was impressed. She would not have expected Lealle to consider the windows of the neighboring house.

"Are you equally certain that no one has followed you? Curious about where you are going? Wondering why you've departed from your usual ways?"

"I told Mamere that my friend Madeleine begged me to go home with her after school today. And she did! I'm going there next." Lealle glanced out the window, where the golden tint of the evening was strengthening. "Oh, dear! I'm probably already late! And I wanted to check how your foot was doing! Antiphonically. And you must have a thousand questions about—about Lord Gabris and his treatment. How—?"

Ohtavie laid a gentle hand on Lealle's wrist, wanting to calm her agitation.

"There's time enough," she said. "You may visit me again tomorrow."

"Oh!" Lealle beamed. "And the next day? And the next?"

"Let's just consider the shorter interval for now." Ohtavie didn't feel any desire to grant her a free rein.

"Oh." Lealle's elation calmed, then vanished. "Oh! But I can't! Mamere is sending me in a hansom cab again in the morning, and fetching me away in the afternoon to help her in the chapel soup kitchen in the evening after my antiphony lesson."

"Very well." Ohtavie's own calm had returned. "Then you will visit me the day after tomorrow. To answer my questions, and assess my foot. Will that suit?"

Lealle pressed her lips together. "I'm going to check your foot *right now*," she said, kneeling to do so.

Ohtavie's slight smile grew warmer. "You needn't," she said. "If you're late . . ."

"I have time enough for this. But—oh, I'd hoped to help you with your supper! Have you eaten? Did you break your fast? Take a bit of luncheon? I know Nurse always said—"

Ohtavie stopped her again with a touch, this time on Lealle's shoulder. "I've eaten. Your adjustments to my crutches"—she nodded to where they were propped against the window sill, beside the books Lealle had piled there—"have made everything much easier. I've done well. Truly."

Lealle smiled back at her. "Oh, good! I'll just check your foot then."

The necessary centering took the girl a moment, and then Ohtavie felt the same soothing warmth that attended the other times Lealle had examined her flesh and bone using antiphony. Lealle said she was simply looking, but Ohtavie couldn't help wondering if she was doing something more. That would explain why the injury no longer grew swollen when Ohtavie forgot to raise it on a footstool when sitting—as she had this afternoon.

When the warmth creeping from Ohtavie's toes toward her heel began to ebb, Lealle's hands fell away and she looked up to meet Ohtavie's gaze. "It's doing really well," she said. "I think the bruising is nearly gone, and the bone is actually beginning to knit."

"Are you surprised?" Ohtavie asked. *She* was surprised. It seemed to be healing too quickly, too well.

Lealle nodded. "When I tripped over the boot scraper at home, it was a sevenday before the bruise started to clear. But . . . I'm glad your foot is not taking so long. It doesn't hurt, does it?"

Ohtavie smiled. "No, it doesn't hurt."

Somewhere outside, a church bell began to ring in the distance.

Lealle's eyes widened. "It must be past the sixth hour! Oh, saints!"

"Go, child," Ohtavie urged her. "You said you were late."

"Are you *sure* you'll be all right?" Lealle questioned.

"Of course," said Ohtavie. "Go!"

Lealle scrambled to her feet, took two hurried steps, and then whirled back to leave a light kiss on Ohtavie's cheek. A moment later the girl was through the library door, her voice floating back on the words, "I'll see you the day after tomorrow!"

Ohtavie sat listening as Lealle's running footsteps faded. A nice child, truly. A nice child, with a generous heart. And one who didn't deserve . . . the possible trouble that might coalesce around a troll.

For the first time it occurred to Ohtavie that Lealle might be in more danger than Ohtavie herself.

She frowned.

Knowledge of truths might change, did change. And when knowledge changed, the laws and mores around it changed, but slowly. According to Lealle, something new had come to light regarding troll-disease, which permitted enigmologists—or antiphoners, as the Giralliyans named them—to slow the course of the malady. And which meant that trolls were no longer sentenced to immediate death upon discovery. At least, it seemed that was what Lealle implied.

And it might well be so. Ohtavie was inclined to believe it was so.

But while knowledge might change, human nature did not. That was the mistake Lealle was making. Understandably. She was young, and kind, and believed that most people possessed her own high ideals. But people . . . were people. Many possessed good intentions, but . . .

When people were scared, they protected themselves, often violently. And trolls were scary. No one would have forgotten that fear in a mere handful of years. And Lealle had said that untreated trolls—trolls like Ohtavie—were still feared and sanctioned. Which meant that if Ohtavie's presence were revealed, the mob she'd feared ever since she understood what her troll-disease meant, might indeed gather. But Ohtavie would be safe inside the Maison de Bellay, while *Lealle* would be perceived as consorting with trolls when she emerged.

Ohtavie's lips pressed flat.

And even if Ohtavie remained secret and hidden, there was the additional danger posed to Lealle by her father's enemies. Ohtavie didn't think Lealle had the least idea how dangerous dissidents could be. She'd not been born when Giralliya annexed Pavelle and could not know how bitter some of Pavelle's surviving defenders might be. Her parents were right to insist she have a protective escort through the streets of Claireau. And Lealle was naïve in eluding that escort.

Ohtavie shifted forward in her armchair, reaching for her crutches. The comforting scent of the leather upholstery wafted upward, but Ohtavie did not feel comforted.

She would need to renew her prohibition on Lealle's visits. It would be only prudent.

The Fourth Day
REINDY—QUEEN'S DAY
Wrongdoing and Rightdoing

Chapter Seven

LEALLE SAT on the top stone step of a half-flight of six.

The stairs connected the front door of the retreat house—where Lealle had just finished the afternoon's antiphony lesson—to the flagway below, and she was enjoying the dappled shade from the tall trees planted along the curb separating the flagway from the narrow cobbled street. The day had been hot and the classrooms at school airless on this last day of the term. It was a relief to be outside, to feel a cooling breeze rising with the advent of evening, to smell the delicate floral scent wafting from the many windowboxes of the brick townhouses flanking the flagways.

A hansom cab driver had stopped his equipage at the old-fashioned horse trough occupying the center of the street to water his horse. A smart curricle maneuvered around this blockage, going the wrong way on the other side of the thoroughfare, while the drivers of several other carriages and a grocer's wagon yelled imprecations.

Lealle watched it all with private entertainment, wondering if her mamere would get caught in the tangle when she arrived to take Lealle to chapel. Although Mamere would be coming in her own brougham-landau, not a hansom. Mamere would see no need to be crammed uncomfortably into a small and stuffy public conveyance when she could enjoy the clean spaciousness of her own carriage.

Where *was* she though? Lealle had been waiting for quite some time. Not that she was in any hurry to ladle giblet broth from a steaming cauldron into soup bowls for the poor. She felt a little guilty, but the shade and the breeze and having a moment to rest beguiled her.

It had been a long day, starting with her ride to school in the hansom, listening to her teachers assign summer reading that no one would do, then another hansom ride to the retreat house, and her antiphony lesson.

She'd practiced the flames-rising movement that was the first of the Phoenix sequence over and over again under Maitresse Aubry's close supervision. It was such a tricky manipulation, involving accurate visualization and precise control. Maitresse had been enthusiastic about these attempts—Lealle's first. Lealle herself had felt a certain exhilaration in the work. But she was *tired* now at the close of the day, and Mamere's lateness, however uncharacteristic of her, bothered Lealle not one whit.

I'll just laze here until the shadows lengthen a bit more, she thought dreamily, *and then wander home on my own.* She could even visit Ohtavie in the Maison de Bellay, if she wished. She'd told Ohtavie that she wouldn't be able to, but if Mamere never came . . . Lealle would have the perfect excuse. "I waited and waited," she would say, "but by the time I realized something had happened, it was too late."

At least Ohtavie had given Lealle permission to visit. She wouldn't be entering the Maison de Bellay against Ohtavie's wishes. That hadn't been comfortable even when Ohtavie had truly needed Lealle's help. Lealle doubted she could have continued to trespass, now that Ohtavie had recovered some, without Ohtavie's permission.

Why was she so fascinated by the troll-witch?

It wasn't just that Lealle wanted to bring succor to Ohtavie's troll-disease, although she did. There was something more than that. Was it that Ohtavie represented a mystery—how had she become a troll? how had she eluded detection for so long?—that Lealle wanted to solve? Was it that Ohtavie was a chance for Lealle to do something on her own, unplanned and unsanctioned by Nurse or Mamere or a teacher?

Maybe.

But really it might be just that Ohtavie was beginning to feel like a friend. And Lealle had never had a friend who was not her own age, who was not a little . . . silly, the way Lealle was silly herself sometimes. Ohtavie saw the world through different eyes—like Papere, like Maitresse Aubry—and yet Ohtavie didn't talk down to Lealle, in spite of her greater age and experience. Lealle liked that. And Lealle liked Ohtavie.

Invading someone's house might be an odd way to make her acquaintance, an odd prelude to friendship, but Lealle did want to be friends.

She became aware that her eyes had drifted closed. She really mustn't fall asleep on the retreat house steps! She might fall down them to the flagway where someone would trip over her. She might sleep all night outside, or at least until the next student coming away from her lesson stumbled upon her and woke her up. How embarrassing that would be!

She should open her eyes. In just another moment, she would.

"Hey, hoity-toity!" came a hatefully jeering voice. "Think the whole town's your bedchamber, do you?"

Lealle's eyes flew open.

∞

Clustered on the flagway at the bottom of the stairs was the least welcome sight in all the north: a clump of grubby boys in faded jackets and knee-smalls, with taunting grins on their faces. On the first step up from the flagway stood Ragged-cap himself. The odors of unbathed skin and unwashed clothing drifted from him on the breeze, and the expression in his eyes looked angrier than that of his compatriots.

Lealle shifted uneasily, but stayed seated. Jumping to her feet would just make her look scared. And she needn't be scared. Not this time, right at the front door of the retreat house where anyone looking out could see the boys in mischief. Where everyone in the street—or walking along the flagway—would witness misbehavior. She was safe here. And staring down her nose while sitting might take the bullies down a peg.

Ragged-cap—what was his name again? Laurent? Something Laurent?—placed one foot a step higher and leaned forward. "Think because you're a citizen"—he dragged the word out, mockingly, citizen—"you can do what you please, wherever you please!" He spat, right on the step below her feet. "Well, you can't!" he yelled.

Lealle wrinkled her nose. The sputum glistened disgustingly in the dappled sunlight. What if he'd spat *on* her shoes? But he hadn't. And she would preserve her dignity by ignoring it.

"You're a citizen, too, you know," she said evenly. "Everyone in Pavelle is a citizen of the Empire."

Ragged-cap sneered. "That's what we're supposed to think," he jeered. "But you know and I know there's citizens and then there's *Citizens*."

The boys on the flagway muttered. "Yeah!" and "You tell 'er, Gaetan!" and "Empire scum!"

Gaetan—so his first name was Gaetan—sniffed and raised his chin, so that he could look down his own nose.

"I wouldn't want to be a Citizen anyway," he said. "I'm a Loyalist!"

He meant he remained loyal to the old prince of Pavelle. But the old prince had died in the civil war that was the cause of Giralliya invading and then annexing Pavelle. Gaetan looked to be no older than Lealle herself. Neither of them had been born soon enough to ever have even seen the old prince, let alone feel personal loyalty to him.

Of course, Lealle's papere was Empire through and through, born in the old Giralliyan canton of Barinia. But Lealle's mamere was Pavanese.

"Like it or not, you're still a citizen," Lealle insisted. "An exemplar elected by all Pavanese represents you in the Chamber of the Orthodoxy, a pauce appointed by the emperador speaks for you in the Chamber of

Paucitors, the nephew of the old prince upholds your interests in the Chamber of Princes and Kings, and the laws of the Empire protect you."

All of that was standard fare from her history and civics lessons.

"What a baby you are, believing those lies," scoffed Gaetan. "All those crooks in Bazinthiad"—the Giralliyan capital—"might represent *you*, but they sure as hell don't know nothin' about what *I* need!"

"They're not crooks," said Lealle composedly. "I've met them myself." And she had. The Pavanese exemplar had dined at their family table just last month.

"Like you could tell. Baby." Gaetan's face looked abruptly adult, and . . . weary? Discouraged?

Lealle frowned, surprised by the nibble of sympathy stirring within her at the sight of his dejection.

The boys on the flagway nudged one another. "Told you she was Empire scum," said one, squeezing closer to the stairs to allow the thickening flow of pedestrians to pass behind him. None of the passersby—clerks and messengers and businessmen—seemed to notice the ugly tenor of the bullies. Were they paying no attention to what was around them? In that big of a hurry to get somewhere? Or did they simply assume the boys were an ordinary and innocent group of schoolkids? Lealle didn't know, but she was feeling less safe than she'd told herself she should. Was anyone looking out of the front windows of the retreat house? *Would* anyone look?

"And those laws?" Gaetan continued. "If your father were ever arrested—which he wouldn't be, because look who he is: cousin to the emperador himself. 'Course no one would arrest him!"

Lealle's frown deepened. Cousin to the emperador? Who had told Gaetan that? And why had he believed them? Her papere was no more cousin to the emperador than he was cousin to the old prince.

"But if someone did arrest 'im, this is how it would go!" pursued Gaetan. "He'd get a private bedroom on the top level of the Fortin de Garde, not some half-flooded cell in the cellars. He'd get breakfast and a luncheon and a dinner cooked by the general's own chef, not one measly bowl of moldy porridge once a day. And when he finally got to the courtroom, he'd get found innocent and get a formal apology from the justice, where my father's gonna get blackballed and thrown in prison, if he's *lucky*! Guillotined, more like!" His voice was loud.

"Yeah!" muttered the boys, in a disjointed chorus.

Gaetan's final words had almost been shouts, but Lealle's sympathy for him strengthened.

Of course he was worried for his father. And if his father wasn't innocent, if he'd done something to deserve arrest—and he must have, or Papere would not have issued the warrant—then he might be found guilty. And depending on what he'd done, the punishment might be severe. Although . . . she didn't think they used the guillotine anymore, except maybe for trolls.

Lealle shivered, thinking of Ohtavie. Was Ohtavie right? Could she be beheaded? Surely not. She was perfectly sane and not dangerous.

"Take that for your laws!" yelled Gaetan, and spat again, this time right on the toes of Lealle's half-boots.

She'd been about to say, 'I'm sorry,' but that gobbet of sputum on the clean leather abruptly banished her sympathy. "Wipe that off," she bade him, glaring.

"Wipe it off yourself," he snarled. "'Bout time you did some of the dirty work your own selves, instead of leaving it to us Loyalists!"

Lealle's heart was thumping so hard, in rage and shock combined, she wondered that it did not leap from her body. She leaned forward, even as Gaetan leaned farther forward himself. They were practically nose to nose.

"Wipe. It. Off," she ordered. "Now!"

"Hoity-toity," jeered Gaetan. "Take that! And that! And that!"

Quicker than she could react to him, he'd reached around to yank the ribbon from her hair, to rip the fichu from around her shoulders, and thrown them down on top of the first gobbet of spit, one step down.

She'd not thought she could be more angry, but she'd been wrong. Almost unable to breathe in her fury, she moved to surge to her feet.

Gaetan's sudden grab for the back of her neck prevented her. Saints, but he was strong.

His fingers were bruising in their force, just behind the hinge of her jaw, as he forced her back down. Her sit bones hit the stone step under her jarringly, but Gaetan did not stop there.

"Lick it off!" he growled, pressing her head down past her knees.

A feather of panic flickered into Lealle's wrath. Dear Thiyaude! He couldn't, could he? Force her to lick his spit?

A driving jab from his other elbow jerked her knee away from its fellow, and her head plunged through the gap.

Now she was well and truly panicked. In desperation, she grabbed for his wrist—breathed in; breathed out; and *reached*. Reaching, remembering how she'd adjusted Ohtavie's crutches, she *squeezed*.

All the pressure let up on her head.

The grip disappeared from her neck.

And she bobbed upright, while Gaetan uttered a sound that should have been a scream, but wasn't. A scream so intense that it went silent? A death rattle? A sob?

He was standing utterly still, his face shocked as he held his forearm before him—his left, the one she'd gripped—and stared at it in horror.

The button in the cuff at his wrist had come off in the struggle, and the sleeve was pushed up to his wrist. Lealle could see exactly what she'd wrought.

Gaetan's elbow was normal, a bit grubby, but it was the elbow any fourteen-year-old boy would possess. The rest—forearm, wrist, and hand—was absolutely *not* normal. Dear Thiyaude, what *had* she done? Forearm, wrist, and hand were grained like wood and immobile like wood, as though carved from that substance. Had she actually turned living flesh to wood? Had she crippled him?

"She's a troll-witch!" gasped one of the boys on the flagway. "Run!"

And run they did, pushing through the passersby behind them and fleeing across the street, much to the disruption of the carriage traffic there.

Gaetan remained a moment longer, staring in horror at his arm, then transferring his horrified gaze to her face. Her eyes must be as big as his own, she thought.

Then he stumbled down the two steps to the flagway and turned, awkwardly cradling his ruined arm and careening around a corner into an alleyway.

Dear Thiyaude. What had she done?

∽

Lealle felt as though she herself were wooden, from top to toe. She couldn't move. She couldn't breathe. She couldn't even think.

The hansom cab blocking traffic in the street had moved on, but the number of carriages had increased to the point where they'd come to a standstill anyway. The yells of the impatient drivers sounded in Lealle's ears along with the rustle of the leaves as the evening breeze picked up, but she heeded them not. Nor did she notice the hard stone step pressing against her sit bones or its edge digging into the backs of her thighs.

All her awareness remained stuck on the last accusation made by the boys before they fled: *she's a troll-witch!*

Lealle almost felt they must be right.

No reputable antiphoner, properly trained and well meaning, would strike out with her antiphony to attack a schoolboy. But that was precisely what Lealle had done—bully or no. And she'd done grievous damage, too.

Only a troll-witch would do something like that. A witch who wasn't trained. A witch who used dangerous *incantatio*, not safe antiphony. A witch who was mad. Or else evil. Lealle shuddered. She herself had done this thing.

Had her radices—the root sources of her antiphonic powers—come unmoored without her ever noticing it? *Was* she a troll? Or had she gone mad, so mad that she didn't know she was mad? Was she evil?

Lealle started breathing again with a gasp, and leapt to her feet. She clattered down the steps, leaving her soiled fichu and hair ribbon behind, as she darted in the direction taken by Gaetan. She would find him.

She would find him and *fix* him.

Her antiphony had not crackled with the strange, acrid light that accompanied *incantatio*. Nor had she uttered doggerel poetry—another sign of troll-magic. She wasn't a troll, and she would not act like one either. She *must* not act like one. She would undo what she had done, what she'd done almost by accident. Dear Thiyaude!

The flagway was so crowded that she couldn't run to Gaetan's aid as fast as she wanted to. Luckily, the press of people were in nearly as much of a hurry as she was. She reached the alleyway where he'd turned and dove between the brick townhouses flanking the narrow opening.

An apronway of gravel scritched under her boots—she was sprinting now—and then gave way to dirt and the muffled thump of her footsteps. She passed a shallow stairwell where four steps descended to a cellar door, and then skidded to a stop, doing a double take.

Gaetan lay at the bottom of those steps, shivering and shaking on his back, still cradling his arm. He'd lost his cap somewhere in his flight. His tousled hair, nearly the same honey brown as her mamere's, bushed out around his head, sweat-dampened.

He tried to push away from her when he caught sight of her looming above him, but there was nowhere for him to go.

"I'm s-sorry, s-so sorry," he stuttered, terror in his face.

Lealle held her hands to either side, palms flat, to show that she meant him no harm—no *further* harm. "No, *I'm* sorry," she insisted. "I want to help you. I want to undo it. I didn't mean to do it. It was an accident."

He didn't seem to take in what she'd said.

"No," he pleaded, "no. I'll go away. I'll never bother you again. I'm s-sorry!" He pushed backward again, and was again stopped by the stone wall of the stairwell.

"Gaetan!" she said, trying to get him to hear her. "I didn't mean it. I want to *help*!"

"Go away," he begged. "*Please* go away!" Two tears started from his eyes, drawing grubby streaks on his cheeks.

She moved gingerly down the steps, half afraid of terrifying him more, half afraid that he might lash out with his feet. He could hurt her badly, if he kicked her.

But he didn't kick. Instead, he squeezed his eyes shut and turned his face away.

She felt awful. She'd felt helpless when he'd shoved her head down between her knees, but she'd also been angry, and that had helped. She'd not surrendered and given up, which was what Gaetan was doing now. She ought to feel glad to see her former tormenter groveling, but somehow she didn't. She hated being the cause of such abject submission. And she *had* to help him. She couldn't just leave him.

He whimpered as she laid hands on his wooden forearm. Saints. It even felt like wood, hard, with ridges marking its grain. But, now that she could examine it carefully, she noticed that there was a transition zone between the wood of his lower forearm and the flesh of his elbow. The upper forearm was weirdly half-wood and half-flesh, showing the patterning of wood grain, but resilient like flesh.

Lealle forced herself not to shudder again.

She couldn't give way to tears. She had to *fix* this. Right now.

She drew in a breath, then let it go. Slower, she told herself. She couldn't focus with quick breaths or on quick heartbeats. She had to center herself. She had to calm down. Or she would accomplish nothing.

Or—horrors!—she might do even more damage. No. Slow. Slow. And slower.

Breathing in and breathing out, she felt the patter of her heart begin to quiet. The silver light of her arcs bloomed in her mind's eye, and she let her eyelids fall closed. The energetic arc within Gaetan's forearm glowed golden. That couldn't be good; it should be silver like her own. And the demi-radix in his palm was slightly orange, not pearlescent white like hers.

She'd squeezed energetically to produce this unfortunate transformation of Gaetan's arm. Logically, she should somehow expand where before she'd compressed. It wouldn't have been possible, if she'd had to do that with crude physical implements. But she didn't. She would do this antiphonically. But somehow an expansive flow of *energea* felt . . . wrong.

It was almost as though the forearm were congested with *energea*, swollen with it. And what she needed to do to bring it relief was draw some of the excess off.

On her next out breath, she allowed a little sound to flow from her throat, humming. With the sound, she *pulled*, instead of *reaching* within as she usually did, and Gaetan's *energea* began to flow from him to her, a trickle of sparks that grew more silvery as they moved, streaming down his forearm and through his wrist and out his fingertips.

But accepting them into herself felt wrong, even dangerous.

With a strange tightening sensation in her palms, she directed the flow down and away, to dissipate in the air.

The golden glow of Gaetan's forearm arc began to fade, shading to an opalescent white and then a cool silver. Lealle could feel the wood that was his flesh softening under her clasp. Was it returning to its proper essence? Oh, but she hoped so, powerfully hoped so.

But she didn't stop the drawing pull on his *energea*. Something told her that it wasn't time yet. She must draw off *all* the congestion.

Gaetan himself no longer tensed at her touch, but lay relaxed. Could he feel the difference? That she was doing him good, not harm? She wished she could open her eyes to look at him with both inner and outer sight. The most skilled antiphoners at the retreat house could, she knew. But she could not. She was still just learning. Oh, if only she could undo what she had done to Gaetan . . .

She'd been so angry. She'd been so scared. But, still! Gaetan might lose his arm entirely, if she could not fix what she'd done.

She continued to draw *energea* out of him.

And heard him gasp in sudden pain.

Oh, no! Was she hurting him?

"Keep on, no, keep on," he answered, as though she'd spoken her worry aloud. Perhaps she had. "It's not wooden anymore, it just looks it," he said.

She kept on, and on. She was tiring, but she would not stop until she'd done this.

Gaetan hissed with pain.

"What is it? Oh, what is it?" she cried.

"Just bruises," he muttered. "But they're fierce!"

And then she felt the balance shift. A moment before, his *energea* had been congested. But now it was draining, and would pass toward meager, if she kept on.

She cut off the flow, and felt her bones sagging into the flagstones of the stairwell in which she crouched next to Gaetan. All the strength had gone out of her.

She let her eyes stay closed a moment. She was so tired. She felt as though she might fall into sleep without even knowing whether she had succeeded or not. But she had to know.

Blearily, she pried her eyelids open.

Gaetan was biting his lips and wincing and squinting at his arm in the long, low light of evening. She followed his gaze with her own, echoing his earlier hiss when she saw the bruises. They were so dark as to be almost black. Which was dangerous. Bruises like that meant—well, she didn't know what they meant. But the foot of one of the gardeners at home had looked like that after the sundial fell on it. Papere said he would have lost the foot to gangrene, if he'd not seen an antiphonic healer right away. Would Gaetan get gangrene?

"You need a real healer," she said.

He swallowed, with difficulty. "Can't," he said.

"Why not? You must!" she insisted.

He just shook his head.

She wondered what she would see if she looked antiphonically. She'd been so focused on the flow of *energea,* and the *feel* of the energetic balance, that she'd not really paid any heed to the background pattern of the flesh itself.

Closing her eyes again was easy. Her eyes wanted to be closed. Opening the inner sight was harder—she wanted to sleep—but she did it. And then the faint spiraling traceries that formed the energetic pattern of his forearm appeared in her vision. They were intact, but slightly blurred.

She swept her attention down to his wrist and into his hand, where the blurring was stronger.

That couldn't be good. Did it mean that he would get gangrene?

She studied the spirals of his fingertips and the roots of the arcs feeding into the demi-node of his palm. Were the spirals gaining focus even as she watched? Was the blurring merely a rebound effect from the wooden state?

"That helps," muttered Gaetan. "It feels good."

Oh, no! Was she *doing* something? She'd thought she was merely *looking.* But if he could feel something . . .

She lost her focus and her eyes flew open.

The bruising on his arm seemed less dark. Had it lightened? Had *she* lightened it? Healed it, a little?

Gaetan nodded. "I'll—I'll be good now," he choked. "You can go."

He hitched himself into a more upright position.

She bit her lip. She'd undone the dreadful thing she'd done to him. But it didn't feel finished between them.

"I—" she began, clashing with his, "It were my own fault."

That startled her, somehow. He'd not seemed like a boy who blamed himself for much.

"Think I go around tormenting girls?" he sneered. "Well, it probably looks that way, don't it."

She didn't know what to say. "You've tormented me three times now," she managed.

He looked away. "Yeah." Then he looked her straight in the eye. "Yeah. I did." He swallowed. "It were wrong."

That was the last thing she'd expected. "Will you do it again?" she asked. "You seemed like you hated me. And your friends did too."

"They'll do as I tell 'em," he said.

"And what will you tell them?" she asked.

"To leave you be." He looked down again, then up. "Look, I—" he started, and then broke off.

"What is it?" It had sounded almost as though he were going to ask her a favor, as unlikely as that seemed, and she felt a strange urgency to know what he would have said.

As she drew breath to say, "Tell me," a young boy's voice screeched her name. "Lealle! I'm here! You're safe! *I'll* protect you!"

She looked up to the top of the stairwell, level with her shoulders in her crouching position, and saw her little brother.

"Remy!" she gasped. What was *he* doing here?

∞

The alley way ran east-west, allowing the strong rays of the lowering sun to flood the narrow space between the two townhouses with light. Remy looked very tall, standing very straight on the lip of the stairwell in which Lealle sat, and glaring down at Gaetan.

"You get, you bully!" Remy yelled. "I saw what you did to my sister, and I won't have it! Don't you ever come near her again!"

Lealle wanted to laugh, and yet she was also annoyed. She didn't need help. Not now. What did nine-year-old Remy think he could do against someone twice his size? And yet he clearly *did* think he could do something.

Her annoyance grew when she saw the effect Remy's words had on Gaetan. The bully looked intimidated and wriggled around behind Lealle to get to the steps up.

"Wait!" she said. She wasn't done. She needed him to stay.

Still cradling his badly bruised arm, Gaetan lurched up the steps to the alley way.

"Wait!" Lealle repeated.

Remy overrode her. "That's right!" he admonished. "You keep going until you're gone, and then *stay* gone!"

"No!" Lealle protested.

Gaetan cringed. "I won't bother 'er no more," he said to Remy. "I swear it." Then he turned to Lealle. "You'll be safe, miss. You needn't fear the streets no more," he said awkwardly.

She felt put off by that 'miss.' It broke the intimacy created by her healing of him. Now she'd never find out what he was going to ask her. Although . . . she'd not find out anyway, because he was leaving, headed between the back gardens into the setting sun.

"Wait!" she called after him. "I want to *help* you!" What was it with her wish to help people who declined her help? First Ohtavie, ordering her to depart. Now Gaetan, whose back stayed firmly turned while he walked away.

She looked up at her brother. "Shun it, Remy! I'd already won! I'd beaten him." She winced, remembering how she'd done it, remembering the feel of his wooden arm under her fingertips. "You didn't need to chase him away!"

"Ooo! You said a bad word!" Remy accused her, gleefully.

She sighed, exasperated, and climbed to her feet. "What are you doing here anyway? You were in the country!"

"Broke my arm," he answered laconically.

"What!" She scrutinized his arm. It looked perfectly normal, covered by his jacket sleeve, with a neat shirt cuff just showing.

Remy grinned. "I fell out of the big apple tree this morning—you know, the one by the old well—and Bon-papy rushed me back to town so that the best antiphoners could mend it. Mamere brought me back to the retreat house in the afternoon, for a follow-up treatment." He shrugged. "I dunno. It feels fine to me, but Maitresse Aubry said it wouldn't be as resil—" he stopped, then tried the long word again "—as resil-i-ent, if they left it with just the basic mend."

"Wait! *Mamere* is at the retreat house?"

"Uh, huh," said Remy.

So she'd been waiting all that time for Mamere, and the whole while Mamere had been inside. Somehow they'd missed one another when Lealle came out and Mamere went in.

Lealle bit her lip and climbed the four steps out of the stairwell. Her knees wobbled a little with her fatigue. Remy looked much shorter when she got to the top.

"How did you see me?" she asked. "If you were being treated?"

"Water closet," he answered. "I peeked out the hall window on my way back."

Lealle snickered. "They're going to think you're taking an awfully long time," she murmured.

Remy shrugged. "We should get back," he said.

As she started walking toward the alley mouth, he fell in beside her.

"Don't tell Mamere!" she said, abruptly urgent.

Remy frowned. "About the bully? And what you did to his arm? And all that?"

"Yes. All that."

"Mamere 'ud forbid your antiphony lessons flat, wouldn't she," he said speculatively.

Lealle nodded. "She would. So keep your mouth shut."

Remy glanced at her sidelong. "I can do that," he agreed. "And I will." He nodded.

Lealle sighed—she was *so* tired—and led the way into a gap amongst the passersby on the street flagway.

Chapter Eight

OHTAVIE FOUND herself in the library again come evening. It was a relief, really.

She pulled the holland covers from all the chairs to reveal the richness of their maroon leather and dragged the floor canvas into a corner. The deep brown carpeting thus displayed, with its rust and golden traceries, felt wonderfully cushioned underfoot. She would *use* this room, rather than preserving it unused. She would take comfort from its carved paneling, from the warm scent of the books, and from the room's history as her papa's sanctum.

The day had been . . . difficult. Although it wasn't truly the day that had been difficult, but that Ohtavie had made it so.

She'd allowed herself the usual daily chores, fixing meals and cleaning up after them. She'd even scrubbed the kitchen sink, gripping its rim with one hand to steady herself while she wielded the scrubbing brush with the other, scouring the porcelain from drain to faucet and then rinsing it down. She'd done the same for the sink outside the water closet in the servants' hall. Today was Reindy after all, and Reindy was when she cleaned the sinks and the water closet.

The water closet she could not manage, not on crutches.

But it wasn't the chores that made the day difficult.

It was that she'd refused to allow herself to pace. The pacing would have been so easy, especially with her crutches, so perfectly sized and so beautifully stable. Pacing was what Ohtavie was used to. It felt natural; it called to her.

But if she were ever to find freedom—be specific, Ohtavie, she told herself—if she were ever to leave this house, she would have to free herself from her embraced reclusiveness. Her habits must change, and *she* must change them. Pacing was one of her most ingrained habits, and the most useless.

So she'd refused herself that comfort.

And it had been hard, but it hadn't been the only hard thing. She'd also forced herself to approach one window in each room she entered and *look out*.

She'd had to trick herself at first, bending her head to stare at the floor as she crutched forward, telling herself that she was merely going to sit in that nearby armchair and rest, but then swerving to the window instead. But then she'd decided that was cheating, and she'd aimed for the window directly, her eyes on her goal.

Her stomach had grown queasy under the strain, but she'd done what she set out to do. She'd stood before nearly every window on the first floor and gazed out on the lanes to each side of the house, out across the back garden with its terrace and lilacs, and out onto Balard Square with its fountain and trees and playing children.

At first, with each window, it had grown harder. She'd almost fainted at the tenth. And, yes, she'd been counting, wondering if she could stop at the fifth or the seventh or the ninth. But after she leaned dizzily against the sash of that tenth window, and then refused to whirl away from it to pace, looking out had gotten . . . not easier, but slightly less fraught.

Sinking into the wingchair by the library window—*after* she'd looked out of it—felt wonderful though, as did propping both her feet on the footstool. Her right foot, the broken one, did not hurt. Nor had it swollen. But challenging her two worst habits, the pacing and the not-looking out, had tired her more than even her ordinary chores would have.

The leather beneath her received her gratefully, and she entertained a smidgeon of hope. She'd won her struggle and won a tiny bit of freedom with it. Perhaps she would win free altogether eventually. But now—now, it was time to rest.

She leaned forward to peruse the stack of books Lealle had left on the broad windowsill. *Pascalina, or Purity Rewarded. Eugenie. The Modern Rosamund.* Truly, the titles gave her little to go by. Which might she enjoy?

About to simply pluck the top book from the stack—*Pascalina,* as it chanced—she noticed that the bottom two books had no titles at all on their spines. She slid the topmost of the two out and opened it.

A flyleaf with old-fashioned handwriting upon its yellowed surface met her gaze. She skipped to the next page, also handwritten, frowning. This wasn't a book from a press at all, but—

She skimmed the first few lines.

Imsterfeldt, 17th Thyaril, 1763

My dearest Berdine,

I simply must, must, give you some account of my first party here amongst my beloved husband's circle. Oh, Berdine! I am so happy...

No, not a story, indeed, but a book of bound letters. Real letters, not fictional ones. Who was Berdine? And who was the letter writer?

Ohtavie settled in to discover the answers.

Hugh is wonderful! Wonderful! Every afternoon he presents me with a fresh token of his esteem, a wristlet of sweet lilies, a brooch for my hair, a fan of Cambers lace. But tonight came the loveliest gift of all. It was after the evening spent at Madame de Valle's.

Oh, Berdine! Everyone was so amazingly kind! I was never left alone and lonely once. The ladies embraced me as one of their own and shared their secrets. The gentlemen danced with me and conversed with me and introduced me. Poor Hugh complained that it was not fair that he should not get even a moment of his bride's attention from start to finish, but it was really all his own fault. He'd begged his friends to make me feel at home, and they did!

I'll tell you more about the party, but first Hugh's gift!

It's a book of poems written in his own hand. He composed them all through his courtship of me, but did not dare share them with me until he'd won me as his own. Oh! Berdine, I cannot tell you how my heart felt in that moment.

Ohtavie read onward, alternately touched by the young bride's emotion and amused by her naiveté. The letter carried on in a similar vein, all the way to its conclusion, where the writer signed herself as *Your rapturously happy, Jovie.*

Ohtavie frowned again. Jovie. What was it about that name?

The next letter was dated a week later, still in Imsterfeldt, and the writer remained equally pleased with her situation, describing an afternoon's excursion to the ruins of an old mooring tower outside the city walls. This time she scribed herself as *Ecstatically yours.*

Ohtavie wondered again about her name. Jovie. Jovie.

Impatiently she flicked the pages back to the flyleaf.

To the Lady Berdine Evrard from the Duchesse Sophia Joviane de Pouilly.

Sophia Joviane de Pouilly. That was Grandmere's proper name, and title. 'Jovie' was Grandmere? But how had that jubilant young bride become the bitter old woman that Ohtavie had known?

Ohtavie bent with renewed attention to the bound letters.

The answer to her question proved absent from that first volume. Longing to know, she dragged the second untitled volume from the bottom of the stack of books, and breathed relief when she saw that the handwriting was the same. What if it had proved to be some entirely unrelated tome?

Dusk was falling in the square outside, and the remaining light in the library had grown dim. Ohtavie lit the candelabra in the nearest wall sconce, forgetting her vow that no lights would shine after dark in the Maison de Bellay, and read on.

But the second volume gave no more clue than had the first. 'Jovie' continued her delighted progress through the social scene of eighteenth century Imsterfeldt, attended by her devoted husband and an increasing number of new friends.

In the very last letter, Hugh returned home ahead of Jovie to his castle in the countryside outside Claireau. Jovie mentioned in her postscript that Hugh had discovered something very curious. *But I'll tell you all about it in my next,* Jovie promised her friend.

Only there was no next!

Ohtavie leaned back in the wingchair, suddenly aware that she was cramped and very hungry. It was full dark outside. She wanted to search the library shelves for more of Grandmere's correspondence, but . . .

She glanced at the cressets burning so brightly at the portals to a few of the houses across the square. The dim glow of her own candles was likely invisible in comparison, but still she should snuff them, fix herself a meal, and seek her bed.

Were she as young as 'Jovie,' she might feel tempted to read on through the night, assuming she could locate the third volume. Assuming there *was* a third volume.

As it was . . .

As it was, she *was* tempted, although she wasn't sure she'd ever been as young at heart as was her great grandmere.

And what an odd thought that was. Grandmere young? But she had been. Once.

∞

By the time Lealle reached the steps of the retreat house, she was stumbling, barely able to keep her feet with the fatigue that weighed her down.

Remy clutched her arm, steadying her as she lurched upward to the front door.

Dully she noticed that her fichu and hair ribbon were gone from where Gaetan had thrown them down. She supposed she should care, but all she wanted to do was sit. In fact, she would just sink down right here and—

Remy didn't let her, hauling on her arm and hustling her in through the stately front door.

Once inside, he dragged her into the front waiting room.

"Where's Mamere?" she asked, vaguely surprised. Why had Remy pulled her in here? Shouldn't he be returning to whatever clinic room he'd been ensconced in for his healing?

Remy snorted, clearly exasperated, and she tried to focus, but the room around her seemed almost to swing in her blurring vision, and she couldn't. At least the solid wing chairs and couches were untenanted by people. Their lacy antimacassars formed pointed triangles on the furniture backs and curving ovals on the arms.

Lealle had a hazy sense that she didn't want anyone to see her right now, like this.

Remy was brushing irritatedly at the skirt of her frock and muttering. "At least you're wearing the pinkish brownish one," he grumbled. "If it was white, you'd be sunk."

Blearily, she realized that he was trying to make her presentable, just the way she had done for him so many times when he'd been playing where he shouldn't be. She must have gotten dirt on her frock when she knelt in that alley stairwell.

Remy's mouth twisted when he left off brushing her skirt to study her shoulders. Then his face brightened. "Ha! This'll do!" he exclaimed, grabbing one of the triangular antimacassars off a chair back and draping it around her neck, crossing the ends over her front, and tucking them into her sash. Then he scowled again. "Mamere will fuss if your hair's down."

He darted a frantic glance around the room, another glance over his shoulder toward the archway into the hall, and then plucked a brown ribbon, tied in a silken bow, from an overly trimmed pillow adorning one of the couches.

"Sit down!" he ordered her.

She'd been swaying and was only too glad to comply, almost falling onto the ottoman that swam into her vision.

She felt Remy's hands in her hair, yanking the strands back from her face and securing them into a ponytail. She couldn't think what he was about.

Then he was in front of her again, urging her to her feet.

"Lealle, you have to, to . . . to be normal," he stammered. "There's no use me keeping my mouth shut about that bully and what you did to his arm, if you make Mamere suspicious. Lealle!"

She pulled her wandering gaze back to his face at the frantic note in his voice. His eyes looked tight with worry. She nodded.

"I can do it," she said.

Remy glared at her. "You better!" he said.

Lealle followed him out into the front hall and up the stairs there. In the upper hall, windows onto the inner courtyard cast rectangles of mellow evening light upon the brown matting covering the polished floorboards. The faint scent of flowers perfumed the air. One of the windows farther along the passageway off the hall must be open, allowing the outdoor air in.

Remy cast an impatient glance over his shoulder, and Lealle jerked into motion again, following him down the passageway and through an open door.

Mamere was seated decorously on a wooden chair, leaning forward to talk with the healer—Maitresse Barbitaine, Lealle noted—occupying the only other chair in the small room. More evening light flooded through the window—large for the small size of the room—to fall on the tall examining table against one wall, and glinting on the coils of Mamere's honey brown hair.

She looked up when her children appeared in the doorway, a slight frown knitting her brows.

"You took long enough, Remy, love," she chided. But her tone was indulgent.

Remy wisely ignored her words. "I found Lealle!" he announced. "She was waiting for us on the front steps."

Mamere's eyebrows rose. "Hardly ladylike, my dear," she pronounced, still complacent despite Lealle's misdemeanor.

Lealle pulled herself together as best she could. "It's such a pretty evening, Mamere," she excused herself.

Mamere repressed a sniff. "No doubt," she answered, "but perching on front stoops is not the kind of behavior I want from you. And we'd not have missed you, if you'd been in the waiting room." She added, "Remy and I came in the Rue Poigny door, not the main one."

That explained how she and Lealle had missed one another anyway.

"I'm sorry, Mamere," said Lealle, stiffening the wobble in her knees. She desperately wanted to sit again.

Mamere nodded graciously, and then turned her attention to Remy, who was scrambling onto the examining table.

"Close the door, will you, Lealle?" requested Maitresse Barbitaine's matter-of-fact voice.

Lealle pushed herself into motion once more, swinging the door to, and then subsiding against it. If she couldn't sit—and just taking the four steps across the room to the chair Maitresse Barbitaine was exiting seemed too much—maybe she could manage not to crumple into a heap if she leaned hard enough on the door. If only Mamere didn't notice her slouching.

Lealle felt her eyelids drifting closed. Maitresse Barbitaine's instructions to Remy on how she wanted his arm positioned formed a soothing murmur that became even more soothing when the instructions transitioned into the chant that accompanied the healer's manipulation of antiphony.

The silver traceries that formed the energy of Remy's arcs bloomed in Lealle's mind's eye along with the gentle blue and green light of safe magic. Lealle couldn't help following the flow sparks that marked the healer's efforts. Watching them seemed to strengthen her own knees somehow, to lessen the sense of her fatigue.

She wondered if she might remember the manipulations well enough later, tomorrow when she was rested, to learn something. Maybe she could find Gaetan and use what she learned to heal his arm more. Maybe . . .

Mamere's voice interrupted her musing.

"Stand up straight, dear. Ladies don't slouch!"

Lealle's eyes flew open. As she withdrew her weight from the door behind her and lifted her chin, she grew aware that she'd lost some time somewhere. Had she slipped into a brief upright nap? Maitresse Barbitaine was giving some last instructions to Mamere for the care of Remy's arm, helping Remy down from the table, and bidding them a very good evening.

Lealle managed to step aside, and Remy twisted the door knob—thank the saints—grabbing Lealle's hand to draw her through once he swung the door open.

"Is something wrong, dearest," came Mamere's voice behind her, a tender tone in it. "Did something happen?"

Lealle's insides sank. She could barely set one foot in front of the other. All she wanted to do was lie down. How on earth was she going to manufacture an explanation for Mamere that would pass muster?

Remy's hand squeezed hers. "She saw some boys tormenting a puppy," he said, still towing Lealle forward. "It really upset her," he added. "She told me when I found her."

"Oh, darling!" Mamere's tenderness increased, and her arm slipped gently around Lealle's shoulders. "How wretched for you. Let's get you home and some supper into you. You'll feel better then."

Some of the tension holding Lealle upright ebbed, and she stubbed her toe on the matting underfoot.

Mamere's grip on her shoulders tightened.

Lealle leaned into her mother.

Mamere might be annoying. She *was* annoying. But she did care. And she'd never much gone for 'I told you so.' And 'I told you so' certainly would have been called for here and now. But Mamere clearly was not saying it.

∞

After her supper, Ohtavie directed her crutches through the shadowy mansion toward her bedchamber. She should go to sleep. She really should. Rest and the horizontal position entailed by slumber would help her foot heal.

But there was something compelling about her great grandmere's letters. It was almost as though they held some personal answer for Ohtavie herself, although how that could be made no sense. In any case, she was curious to know what Grandpere had found that had so thrilled Grandmere.

I'll just go check that bottom shelf where Lealle found the first two volumes, she told herself, knowing she was lying. If she found a third volume . . . would she really set it aside to read in the morning?

Hardly.

She did pull the drapes the instant she entered the library. It was one thing to be self-indulgent regarding her bedtime. It was another entirely to risk her safety by flaunting candlelight at the windows.

Only after she dragged each set of drapes completely closed did she light candles—a round dozen. Her eyes squinted, adjusting to the sudden radiance after gloom, and the gold threads in the folds of the brown brocade drapes glinted. She would need good light, if she were going to stay up late reading.

Crossing to the bookshelves with the poetry, Ohtavie swung the glass fronts open and lowered herself to the floor. She was surprised at how easy it was until she realized she'd allowed a little weight to rest on her casted foot. It hadn't hurt at all, but she'd better be more observant going forward. Lealle's enigmatic scrutiny might have speeded her foot's healing, but it couldn't possibly be ready for standing.

Lealle had removed enough books from the bottom shelf that the remaining volumes had toppled sideways. Most of them had no titles on their spines, which was promising, since the first two collections of Grandmere's letters had been titleless as well.

Ohtavie pulled out the topmost and checked the flyleaf.

To the Lady Berdine Evrard from the Duchesse Sophia Joviane de Pouilly, 13th Jubiante through 11th Bricember, 1763.

A third volume! Or was it a fourth? The previous collection had ended with a missive from the month of Joiesse, hadn't it? Where were the letters from Labresse?

Ohtavie turned the page.

Claireau, 13th Jubiante, 1763

My dearest Berdine...

So Grandmere had returned home from Imsterfeldt. What did that mean?

I remain rapturously happy! Hugh's mother received me in the kindest way and is turning over the management of the household staff almost faster than I can learn what I need to, in order to do it properly! If the housekeeper were not so willing to help such a novice as I, I'd be sunk!

Ohtavie felt a little buffeted by all the exclamation marks. Clearly Grandmere continued as the enthusiastic bride even once she was settling into her husband's estate.

But, oh, Berdine! I have even more exciting news! Docteur Moineux says I am to become a mamere in Bricember! Hugh is as excited as I am. If it is a boy, we will call him Henri. If it's a little girl, she will be Apolline.

Well, it would be a girl. Ohtavie knew that. A girl, and an only child. And *not* called Apolline. Heavens, what a name! Ohtavie had never met her mother's mother. Yvette had died the year before Ohtavie was born.

She skimmed ahead. There was something important in these letters, she was sure of it. What that something was, she was not sure.

But it wasn't going to be Grandmere's burbling about her 'interesting condition,' as they called it in those days.

But, Berdine! I have used you monstrously, to be sure. I promised you news of Hugh's discovery in my last letter, and then gave you neither news nor even a letter! I do apologize, my dear friend! Say you forgive me, do! I shall make up for my dereliction now, I promise!

Ohtavie suppressed a smile. Well, get on with it, she thought, still bemused by the youthful Jovie.

This is what happened, Berdine.

You know my darling Hugh has a passion for antiquities, do you not?

Well, maybe you don't, but he does. Almost as great as his passion for me, but not quite. (I'm laughing, my dear friend, in case you can't tell!) Anyway! Hugh inherited some wonderful things from his father, who also collected antiquities, but was not nearly so careful about what Hugh calls provenance. *Which I don't quite understand, but which Hugh assures me is important. He says that if you don't know what something really is or where it came from, it's not nearly so valuable — or* interesting — *as if you do. (I think Hugh cares more about* interesting *than he does about* valuable.) *So!*

What Hugh came across in Imsterfeldt was an old scroll from the days of the airships! Can you imagine! Airships! And the scroll explains what that strange, black pebble in his papere's collection really is! It's an energea-*stone!*

Ohtavie sat back. How odd. She'd been learning about *energea*-stones in the book she'd read just before encountering Jovie's letters. The old mages of Navarys had used them to magnify their magery. Encountering the term again, in her great grandmere's account, seemed oddly significant. But significant of what?

She became aware of her knee aching, curled to one side with the other and pressed down by her casted leg. She hadn't meant to sit on the floor reading. The light wasn't as good here either. She'd get eyestrain and a headache and who knew what else, if she stayed put. She should move to the comfortable leather chair she'd occupied in the afternoon.

She glanced at the other volumes on that lowest shelf. There were quite a few. Had all of Grandmere's letters to Berdine been preserved and bound?

No matter. She couldn't read them two at a time, and if she skimmed too quickly, she might miss . . . whatever it was she wanted to find in them.

Tucking the Jubiante-Bricember volume into her apron pocket, she hauled herself up her crutches to her feet. Her whole body felt stiff from hunching to read. She touched the lump of her pendant under her blouse before crutching over to the chair in front of the curtained window, its drapes hiding Balard Square and any bright-shining cressets from townhouses holding evening entertainments.

The comforting scent of leather rose around her as she settled onto the armchair's cushions. Ah, this was much better than the floor.

She reopened the book of Jovie's letters. She felt like she knew Jovie, but she still balked at considering Jovie and Grandmere as one and the same. They were, of course. What had happened to the blushing bride, that she became the severe and joyless old woman?

But, Berdine, here's the really exciting thing! The scroll not only identifies that black pebble as an energea-stone, *but it explains how to turn an* energea-stone *into something called a lodestone. A lodestone is much more powerful than a mere* energea-stone! *And dear Hugh has always felt troubled by the smallness of his own magical gift. With a lodestone at his command, his gift could be much more! And as a scholar, which he is much more than a mage, replicating the technology of the ancients gives him such a thrill.*

That *is why my letters to you ceased so abruptly in Joiesse, dear Berdine! Hugh was determined to return home willy nilly, so he could dive into his workshop there and get to work! Which meant I was plunged into learning from the dear dowager, with little time for letters! But I promise to keep you apprised going forward. This fall is going to be so exciting!*

Ohtavie sat back again. *Energea*-stones. Lodestones. A small black pebble. Was there any connection to the small black stone held within the delicate silver cage of her pendant? Was this why she wanted—needed—to read Jovie's letters?

She bent her head again to the bound volume.

Jovie did keep her promise to write her friend more often, although the frequency of her letters was not apparently to her own satisfaction, because she apologized profusely in nearly every one for not writing more often. Looking at the dates, Ohtavie could see that she had written every two or three weeks, rather than every week, as she had in Imsterfeldt.

Hugh's research did not go as quickly as Jovie had envisioned, but Jovie described every step of the process, dwelling particularly on all the obscure methods her husband tried in his efforts to chill the black pebble sufficiently.

Ohtavie wondered if he had been aware that his wife was leaking his secrets to her friend. Didn't most scholars guard their discoveries from their competing peers until after their scholarly treatises were published? Ohtavie wasn't sure, but she wondered if that was the real reason Hugh eventually banished Jovie from his workshop.

Jovie claimed it was because he was worried about what the next step of the process—percussive force applied repeatedly along with enigmatic (magical) force—might do to their unborn child in Jovie's womb.

Ohtavie fingered the lump of her pendant. Excluded from Hugh's workroom, would Jovie still report on his researches to Berdine? Ohtavie hoped so. She was more and more sure that it was Hugh's researches she needed to learn about. Surely Hugh would tell his wife of his progress. And she would tell Berdine in her turn. Unless Hugh did indeed know of—and disapprove of—Jovie's indiscretion.

Ohtavie turned the page and read on.

Dearest Berdine,

Hugh spends more and more time in his researches, which means I miss him a bit during the day. He does not walk with me in the gardens as he used to, nor escort me to society luncheons, but it is all worthwhile, because in the evening over dinner we trade stories.

He tells me all about how he is having difficulty generating sufficient enigmatic force. And I tell him about how many times Baby turned somersaults within my womb and kicked my ribs from the inside! He loves hearing of all my doings, and of course I love hearing of his!

Oh, Berdine! I never guessed that being in love with one's husband could be this wonderful! I am the luckiest bride alive!

Jovie's enthusiasm continued unabated as her letters went on, but Ohtavie couldn't help but notice that Hugh appeared to grow more taciturn as time passed. Jovie herself seemed not to notice. Their daughter was born, and Jovie complained that Hugh didn't visit the nursery every day in the same breath that she spoke of his fatherly devotion.

To Ohtavie, he came across as increasingly preoccupied with his enigmatic research, frustrated that its progress had slowed almost to a halt, and convinced that he would have more time for his family once he made a breakthrough on his *energea*-stone. Ohtavie suspected . . . that he was wrong about that. Habits formed over months and years of months could be very hard to break. She was learning that herself. Looking out each window of her home this morning and this afternoon had been hard. Not pacing . . . had been harder. She still was entirely uncertain of the outcome in the battle between herself and her habits.

Would Hugh break his? Would his enigmatic breakthrough even arrive? Or would he withdraw into his workroom more and more? Ohtavie thought she knew the answer to those questions. No, no, and yes. She was likely witnessing the origin of Grandmere's bitterness even as she read.

Setting the open book down on her lap, Ohtavie pulled out the pendant from beneath her blouse and studied it. The candlelight gleamed on the dainty links of the platinum chain and the delicate platinum prongs enclosing the matte black stone within their abstract swirl.

The texture of the stone over most of its surface was almost like velvet, smooth but with a subtle catch to it that she could just barely feel through the spaces between the cage prongs. But one edge of the stone had been broken away, leaving an ugly and jagged face.

That damage had made her doubt her initial suspicion that her pendant was Hugh's *energea*-stone. Jovie had described Hugh's stone thoroughly, and it was perfectly smooth, with no breach in its smoothness. But now . . . now she believed that some accident would happen to Hugh's stone, making it the twin of hers.

She needed to know what that accident was. It held answers for her, she was sure.

But what time was it? How long had she been sitting in her papa's library reading? She was near the end of this third volume of Jovie's letters. Was it very late?

Closing the book, she leaned forward to place it on the window sill, and then leaned forward yet more to pull the drapes slightly apart where their halves met, and peer out the crack.

No cressets burned in the square, but the moon rode high and full, shedding silver light on the stilled fountain—turned off for the night— and the tops of the shadowy trees.

Ohtavie let the drapes fall closed.

She doubted the last pages of this third volume of Jovie's letters would hold Hugh's yearned-for breakthrough. She wasn't going to find out what had happened tonight. And it was long past time for bed.

The Fifth Day

Hunting in Book and Street

Chapter Nine

OHTAVIE AWOKE very late the next day. She could tell the instant she opened her eyes.

She'd not closed the curtains in her bedchamber the night before, undressing in the dark, and beyond the windows the sun now shone high in the sky, casting only a sliver of shadow below the shrubbery at the side of the house. The light was very bright.

It must be nearly noon!

Her morning routine was almost too easy, although she supposed she ought not call it a *morning* routine, given the time. Her *awakening* routine of washing hands and face, dressing, even making her bed was too easy. She kept forgetting to favor her casted foot, touching it down whenever it was convenient to help her balance and—once—starting to step forward with it. She remembered before her weight transfer was complete, thank the saints, but she grew frustrated with herself. Did she want her foot to heal properly? If so, she couldn't afford to be careless.

She was eager to get back to her Grandmere's letters. Today, surely today, she would reach Hugh's breakthrough and find out . . . something.

And one side benefit of her interest would be that her temptation to pace should be greatly reduced or even absent altogether. Last night, she'd not once longed to leap up from her chair and start walking about the house. Saints willing, it would be the same today.

She'd already noticed, on her trip to the water closet in the servant's hall, that she was looking out of all the windows . . . not routinely, but with only a slight queasiness in her stomach. She'd need to persevere, and she suspected she'd need to be vigilant about not falling back into her reclusive ways, but maybe the worst of it—the lightheadedness, the panic, the hammering heart—was over. She felt more sure of herself, that she would win out over her bad habits.

And maybe Hugh de Pouilly—her great grandpere—would win out over his. And maybe his wife, Ohtavie's great grandmere, would remain happy for longer. Perhaps it would be Grandpere's death, not his neglect, that would embitter Grandmere.

Ohtavie hoped so, as she made her way on her crutches toward the kitchen.

It might be noon, but Ohtavie still needed to break her fast before she dove again into reading.

As she passed into the passageway beyond the butler's pantry, she came to so abrupt a halt that she nearly fell. Lealle, dressed prettily in a print frock of green and cream, was just climbing the last few steps up from the cellars.

Ohtavie's heart slammed into sudden pounding against the inner wall of her chest—with fear. But it was not fear *of* Lealle that she felt; it was fear *for* her. A dreadful thing, *the* dreadful thing had happened to Ohtavie in those cellars. Was Lealle all right?

Ohtavie catalogued Lealle's features in one frantic glance: eyes bright and wide, nose straight and small, color good, head held high. The girl looked . . . fine. And Ohtavie knew that her fear was irrational—it was not the cellars themselves that had wrought the damage—but she couldn't help associating disaster with the underground spaces.

Why had Lealle been down there anyway? She shouldn't have been! This was not her home that she should wander it freely. How dare she?

"How dare you descend there again?" Ohtavie grated out. "How dare you!"

❧

Lealle, when she awakened in the morning, barely remembered the previous evening's drive home from the retreat center in Mamere's brougham-landau. The dust of the street air had tickled her nose. The crushed velvet of the seat back had felt hot and plushy under the pressure of her cheek as she slouched against it. And Mamere had not reprimanded her for failing to sit up straight. Lealle remembered that, but she didn't remember being put to bed or even being driven under the always-raised portcullis into the narrow courtyard of her castle home. Had Papere carried her up to her bedchamber? Surely she was too big to be carried?

But somehow, she'd reached chamber and bed, where she'd slept straight through to dawn.

Her idea upon waking, with the cool gray light before sunrise flooding through her windows, was that this was the perfect time to slip off to see Ohtavie. Mamere's plans—and then Lealle's own exhaustion in the wake of returning Gaetan's wooden hand to flesh—had kept Lealle away from Ohtavie's mansion. The troll-woman had seemed much better the last time Lealle saw her, better both physically—her foot was healing—and in spirit. She'd been composedly reading. And Lealle had found her a bunch of good books to read.

But still . . . Lealle felt uneasy.

A whole day had passed. What if Ohtavie had taken a turn for the worse? Lealle wanted to check on her. Besides . . . Ohtavie was *interesting*. Lealle was looking forward to their next conversation.

Unfortunately for Lealle's idea for her Beldaine morning, Mamere had different ideas.

She bustled into Lealle's room, skirts swishing, determined to whisk Lealle off on an errand of beneficence.

"Remy's broken arm meant we both missed helping out in the chapel soup kitchen!" she announced. "And you'd particularly wanted to, hadn't you, darling?"

Well, yes. Lealle had *said* she particularly wanted to when she was trying to come up with reasons not to be sent out of town on a visit to Bonne-mémé and Bon-papy. But repudiating that expressed wish . . . seemed unwise. Mamere's voice held an unusually tender note.

And so Lealle was whisked away—to the soup kitchen held by Les Dames de la Princesse, another of the charities patronized by Mamere.

But really it turned out very well. At such an early hour in the morning, they were serving breakfast. Which meant that when breakfast was done, it was merely late morning, and Lealle managed to elude further supervision by claiming that she was tired and needed to rest, since she wanted to be fresh that afternoon when she went to take tea with Tiffanie Mercier.

Said tea *was* on her schedule, but her ploy nearly miscarried; Mamere's brow creased slightly at Lealle's claim of fatigue.

"Dearest, you're not still upset by the puppy, are you? You needn't be, you know. Shall we talk about it? Will that help?"

Almost did Lealle blurt out, "Puppy? What puppy?"

Just before she spoke, she recalled Remy's excuse for her exhaustion yesterday and converted her confused question into a restrained, "No, not at all, Mamere. Truly. In fact, I'd rather *not* talk about it. I'm just tired. All those crippled old men, from the wars, made me sad." Which they had, but her sadness had not translated into physical weariness as she pretended.

Mamere touched a light kiss to the tip of Lealle's nose—which made Lealle blink—and acquiesced. "Very well, darling. Go rest!"

And so Lealle retreated to her room, staying there long enough to be sure Mamere was well out of the way, and only then sneaking out to walk to the Maison de Bellay.

When she let herself in through the kitchen door, the mansion seemed very quiet, too quiet. Which didn't really make sense. How could a house be any quieter than when its sole occupant was sitting in the library reading? But it was.

Lealle peered into the scullery, but she couldn't tell if Ohtavie had eaten breakfast or not. The clean dishes were adding up, since Ohtavie had decided not to worry about putting them away until her foot was better. Lealle felt her brows knitting. She sniffed the air delicately. The scullery did have that fresh smell, as though cold water had been running recently. But it had smelled that way every other time Lealle had entered it, so that didn't really mean anything.

She found herself tiptoeing as she moved through the passage to the butler's pantry and on to the rest of the house. Somehow she wasn't surprised when she reached the door to Ohtavie's sitting room and found it closed. Was Ohtavie still asleep?

Lealle jittered there before the closed door. She wanted to go in and check on her friend, and yet it didn't seem quite right to invade Ohtavie's privacy like that, without even a knock. And Lealle didn't want to knock if Ohtavie *was* asleep.

What to do? What to do?

Lealle's forefinger tapped against its neighboring finger in her indecision.

I'll wait a little while, she decided, and then if Ohtavie's still not up, I'll go in and check.

She retreated to the kitchen, quickly grew bored with sitting at the central worktable there, and started to put away the clean dishes resting on the scullery drainboards. After her second trip from scullery to dish pantry, she realized that even helping Ohtavie in this way was a little intrusive. She'd not asked Ohtavie after all, and Lealle didn't know if she might be messing up the troll-woman's system, whatever that was.

Lealle sat some more, and found her thoughts turning to Gaetan, her other self-imposed charge. She had to find him and check his arm. She thought she'd eased the bruising enough that it would heal. But it had to be painful. And . . . a responsible person would check. Just look at Remy and his broken arm. Maitresse Barbitaine had made the bone whole yesterday morning and then checked on her work and done follow-up healing that very afternoon.

Lealle simply had to find Gaetan. And soon. Today, by choice.

But what would she do, when she found him? She wished she knew more about the effects of her magery. Gaetan's arm had been badly bruised, but was there more to it than that? Was there any way she could find out? Or figure it out?

She straightened in the kitchen chair abruptly, and then jumped up from it.

If she returned to the scene where she'd discovered the antiphonic technique she'd used, first triumphantly on Ohtavie's crutches, and then so disastrously on Gaetan's hand and arm, maybe she could learn something that would help.

Clattering out into the passageway, she dashed for the stairs down to the cellars.

Descending into the shadows felt a little spooky. The ground floor of the mansion was so bright and airy with its large windows that the cellars seemed especially dark in comparison. Although, really, the cellars were very well lit for underground spaces. At least the rooms on the outside edges were, with the parade of half-circle windows all along the outer wall. Or maybe Lealle's eyes were just adjusting.

The scent of the cool stone and the sound of her shoes slapping the flagstone floor somehow combined to create a friendly feeling to the cellar passage.

In the workroom where she'd fixed Ohtavie's crutches, she paused to study the pegboard hung with all the tools. They were very dusty, and most were beyond Lealle's understanding. But the jagged teeth of the saws and the sharp edge on another tool with a strange pommel looked . . . dangerous.

She turned away from the pegboard to scrutinize the clamp that had held each of Ohtavie's crutches steady while Lealle had sawed them shorter.

She reviewed the process in her mind's eye: sawing each stalk of wood, the great splinter that had detached from the first, the more careful sawing of the second, the way the rubber cap had been too small for that second, and then how she had *squeezed* the wood antiphonically.

She couldn't help shuddering a little at that memory. It called up too vividly the sensation of squeezing Gaetan's arm.

She nibbled her lower lip.

Reviewing what she'd done to the crutches—and to Gaetan—wasn't helping. What she needed was not a better understanding of what she'd done. She knew what she'd done. She needed to know more of how to heal him. And that . . . would take years of lessons. Probably.

What if she focused instead on what Maitresse Barbitaine had done for Remy yesterday afternoon? Lealle had seen the antiphony for it. In fact, that was the only thing she'd seen, since her eyes had been closed at the time. Could she reconstruct it now?

She straightened, not in the stiff way that Mamere prompted her so often, but in the comfortable way that antiphony required, the way that Maitresse Aubry instructed her. Leveling her chin and lifting her crown felt good, as did the relaxation that came from allowing her shoulders to drop. Softening her knees permitted her hips to drop slightly as well, and then her feet felt better grounded against the stone floor.

She drew a slow breath in and allowed it to flow even more slowly out.

Maitresse Aubry had followed a similar discipline yesterday. Every antiphoner did when preparing for antiphonic work. But what had she done next?

Lealle took another gentle in-breath. As she let it go, the cool arcs of silver and blue sparks from Remy's healing moved through her memory. First had come the discipline called Breath of the Pegasus, which was just looking, perceiving, without any attempt to manipulate the physical reality.

But what had come next?

The dance of cool antiphonic sparks moved on in Lealle's memory, familiarly. Surely she recognized that pattern? Oh! She did! It was the Zephyr's Gavotte, one of the earliest patterns she'd learned. And practiced. Saints, but she'd practiced it, over and over again. She *knew* the Gavotte. She knew it and could perform it without flaw.

Her eyes flew open, and she started toward the workshop door.

She would see if Ohtavie was awake yet. If she was, Lealle would see how she was doing. And if she wasn't . . . if she wasn't, Lealle would go in search of Gaetan. Ohtavie was probably all right. Gaetan . . . wasn't. And it was Lealle's fault he wasn't. She *wanted* to see Ohtavie. She missed Ohtavie. But she *needed* to see Gaetan. To see him and to help him.

Quickening her pace, she took the first few steps up from the cellars two at a time. She knew what to do now, and it felt really good.

Up, up, up.

She had to slow as her legs tired, but her excitement increased. *This can work,* she told herself.

As her gaze cleared the top step, she saw Ohtavie passing through the doorway from the butler's pantry and into the corridor where the cellar stairs debouched.

Ohtavie was moving easily and looked good.

Perfect, thought Lealle. Then she saw Ohtavie's face: tight and angry.

"How dare you!" grated the troll-woman. "How dare you risk yourself again!"

～

Lealle teetered on the top step, nearly tipping backward in a fall. Then she clutched the hand rail and saved herself.

"I didn't," she protested, confused. What was Ohtavie talking about?

"You knew I didn't want you in the cellars!" Ohtavie was actually yelling. Emphasizing her point, she raised her right fist, clenching it and shaking it. Her right crutch clattered to the floor.

Still puzzled, Lealle dove after it. Had Ohtavie really forbade Lealle the cellars? She retrieved the fallen crutch and offered it back to the troll-woman, who refused it.

"You enter my home uninvited!" Ohtavie continued her tirade. "You refuse to return me my privacy! You pop up under my elbow again and again! You endanger yourself merely by being here! And now this! A deliberate return to the exact place in this house that you knew I didn't want you in!"

Lealle gripped the refused crutch, her surprise at Ohtavie's anger giving way to a different sort of puzzlement. What should she do? What *did* one do when someone was shouting the way Ohtavie was shouting?

Mamere got cold and severe when she was angry, which made Lealle feel about two feet tall, but Mamere didn't shout. In fact, she didn't raise her voice at all; she lowered it. Nurse got fussy and querulous when she was irritated, and Lealle always felt guilty for upsetting her. Her teachers at school didn't bother to be angry. They just meted out a set number of strokes from the rod or so many minutes standing on the platform before the class—although not to Lealle. She was well-behaved in school. And Papere . . . was more inclined to laugh at childish misbehavior than to punish it. Although he would take steps when he deemed it necessary. But like her teachers, he didn't get mad.

So what did one do in a situation like this? When someone yelled? Lealle's brows knit and her index finger tapped the knuckle of her middle finger.

Ohtavie fell silent, her chest heaving as she panted.

Lealle found herself glaring at the troll-woman.

Ohtavie glared back.

Lealle's mouth opened, and it almost seemed that it was Mamere's voice issuing from between her lips. But it wasn't. It was Lealle's own voice and Lealle's own words. Except they seemed like Mamere's words also.

"You are overwrought," she stated, her tone chilly. "If you cannot rein in your emotion to civility in company, you had best not have it. I shall give you the solitude you require in which to contemplate your behavior!"

Despite her cold demeanor—and, oh, she was cold—a hot feeling was growing in Lealle's chest. How dare Ohtavie claim Lealle was there uninvited! She had been at first. But Ohtavie herself had granted Lealle permission to visit the very last time they'd spoken. To claim that Lealle was trespassing now was wholly unreasonable.

Lealle lifted her chin. "I shall leave you," she declaimed, still collectedly, but with a bit of a ring to her voice. "I shall expect an apology upon my return!"

And now it was time to go. She wasn't sure she could maintain Mamere's sort of dignity, if she stayed. And what if she started yelling like Ohtavie had? That would be *so* embarrassing!

Turning sedately, she leaned the crutch she still held against the banister guarding the stairwell, and paced toward the kitchen—and its side door to the lane—with a measured stride.

There was only silence behind her.

❧

As Lealle walked away from her down the passageway, Ohtavie fought tears.

Why had she lost control like that? How could she have uttered such unkindness? Why had she raised her voice like that? Why hadn't she simply bitten her tongue until she could speak civilly?

Lealle was right. Ohtavie had been overwrought, and she assuredly owed Lealle an apology.

Teetering a little on her one leg, supported by only the one crutch, she reached her free hand after the girl as Lealle turned the passageway corner.

"Lealle?" she husked, her voice barely a whisper.

The measured tread of Lealle's half-boots on the kitchen flagstones echoed distantly. Then came the sound of a door closing, a lock turning.

Lealle was gone.

"Oh!" gasped Ohtavie. "Oh!"

She wished she could run after the girl and bring her back. She wished she could retrieve her own unkind accusations before ever she spoke them. She wished she could do the last few minutes completely over. But she couldn't.

She could not run. She dared not leave the house. And she assuredly could not unspeak spoken words or rewind time.

Instead she hung on one crutch, wishing, while unaccustomed sobs shook her ribs and shoulders, and hot tears ran down her face.

What was wrong with her? She never cried. But she was crying now.

After an interval, the tears and the sobs stopped. She mopped her wet face with a corner of her apron, then gathered in the other crutch from where it leaned on the stairwell bannister. Tucking it beneath her free arm, she took a few slow swings toward the kitchen, paused, and then turned back toward the butler's pantry and the loggia beyond it. She wasn't hungry, and she needed to think. To think and to move.

Was her loss of control with Lealle due to her inexperience in dealing with people, the natural consequence of her long solitude? Or was her troll-disease overtaking her? Dear Thiyaude! Let it not be that!

❧

Lealle held herself very tall as she stalked through Claireau's streets, her face stiff and her glance disdainful. She was cold, oh, very cold. At least that's what she told herself. But the inside of her chest felt hot still, and she seethed.

How dare Ohtavie accuse her of being a nuisance like a little kid! 'Popping up under her elbow' in Ohtavie's words! How dare she assert that Lealle had destroyed her privacy! Invaded her home!

"I did nothing wrong!" Lealle growled to herself, and then blushed. Not only did ladies not mutter to themselves while walking abroad, but neither did sane people, whether they were ladies or charwomen or gentlemen or even little boys.

She glanced around her. Had anyone heard her? Where was she anyway? She hadn't been paying attention.

But the nearest person to her was a housemaid, shaking out a small rug on the front stoop a few doors down in one of the modest rowhouses lining the street. A cluster of little girls with hoops chattered to one another on the corner beyond. No one had heard her. No one was even paying attention to her. Which was good.

A gentle breeze rustled the leaves of the young trees shading the street, creating a swaying pattern of sun-dapples on the brick flagway. The air was very soft and that comfortable cool-warm typical of summer shade. The sweet scent of honeysuckle drifted from somewhere, maybe a back garden.

Lealle felt the hotness inside her ebbing, giving way to the beauty of the day.

An unexpected thought sprang to mind: *I think I scared her.*

Was that right? *Had* she scared Ohtavie?

Ohtavie couldn't have known Lealle was there. Lealle hadn't called out, or knocked, or indicated her presence in any way. How would Lealle have felt, if she'd been in Ohtavie's shoes?

I'd have jumped as high as that style in Bon-papy's far meadow, she admitted. And then what? *I'd have been angry,* she further admitted. *I might even have yelled.*

Lealle sighed. She suspected she owed Ohtavie an apology. No, she knew she owed her one.

Passing the giggling group of little girls with hoops, she noted the street sign adorning the brick wall of a small front garden: Rue Tulipe. She'd come clear across town in her rage. It had been rage, she admitted.

She'd been pretending it wasn't, but it was. And now that she wasn't raging . . . she'd better turn herself right back around and go make that apology to Ohtavie.

The sooner, the better.

She didn't want to live with this uncomfortable feeling in her tummy one minute longer than she had to.

Chapter Ten

PACING ABOUT the mansion, Ohtavie thought.

Her crutches—the crutches *Lealle* had fixed for her—made pacing so easy. And Ohtavie couldn't bear to sit still.

She'd lost control. (She was out of control now.)

She'd shouted.

She'd accused her young benefactor of bad behavior and poor choices.

Was it because of her troll-disease? How would she know? Was there some sign that would tell her? What should she look at in order to know?

That last question made her wince. She knew, of course, exactly what she could look at to discern any increasing incursion of her troll-disease. All she had to do was stop pacing, stand quietly, close her eyes, settle her breathing, and allow her inner eye to open. Then—

Then she would see the soft glow of her crown radix, hanging lower within her skull than it should, because it had been torn from the anchoring that would keep it properly positioned. And she would see the equally soft glow of her root radix, floating higher in her pelvis than it should, because it too had been ripped from its proper mooring. Every radix in between—belly, plexus, heart, throat, and brow—would be malpositioned. And each of the enigmatic arcs connecting her radices would be overly bowed, unable to take the straighter curve that was healthy, because of the diseased position of the radix at each end.

But how high did her root radix float? How low had her crown radix sunk? And what color would they be?

Would the crown radix still hold its proper violet light? Or would it have gained a sickly reddish tinge? Would it be fully magenta?

She shuddered. Dear saints, no!

Did her root radix maintain its correct silvery radiance? Or did it glow amber, or even worse pure red?

She could look.

But she wouldn't.

On the day that her radices tore loose, she'd vowed she would never touch enigmology again. And she hadn't. Not once through all the long years since. Neither would she do so now. She could remember that terrifying ripping sensation within her, as though her very bones had been sundered, one from the other, and the flesh around them torn apart with that sundering.

She'd been attempting the Burning Wings pattern—advanced work—because she'd actually gotten very good at enigmology. Taking her governess' words to heart, she'd practiced and practiced and practiced. Almost always in the cellars, to make sure Grandmere would not see her.

She'd practiced her way through the basic sequences, and then through the intermediate ones until she'd reached the advanced ones. At the advanced ones . . . she'd nearly halted. She could handle their intricacy and subtle angles. The thing that stopped her was the power they required. She didn't have it. Which galled her. If she'd not been able to master the complexity of the advanced patterns, that would have been one thing. Many practitioners could not. But to be able to get the patterns exactly right and then lack the enigmatic power to fill them was just . . . heartbreaking.

She hadn't given up easily. Practice had gotten her through so much. Surely it could get her through this, too.

So she'd practiced and practiced, making no headway, but determined nonetheless.

And in the midst of all her practicing, she stumbled upon an unexpected resource. If she bounced her enigmatic flow against the black pebble of the pendant she hid beneath the neckline of her blouse, the flow was redirected with nearly double the power she'd invested in it!

Using that trick, she made progress once again, blowing through the Flaming Song, Smoldering Dip, and Incandescent Reach patterns.

But the Burning Wings stopped her again.

How she wished it had stopped her permanently, that she'd never had her marvelous idea, that she'd never pushed the boundaries so extremely. But she had, oh, she had.

Instead of bouncing the silvery sparks of her enigmatic power off her pendant's black stone, she'd channeled it right through the stone, and then everything had gone amiss. As the curling scroll of force emerged from the rock—right where it was chipped—the healthy silver sparks flashed searing gold, and the gentle curve bent sharply. With the flash of gold, the intense curvature, had come the pain deep within Ohtavie's core, as though the essential structure of her body were bent until it ripped.

She'd fainted from the pain. And then awakened to yet more of it. She'd had to crawl toward the more tenanted portions of the cellars— the laundries, cold storage, and workshops—and then fainted once again when she reached them.

Someone had found her, because the next interval of nightmare had transpired in her own bed, a slow and sickening pendulum swing between blurred muzziness and black unconsciousness that went on and on.

When she'd emerged to a clarity marred by weakness in all her extremities, she'd thought the worst of it over. But, oh, the worst had only begun.

Then it was that she'd learned what had really happened: she'd torn her radices from their anchorages; troll-disease had claimed her and would go on to claim more and more of her as time passed, until at the last only complete physical debility and madness remained.

Still a child, not really understanding, she'd begged her mamere to make her better, and Mamere had wept. Papa had cradled her in his gentle embrace, explaining that they would protect her, hide her disease so that no one would know. Only Grandmere had raged, and after her first rant, Mamere and Papa had kept her away from their daughter's sickbed.

Once Ohtavie was stronger, no longer confined to bed, it was impossible to prevent Grandmere from having her say. And, oh, had she said it. No words were too harsh. Ohtavie was a mistake, a blot upon the family honor, disobedient and defiant, greedy and selfish, stupid and ill-judging, and—especially—overly curious. "You should never have found that accursed stone!" she'd hissed, pointing at the pendant that still graced Ohtavie's breast. Finally Mamere had told Grandmere that she would have to live in the dower house on the country estate, if she could not rein in her tongue.

Then Grandmere had kept silence with a vengeance, but her glances conveyed all the disgust that her stifled words did not.

Ohtavie still felt guilty for the relief that Grandmere's death, a year later, had brought.

Aside from Grandmere's intensified disapproval, Ohtavie's life had not changed immediately. Her troll-disease did not manifest visibly in her face or body for a long time. Her family let it be known that she was 'delicate,' and began to keep her closer to home, but her complete confinement to the house happened gradually, over the course of several years. And her sequestration from all visitors took even longer.

She sometimes wondered if they'd been right in their decision to hide not only her troll-disease, but her very person. Maybe it would have been better to live normally, it for less time, but to *live*, rather than occupying the shadows and edges of life. But when she was old enough to decide for herself, she'd continued the policy started by her parents. She'd skulked and made her life smaller, and smaller.

And now, after decades of hiding, she was sick of it. Yet she lacked the courage . . . or the will? . . . or the imagination? . . . to do anything else.

Or did she?

Today . . . this moment . . . was a setback. But she'd been making changes in the last few days. Meaningful changes. Successful changes.

Right in the middle of her thinking and pacing she stopped dead, teetering slightly on a wide step in the abbreviated flight down from the central hall to the foyer.

I'm being inexcusably self-indulgent, she realized abruptly, *almost childish.* This wasn't troll-disease at work, or any other agency that might be blamed. The memory of her old trauma—the onset of troll-disease—had reached out of the past to unbalance her. She'd allowed it to panic her. She'd lost her temper and yelled at Lealle, which unbalanced her further. And then she'd simply been wallowing in angst.

How absurd.

It was past time to rein in her own self, much as Grandmere had managed to rein in her temper all those decades ago. Although Ohtavie hoped she might manage more gracefully than had Grandmere.

She would stop this ridiculous pacing.

She would stop this useless obsessing.

And she would apologize—thoroughly—when Lealle returned.

Until that time . . . it was Beldaine. Normally she would bathe on Beldaine. She doubted she could manage a tub bath with a casted foot, but surely she could take a sponge bath and greet the new week moderately clean.

She nodded to herself and turned, headed bathward.

∽

Lealle was just crossing Rue Allongé, and composing her sixth version of an apology to Ohtavie in her head, when the flicker of . . . something . . . caught the corner of her gaze.

What had she seen?

Rue Allongé was exceptionally narrow, so much so that the apple trees in the back gardens of the pair of rowhouses flanking its entrance cast the lane itself entirely into dappled shadows.

Lealle almost kept going. She needed to get back to Ohtavie. She needed to get her apology over with. Besides . . . what if it was Gaetan and his gang? She needed to find Gaetan, but she wasn't sure she trusted his promise to rein in the bullies in his string.

What if they found her here? And what if she did something even more awful while defending herself? She had to get on.

In spite of that decision, she paused on the curb of the flagway, peering past the two flanking rowhouses into Rue Allongé's shifting shadows.

It was Gaetan all right, but Gaetan alone. He was shuffling along the lane toward Lealle, kicking up dust with his scuffing, and staring at his feet. He wore his usual ragged cap, patched trousers, and stained shirt, but no jacket. The sleeve of his left arm was rolled up past the elbow—did the touch of the fabric hurt too much?—and he held the arm itself gingerly away from his body. Even at this distance, perhaps thirty paces, it looked bruised.

Gaetan stumbled while Lealle watched, wincing as his stumble jarred his arm.

Oh, saints, she had to help him. She had to help him right now. But would he run away again? At least Remy was nowhere near. But it had to be Lealle Gaetan feared. She was the one who'd turned his arm to wood, after all.

Stepping slowly from the curb to the cobbled apron of the Rue Allongé, she picked her way along it. She reached the spot where the cobbles gave way to dirt before Gaetan did. He still had not noticed her, all his attention for his dusty boots.

She waited.

Just before he must have noticed *her* boots with his downturned gaze, she spoke. "Please let me help you, Gaetan. I feel terrible about what happened."

His head jerked up, eyes wide.

Lealle clasped her hands behind her back.

"Your arm felt better after I did Breath of the Pegasus yesterday"— just looking—"didn't it? I could do that again, only looking and nothing else." Although she'd sure like to try the Zephyr's Gavotte, if she could persuade him to let her. She knew she wouldn't mess that one up. And it was what Maitresse Barbitaine had used on Remy's arm.

Close up, Gaetan's arm looked terrible, a mottled expanse of blue and purple with narrow fringes of greenish yellow.

But his jaw tightened at Lealle's suggestions.

"Why you bein' nice to me?" he muttered, his face sullen. He looked like he was about to turn on his heel and walk away.

Lealle hurried into speech. "Because it's my fault your arm is hurt. I'm *not* a troll." Her voice went a bit sharp on the word. "But I should have had better control of my antiphony. I take lessons from Maitresse Aubry and—" Lealle gulped "—she'll give me such a scolding when she hears about this." Lealle was realizing that she'd have to tell her teacher what had happened, however much she wished she could keep it a secret.

Gaetan shrugged. "I deserved it."

Lealle bit her lower lip. "You deserved *something*," she agreed, "but not—" she winced, remembering the feel of his wooden arm under her touch "—not that. No one deserved that!"

"Look," growled Gaetan, "I done told my friends to leave you be. And they will, or I'll learn 'em th' hard way. You don't have to worry on that, if that's what this is about."

"Thank you," gasped Lealle, a little intimidated by his tone. "I'm— they scared me, s-so I'm glad they'll leave me alone."

"Well, they will," said Gaetan. "Artois and Denis promised me they'll keep the others in line."

"Thank you," Lealle repeated.

Gaetan scowled. "So, we done here? We good?"

Lealle struggled to pull herself together. "I really do want to see to your arm," she said firmly. "Hand it over." She held her palms out, invitingly.

Gaetan stared at her, his gaze suspicious. "I don't get you!" he burst out. "I torment you every time I see you, and now you want to help me. That's crazy."

Lealle inclined her head slowly, then lifted her chin again and gestured with her open palms.

Gaetan snorted, but laid his bruised forearm in her hands.

He didn't give her the weight of it, however.

She lifted her eyebrows, and then he surrendered it. It was surprisingly heavy.

Lealle strengthened her support, closed her eyes, and started the antiphonic centering process: slowed breaths, straightened posture, opening the inner sight, reaching deep within, and then guiding the silver sparks that flowed from her radices in the lacy curls of Breath of the Pegasus.

Gaetan's energetic structures within his forearm still looked blurred to her perception, but as her own energy entered his elbow and chased down through his wrist and out his fingertips, he sighed deeply. Relief? Lealle continued her antiphonic scrutiny.

Gaetan's arcs were properly silver, but seemed to have a nimbus of pale gold. That couldn't be good. Gold was never good, when it came to antiphony. Gold and the other warm hues went hand in hand with troll-magic.

Lealle transitioned almost without realizing it from the smooth Breath of the Pegasus into the pulsing Zephyr's Gavotte.

"Oh, that's good," murmured Gaetan.

Lealle kept on, and on.

A breeze rustled the apple boughs above them, the moving air cool against Lealle's face. Somewhere a dove cooed. In the distance, a woman called. The scent of mint wafted from nearby.

A slight weariness began to drag at Lealle's core.

Reluctantly, she allowed her antiphonic manipulations to cease and opened her eyes.

Gaetan was staring at his forearm, his mouth partly open.

The formerly blue and purple bruises were now yellow and green.

His gaze lifted to meet Lealle's. She smiled primly. "Better?" she asked.

"Why did you help me like this?" asked Gaetan, taking back his more-healed arm.

Lealle took an impatient breath, gearing up to repeat her previous explanation.

Gaetan shook his head at her and waved his good hand, as though brushing away her unspoken words. "Really why," he demanded.

Lealle frowned. She had told him her real reasons, but she sensed there was more to it than that. And Gaetan . . . deserved the full truth from her somehow. She wasn't sure why he did, but he did. She felt it.

"I—I like solving problems," she essayed. "But not just any problem. I like solving the ones that help someone who really needs help. Like Ohtavie." Oh, she shouldn't have mentioned Ohtavie's name. "And my brother sometimes. Sometimes even Papere. I'll say something that gives him an idea, and I can tell the idea's really important, even though he doesn't say what it is."

"Hmm." Gaetan searched her face. "You really mean that, don't you?"

Lealle nodded.

"You love your papere, don't you?" he pursued. "And your brother."

Lealle nodded again.

"Do you think your papere is fair?" asked Gaetan.

"Yes," answered Lealle. "I do. He is."

"Will he give my da a fair trial?" Gaetan sounded belligerent, but his eyes looked scared.

Lealle nodded firmly. "Yes. He will. My papere believes in justice. He would never want anyone wrongly imprisoned. Ever. Even if it was someone he disliked."

"I think my da might be guilty," whispered Gaetan.

Lealle frowned. "What did he do?" she asked.

Gaetan glared at her. "It were something I heard," he said, his tone curiously humble, at odds with the expression on his face. Would his voice and face always be mismatched? One angry, the other pathetic? And vice versa?

Gaetan continued, "Da was talking to my L'Oncle Bardot, talking about how they could best outlay the money, but something he said made me think he'd stolen it. Maybe stolen it from the town treasury!"

Now Gaetan sounded appalled. It was strange, hearing moral conviction in one who she'd been sure was bad through and through just a few days ago.

"But that wasn't the only thing. I think he and Uncle were planning something even worse. And—and I'm afraid Uncle might do it even though Da's in jail, and—"

Gaetan's head came up from its hunched position.

"I gotta go," he said abruptly.

"Wait!" Was he about to tell her the thing he'd almost told her yesterday when Remy popped up? "Please!" she urged him.

"I gotta talk to you again!" he muttered.

"Yes!" she agreed.

"But not now!" he insisted.

"When? Where?" she asked.

He patted her shoulder. "I'll find you!" he said, and then dashed away under the arch of apple boughs, back the way he'd come.

Lealle sighed in irritation. What had spooked him this time?

She stood a moment chewing her lip. Go after him?

No.

Let him pick the time and place?

Not much other choice, really.

So what should she do next? Was there still time to get back to Ohtavie before she was expected at Tiffanie Mercier's for tea?

"Lealle!" piped Remy's little boy voice behind her. "Were you scaring Gaetan? I wish you wouldn't!"

Lealle whirled, and sure enough, there was Remy just starting into Rue Allongé, while an armiger crossed the street behind him.

"You again!" she burst out. "Every time I make progress with Gaetan, you show up and spoil it!"

"But I didn't!" protested Remy. "I wouldn't! I was making friends with him this morning."

"What?" she protested in turn. "You were all ready to defend me to the death from him yesterday."

"Yeah, but then I thought about what you said. And what he said. And I figured that if he really meant it about calling off his friends, that would be better. And if I was friends with him, I could make sure he called them off!" Remy grinned.

"Oh, Remy," Lealle sighed. "But he was just going to tell me something important. And now he's run off again. Because of you!"

"Not 'acause of me. He's afraid of the armigers. They always run off the raggedy kids. He says." Remy nodded.

Lealle sighed again. Remy was probably right about that. But why had Remy turned up again under her elbow? "Are you following me?" she demanded.

Remy looked all hurt innocence. "O' course not," he insisted.

"You *are* following me!" she exclaimed.

"W-e-e-l-l. Yeah. Papere said there were diss-i . . . diss-i-dents" — Remy tried again— "dissidents around, and it might be dangerous. And you shouldn't be wandering all over town alone. You promised Papere you wouldn't. But you are. So I'm protecting you!"

"Well, don't!" snapped Lealle.

"Well I will!" Remy snapped back.

"Go away!" ordered Lealle.

"No!" answered Remy.

"You, you—!" Lealle broke off and stomped back toward the Rue Tulipe. "Fine! Escort me to the Mercier's then. But *you* weren't invited to tea, so don't you dare come in!"

Remy smirked. "I won't," he said breezily. "*I'll go find Gaetan!*"

∽

Ohtavie's sponge bath was quite successful. She followed it up with a modest meal, and then washed up her plate, bowl, and tumbler.

What she truly wanted to do next was apologize to Lealle, to make things right with the girl. Truly, she owed Lealle several apologies. Which she would make. But . . . there was no knowing when Lealle would return.

Ohtavie trusted the girl's judgment, as well she should. Lealle had earned that trust the hard way. She wouldn't repudiate her friendship with Ohtavie because of their quarrel. But it might take her some time to deal with her own feelings. Lealle had been angry, too. With reason. And—even more likely—Lealle would have to juggle all the rest of her life in order to find a safe interval in which to visit.

So Ohtavie would read more of Grandmere's letters.

Nodding firmly, she crutched her way easily to the library and ensconced herself in the comfortable leather wingchair by the window, with another half dozen of the books with blank spines piled on the deep sill.

They were not exhilarating reading.

Hugh de Pouilly—Ohtavie's great grandpere, she had to remind herself—burrowed ever deeper into his workshop and grew steadily more neglectful of his wife and daughter. Jovie de Pouilly followed a connected progression: from proud and patient to proud and weary; from proud and weary to just weary; from weary to sad; from sad to mad; from mad to bitter.

It was no longer difficult to recognize Grandmere as Jovie in those bitter, bitter passages.

Ohtavie wondered what Berdine's answering letters had contained. Had Grandmere saved them? Returned them to Berdine's descendants? No, that especially was unlikely. Grandmere had revealed far too much. No doubt it was she who had requested that her own letters be returned. The only real question was: why had Grandmere not burned them immediately?

Hugh's breakthrough occurred the year his daughter was married, twenty years after his own wedding to Jovie.

Jovie was able to recount the events, not because Hugh shared them with her—such sharing had long since ceased—but because she'd bored a hole in the paneling of his workshop through a wall with an unused closet on the other side. When Hugh immured himself away for work, Jovie hied herself to the closet, where she spied on him.

Jovie's report of Hugh's success was ugly reading.

My dear Berdine,

No doubt you look back on my letters to you in the first flush of my marriage as the ravings of a romantic madwoman. I certainly do. When I think of my old joy, I want to choke. And when I think of my pride in Hugh's scholarly prowess, I want to strangle myself. And him. Saint's failures! Would that I could.

No doubt you are wondering what brings on this spurt of rage. I've been rather sedate over the last few years. Why rage now?

Pausing a moment in her perusal, Ohtavie planted a finger to hold her place. She supposed 'sedate' might be one word for Grandmere's written effusions to her friend, but it wouldn't be Ohtavie's. Swallowed rage didn't come across as sedate; more like black ice miraculously intact over searing steam. When it cracked, the escaping heat would be lethal.

Ohtavie touched the lump of her pendant before reading on.

Well, I have good reason, continued Grandmere. *No doubt you'll remember that at one time I thought that Hugh's success would release him from that damned workshop of his and return him to being the old Hugh, the Hugh I loved and who also loved me. What a naive idiot I was. For success has come at last, and what will be the end of it I do not know. I almost do not care. But I do know that even if Hugh is released from that workshop, I don't want him back.*

Hah! I can almost see the sympathetic look on your face, Berdine. But don't be too sympathetic. I'm a nasty old woman—Ohtavie's mouth twisted; Grandmere would have been all of thirty-eight when she penned this missive, not old in Ohtavie's opinion—*worse than Hugh himself, in all honesty. You should be berating me, not sympathizing. And yet*—Ohtavie could almost hear Grandmere sighing—*I am grateful for your sympathy.*

But once again I trespass upon your patience.

This is how it happened.

Hugh got hold of another energea-stone *from ancient Navarys and channeled his own enigmatic force, such as it is, through that second stone, from which it emerged strengthened. I've already told you how he learned to sequester the original* energea-stone *upon which he worked in the icehouse for a full sennight before he withdrew it to a shaped pedestal of ice. Thus the thing acquired and retained its necessary chill.*

And I've also described the geared contraption that administered regular hammer taps to the energea-stone, *freeing Hugh's hands and concentration for his enigmatic manipulation.*

Both of those methods were in use for this last disaster.

You know that I disapprove of enigmology as much as anyone can, but I opened my inner sight to observe. How else could I keep tabs on Hugh's progress, I ask you?

But, oh, Berdine! It's not true. I love him still! Oh, how could he? How could it? It all went so very, very wrong.

Ohtavie swallowed. Were those ink blots the result of falling tears?

I watched the narrow arc of sparking green light flow from Hugh's heart through his arm and out his palm. It looked good; it looked safe; it looked the same as ever it had for years. Hugh's control was superb, I swear it.

If I'd known, if I'd even suspected, I swear I would have burst from that closet to stop him. But I didn't know, I didn't suspect, I didn't expect anything other than all the other useless failures. Oh, but I would take those by the dozen now, if only I could.

Because, Berdine, that modest curl of enigmatic power emerged from the augmenting energea-stone *— the new one — so much fatter, so much denser, so much faster, and with so much more intensity — how could it do anything but damage the first thing it hit?*

But it didn't hurt Hugh's energea-stone *at first, the one he wanted to transform into a lodestone. Instead it was almost sucked into the stone, the way black ice swallows sunlight. And Hugh did something amazing with its configuration, creating a veritable snowflake of enigmatic power, delicate and intricate and perfect. And I swear he was still in control, upon the very brink of the scholarly success he'd been pursuing for two decades. Oh, Berdine, all my foolish pride in him surged anew. And then . . .*

That blasted little pebble cracked, a chip flying off one side and turning to pulverized dust, leaving a jagged face behind.

But it wasn't the breaking of the stone that mattered, save that it broke the enigmatic pattern Hugh had formed. One projection of his snowflake was ripped away with the chip of stone, and the whole pattern flashed searing gold, not only the snowflake, but the arc connecting the two energea-stones, and the arc connecting the stones to Hugh. The extra energea-stone exploded into dust, just like the damned chip off the original one.

And he screamed, Berdine. I thought my heart would burst. And I tried to batter through the closet wall, but of course I could not.

Oh, Berdine, if only I could have. If I'd gotten to him sooner, could I have saved him? But I had to go out through the closet door, through that spare bedchamber, around through the corridor, and then into the workshop.

He wasn't breathing when I got there. I had to pound on his chest and raise his arms three times before he coughed. And even so, I could see he was already a troll. Oh, Berdine, my darling Hugh! No man could deserve such a fate.

He is so ill now. I write this at his bedside. He is sleeping, but restlessly, or I could not be so occupied. But I had to tell you what had happened. You've kept all my secrets so well. I pray you keep this one as well. And pray for me, dear friend, for me and for my precious husband.

Ohtavie sat back, her heart pounding.

This confirmed every one of her suspicions. Her pendant was Hugh's lodestone—or *energea*-stone—she didn't know which. The accident which had created the imperfection in its velvet smoothness had grievously injured her great grandpere. The same imperfection that had made him a troll had done the very same to her. And Grandmere's bitterness . . . actually seemed reasonable in the wake of her husband's long neglect and then fatal—was it fatal?—accident. What woman would not be warped after such a travail? Ohtavie could not say that she would have survived it all intact. She could not say that she had survived her own trials . . . all that much better than Grandmere had survived hers.

Ohtavie gazed out the library window.

A small rainbow shimmered in the spray of the square's fountain, formed by the slanting gold of what must be evening light. A few nursemaids were gathering their charges, marshaling the children toward home and supper and bed. A young woman bent over one of the flowerbeds, holding a blossom to her face. Another sat on one of the benches, reading. But the square was emptying.

Ohtavie glanced back at the book in her lap.

She felt . . . full. Full of revelation. Full of feeling, although she could hardly put a name to her feeling. She felt full of new information, because knowing was—it seemed—quite different from suspecting.

But what did it all mean? For her. For her decisions going forward.

She needed time to digest what she had learned.

The Sixth Day

SAIDY—THE SABBATH

Moment of Truth

Chapter Eleven

LEALLE HAD JUST finished dressing for chapel the next morning when Mamere entered Lealle's bedchamber on a waft of lily-of-the-valley perfume—an aroma much too sweet in Lealle's opinion, overpoweringly so in large quantities, bearable in the discrete dabs that Mamere applied. Mamere would never be guilty of the vulgarity of drenching her person in scent. Of course not, thought Lealle, hiding a grin.

"Oh, good," pronounced Mamere, satisfaction in her tone. "You're wearing your pretty lace frock. Chaplain Rousseau wants you to read the Third Lesson, so I especially wish you to look nice."

Lealle controlled the frown that wanted to draw her brows down.

"But, Mamere, I haven't practiced it," she protested.

"Naturally not, darling." Mamere smiled. "That's why I've brought you *Bouilly's Catechism.*" She brandished a small booklet. "You'll just have time to read over it before you go down to breakfast." She nodded, then continued, "But, dearest, where were you all yesterday afternoon? When I came to wake you from your nap, to make certain you would not be late to tea with the Merciers, you were not in your room." Mamere directed a straight glance at Lealle's face, brief, but scrutinizing.

Lealle restrained a sigh. Really she should have expected Mamere to check on her. Mamere tended to hold a looser rein during the school year, when Lealle sat under the eyes of her schoolmasters for most of the day or else was busy with home lessons the rest. But last summer, she'd rather taken Lealle over. And now it looked like she might be ready to do the same again. Lealle controlled another sigh. Figuring out how to escape Mamere choreographing Lealle's every move was definitely going to be a problem, but right now she had a more immediate one: making sure Mamere didn't discover Ohtavie.

"I went to the Mercier's early," Lealle answered. "Tiffanie had asked me to spend an hour with her before the family gathered for tea." All of which was true. Tiffanie *had* asked her. And she *had* gone early, because of Remy insisting on providing escort once he'd encountered her on Rue Allongé. No need to tell Mamere that she'd gone early to the Mercier's from Ohtavie's home rather than her own.

Mamere's face lightened. "I'm so glad!" she said. "I told you you'd like Tiffanie, if you only gave her a chance." Then Mamere tamped her smile down. "But, darling, I doubt you took a hansom cab all on your own, and I know my brougham-landau did not convey you, because Gauchand Coachman delivered *me* to my board meeting. Which means you walked."

No sliding out of that accusation, but Lealle could make her voice light at least. "I did walk, Mamere. It was such a beautiful day, I wanted to be out in it. And nothing happened to me."

Mamere repressed a sigh of her own. Did she sympathize with Lealle?

"Yes, darling, of course. But your Papere especially requested of me that you always be escorted, or conveyed by carriage, if you were going to remain in town rather than go to your Bonne-mémé and Bon-papy. And I promised him that I would not break his trust." Mamere's face was troubled, and her voice held real distress. "But, darling, I need your cooperation to make that happen. Promise me you won't slip out again." Her gaze grew beseeching.

Lealle started to promise, opening her lips on assent, and then she stopped. She *couldn't* promise. Not truly. And she refused to give a lying assurance. But Mamere wasn't going to let this go. Lealle could see that.

"I'm sorry, Mamere," she temporized, real contrition in her words, because she *was* sorry. She just was not going to give up her secret. Or her freedom. "I didn't mean to cause you alarm. Really I didn't."

"Tell me you'll be more careful going forward," said Mamere.

Now *that* she could promise. "I *will* be more careful. I promise," replied Lealle.

Mamere's face brightened. "Thank you, darling." She smiled and proffered the booklet in her hand. "Now I'll take myself off, so that you can practice the reading!"

Lealle accepted both *Bouilly's Catechism* and a kiss on her cheek, and then Mamere swept out, leaving the scent of lily-of-the-valley on the air behind her.

Lealle allowed the frown she'd been fighting to knit her brows. She'd not lied outright, no, but her disingenuous handling of Mamere— yes, it really had been handling, disgracefully so—was beginning to feel too dishonest. She wasn't sure what she would do about that. As long as she continued to visit Ohtavie secretly, she would have to lie to Mamere. And, extending that line of reasoning, disobey Papere.

Was Papere right? Were the streets of Claireau dangerous? Mamere clearly didn't think so, but she loved and respected Papere, and thus intended to comply with his stated wishes.

Lealle had agreed with Papere—at least a little—when she was still dodging Gaetan and his bullying friends. But now? In the wake of Gaetan's promise did she feel safer?

She did feel safer, she decided, but it wasn't truly because of Gaetan's promise that he and his friends would bother her no more. Oh, she believed him. But that wasn't it.

She felt safer because she'd defended herself, and done so successfully. As horrific as turning Gaetan's arm to wood had been— and she was still horrified—it had changed her feeling of vulnerability to a feeling of . . . what? Power? Not exactly. Self-sufficiency, she decided. She hoped she wouldn't do anything so awful as destroying a boy's arm next time, if there was a next time, but she knew she could do something. She was not helpless, would never be helpless again. Not like before.

But Papere was worried about grown men. Would Lealle be able to defend herself against Laurent Senior's friends, if it came to that?

It felt arrogant to think it, but she suspected she could. Antiphony was *powerful*. Besides, she wasn't sure Papere was right about dangerous men lurking in the streets of Claireau. She'd seen no sign of them. It seemed that Mamere might be more right about this than Papere.

She looked at the little booklet in her hand, tracing its title on the plain leather. *Bouilly's Catechism*. Her fingertip at the end of the final letter, she glanced out her windows where the river glimmered in the bright morning sunlight. A group of boys gathered atop the wall across the water, baiting their fishing lines and laughing. She could just hear them—barely—through the glass panes. *They* clearly were skipping chapel, but Lealle could not. Which meant she had some reading practice to do.

But she also had one more thing to consider: Remy.

Sinking down onto the end of her bed, she considered. Remy had admitted he was following her, convinced that she *did* need escort and equally convinced that he could provide it.

The question was: had he deliberately sought her yesterday and found her? Or had he stumbled upon her by chance and then claimed the duty of accompaniment because it made him feel important?

It didn't matter, she realized. Whichever it was, he'd attached himself to her and it would be at least a day or two before he got bored of following her around. Which meant she had to make sure she eluded him, if she went to visit Ohtavie. And she *had* to visit Ohtavie. Well, she didn't *have* to, but she really, really wanted to. She still hadn't apologized for startling the troll-woman, and it made an uncomfortable lump at the back of her thoughts.

Once across the bridge, there were lots of twisty streets and alleys.

All she would need to do was take a few loops through them, making lots of turns, and Remy would have no idea which way she'd gone. In fact!—Lealle's forefinger tapped its fellow—if she went around a block fast enough, she could come up behind Remy herself and watch *him*, making sure he really had lost her trail. Yes!

She nodded. After chapel then, once everyone was home, she'd make her break.

In the meantime . . . she didn't really need to practice reading the selection for the Third Lesson aloud. She'd gotten lots of elocution practice in school this past year. But she did need to cast her eye over the words, so they'd be familiar.

She nodded again and opened *Bouilly's Catechism*.

❧

Ohtavie had hoped to awaken to clarity, but she didn't. She felt muzzy.

The dawn light creeping around the edges of the curtains held the warmth of the summer season. The bedding around her shoulders matched the sunshine's comfort, as did the still air against her face.

What day was it anyway? She did a brief reckoning on her fingers. Should she read the *Holy Book of Thiyaude's Hours*? It was Saidy, the sabbath, and she almost felt she ought to, but . . . no. She wanted to read more of Grandmere's letters.

Ohtavie hurried through the washing of face and hands, the brushing of teeth, dressing, and breaking her fast.

Yesterday evening she'd broken off from Grandmere's book of letters, feeling she needed to digest what she'd learned before she learned more. If there even was more to learn. Hadn't she discovered everything pertinent to herself: the full origins of the pendant that had been so disastrous to herself?

Reading of Grandmere's tragedy had been . . . painful. Her heart ached for Grandmere's losses.

But maybe she'd stopped too soon.

Maybe she needed the next events of Grandmere's life, however heartbreaking they might be, to produce her own clarity about . . . whatever it was she needed to be clear about. Maybe it wouldn't even be anything big. Maybe some small occurrence, some seemingly insignificant thought, would make everything fall into place, and her personal enlightenment would arrive.

Her lips puffed out in a silent laugh. Enlightenment? There was a grandiose term. But she wanted . . . something. And maybe Grandmere's letters still held it, whatever it was.

Hopeful, she headed to Papa's library.

She'd drawn its heavy drapes closed last night, so the room was dark, but the warm scent of its leather chairs brought her a sense of ease and comfort as she groped her way through the dimness. Her chair by the window awaited her, along with the pile of blank-spined books, most of which she'd read, all but the very last one.

When she pulled the drapes open, daylight flooded in.

The waters of the fountain in the square sparkled gaily, but no loiterers sojourned there to enjoy its beauty. Ohtavie could have it all to herself, were she brave enough to step outside. She tamped down an incipient shudder. No, she would not be stepping outside, no matter that all the residents of the square were gone to their respective places of worship. A troll-woman hiding her troll-disease . . . belonged indoors.

Ohtavie sniffed. That was enough of that; torturing herself with thoughts of improbabilities was not sensible. Although Lealle didn't think going out was so improbable. And Lealle might be right.

But that was no help now. Ohtavie would ask questions once Lealle was present. In the meantime . . . she had Grandmere's letters.

Oh, Berdine!

I'd not imagined I could possibly be more angry, but I am.

You must know by now that Hugh has died the death and his remains been laid to rest in the family mausoleum. Indeed, you must have seen the mortal announcement. It was in all the papers.

Ohtavie frowned. What was the date on this letter? *13th Sanember 1804.*

So . . . Grandpere had not died upon the onset of his troll-disease, but lingered another two decades—gracious! twenty years!—with whatever symptoms it had brought him. Had they been similar to her own? She found herself wishing that Jovie, so prolific a letter writer up until now had not—apparently—skipped over such a great span of time. Perhaps she hadn't. There was really no knowing what might have happened to the whole of her correspondence. It was a minor miracle that so much of it had been preserved.

Ohtavie read on.

I find I miss him dreadfully, in spite of how angry I feel. How is it possible that I want both to murder him, if only he were alive for me to do it, and to drag him up out of the grave and breathe life into his stilled lungs? For I do.

But it's not the long years of neglect, or even his foolish pursuit of a scholarly triumph destined to end in disaster, that has me so irate now. It's Hugh's last words—and his last actions—that have me fuming. For this is what he has done: he commissioned a jeweler to make his devilish lodestone into a necklace! For me! And he bade me wear it always in memory of his achievement. His achievement! As though there were any achievement. Death and disease and the dishonor that comes with troll-disease. Oh! I hate him all over again!

Evidently he did succeed in transforming the original energea-stone *into a lodestone, although what good a lodestone will do him now he's dead, I entirely fail to see. And what good it will do me, likewise. And furthermore, it's a damaged lodestone, which damage makes it superlatively dangerous, should anyone be stupid enough to use it.*

But I am supposed to drape the damned thing around my neck as a pendant in memory of Hugh. Well, I won't, and that's final.

Ohtavie leaned back in her armchair, feeling slightly breathless.

She'd not needed to know how Hugh's *energea*-stone—Hugh's *lodestone*—had come to decorate the pendant she herself wore around her neck. She'd not doubted that its matte black pebble, marred by a chip, was one and the same with Hugh's treasure. But the story explained something Grandmere had said when she visited Ohtavie's sickbed that last time so long ago.

Grandmere had rustled up to Ohtavie's bedside, her stiff black silks gleaming and smelling of the musk Ohtavie hated. Grandmere's face had been very cold and imperious, her lips thin. "So," she'd said. "Your grandpere would be truly pleased. His trophy adorns a feminine neck after all. But whether he'd be pleased with all its consequences, I cannot believe. Even of him!"

Ohtavie the child had not known what in the north Grandmere had meant. She'd not known the pendant from the cellars was Grandpere's. She'd not known that Grandmere blamed Grandpere for Ohtavie's troll-disease. Now it was very clear.

But what of Grandmere's other mysterious remark? She'd turned her back to Ohtavie's sickbed, muttering, "Too late for an infant ring to save her now, damnation. Would that I'd secreted anything else!" Grandmere had never sworn, and this one instance of profanity on her lips had stuck in Ohtavie's memory. Did her letters hold an answer to that as well?

Ohtavie bent her gaze to the book of letters again.

The remainder of the missive describing Hugh's deathbed choices held little more than Jovie's ranting. The energy of it reminded Ohtavie of the Jovie of the early letters, departing from the more controlled acerbity of the Grandmere of the later missives and of Ohtavie's own acquaintance. Her anger gave her words an animation similar to that evoked by her joy. Somehow it made Ohtavie even more sad than had the bitterness. The bitterness was unpleasant, very much so. The impassioned fury . . . showed the bitterness to be what it was: a tomb for the living Jovie, in which she buried . . . everything, Ohtavie realized.

Zest, joy, engagement, disappointment, grief, wrath, and . . . love—they had all been gone by the time Ohtavie knew her.

She read on, and in the very last letter of all she found two items of especial interest.

My dearest Berdine,

I am calm again. No doubt you thought me demented in my ravings about Hugh's necklace. Indeed, I think so myself. But my sanity has returned, along with a solution.

You may recall that I'd tossed the damned thing into the bottom of my jewelbox. I make no apology for my adjective. That thing destroyed my darling husband. (Yes, I can still call him that, for I love him yet, despite everything.) It destroyed my marriage. It destroyed my happiness. I've called it 'damned' before, and I stick by that choice. It is damned. But I digress.

Anyway, I threw it in my jewelbox, and there it lay, all through my mourning while I wore no jewels, and all through the transfer of the estate to Hugh's heir—a distant cousin—and all through my remove from my own home to my granddaughter's mansion.

Ohtavie flipped back a few pages to check the date—*9th Ionaber 1807*. Yes, Ohtavie's mamere—Grandmere's granddaughter—really would have been grown and married by then. In fact, Ohtavie herself had been born, was an infant then. And Grandmere's own daughter, Yvette, would have been dead. Why had not Grandmere written about that? Wouldn't it have been agonizing, more so even than Hugh's dereliction? Too agonizing to write about? Or maybe, Ohtavie realized, merely less complex. Losing Yvette would have been grief straight up, rather than grief mixed with everything that Grandmere's marriage provoked.

Grandmere's last letter continued.

I'd thought of the thing every day since Hugh's death. How could I not? It had been his death. But I'd not set eyes on it since it landed in my box. Why would I dig to the bottom, even once I resumed jewelry? All I wanted was the grisaille mourning brooch with my dear Hugh's profile.

Well, I dug to the bottom today. I wanted that sweet child's ring for darling Ohtavie.

Oh, Berdine! She is the sweetest, most precious little babe. And she holds her arms out to me like such a little love. I'd believed nothing could ever make me happy again. But little Ohtavie has!

Ohtavie sat back again, stunned by this effusion. She would never have guessed Grandmere could feel this way. Why had Grandmere never said anything of the sort to Ohtavie herself? Had she forgotten how, after all the years of ranting about Hugh? Or was it Ohtavie's study of enigmology that had staunched Grandmere's adoration?

I couldn't find the ring, but that damned pendant leapt at my hand, as though it were a viper in hiding. I jumped, I swear I did, Berdine. You see, I'd forgotten it was there. Oh, I'd not forgotten the pendant. How could I? I'd just forgotten where I put it.

I nearly threw it to the floor and crushed it underfoot. But remember what it did to Hugh! What if it did something equally dreadful to me? I couldn't risk it!

I imagined tossing the thing to the bottom of a well. Surely it would hurt no one down in the dark and the cold and the wet. But what might it do to the water? What if the pendant poisoned the water? Even if I could find an abandoned farmstead, it might not stay abandoned. And then an innocent family might drink the fouled water.

I wished I could throw it away into a crossroad, but that posed all the same problems and more. Someone would find it, and harm would ensue. Even the city midden would be unsafe.

But then I had the most marvelous idea!

Berdine, you've never visited Claireau in all the years since you've married, never entered the Maison de Bellay, my current home with my granddaughter Sophia. (She was named after me, you know! You'll not be forgetting I go by my middle name, will you?) But the De Bellay mansion was built upon some very strange, very old ruins. Oh, I don't mean recently, of course! The mansion is very old itself. But the ruins beneath it might be three or four thousand years old. Imagine it! And some of the ruins form part of the mansion's cellars. But no one goes there. I'm going to hide the pendant there. I found the most perfect place. No one will ever see it again.

Ohtavie swallowed. Hard.

Grandmere must have been . . . Ohtavie couldn't imagine how Grandmere must have felt when she realized that her great granddaughter had found Grandpere's pendant, found it and been turned into a troll by it.

No, that wasn't true. She knew exactly how Grandmere had felt. Every word that bitter old woman had hurled at Ohtavie—*a mistake, a blot, defiant, selfish, stupid, ill-judging, prying*—had been meant for another target. Grandmere . . . blamed herself.

Ohtavie swallowed again. She'd never imagined herself forgiving Grandmere. Grandmere might have adored Ohtavie the infant, but she'd never expressed a speck of that affection to Ohtavie the girl. At least, not when Ohtavie could remember it.

But now . . . could anything worse happen to a woman than to be responsible for her great grandchild's doom? Perhaps, but Grandmere's fate seemed an extraordinarily bad one. Ohtavie's heart ached all over again for her. And, yes, her heart held forgiveness. Almost against her will did she feel it, but she did indeed feel it.

Grandmere had penned her full name to her last letter, uncharacteristically. *Sophia Joviane de Pouilly.* Many of those preceding it had ended with simply the word *yours.*

But then, following the signature, she'd appended a postscript—a dated postscript—some twelve years after the date on the letter.

12th Nerich 1819. Ah, Berdine, I am a fool. Perhaps if I'd actually sent these letters to you, and you'd been stalwart enough to read them, and to answer them, everything might have been different. You would have given me advice, very good advice. You were always so wise, my friend. And with your good counsel, I might have done better. No, I would *have done better. I know I didn't handle Hugh rightly. I wanted to punish him even more than I wanted to straighten out what lay between us. If I'd been stronger, committed myself to the high road of forgiveness and self-honesty, not fallen for the lower road of vengeance and manipulative weakness—if I'd realized that I could be the author of my own happiness, if I'd not insisted that* Hugh *must make me happy—*

Oh, Berdine—why am I pretending that I write to you? It's been decades since I put my last letter to you in the post. Clearly I write only to myself. I don't even know if you are yet living. And yet habit is strong. I must *write to you, because, oh, because I know you love me. And I love you. We were like sisters. Why did I ever forsake our correspondence? Was I ashamed? Or had I simply given up? I don't know.*

But I do know that my cherished great granddaughter would be whole and healthy and unharmed, if I'd sought your advice.

Oh, dearest, sweetest Ohtavie, forgive me. I am culpable of so much, so very much toward you.

S.

A drop of water spattered down upon the faded ink of Sophia Joviane de Pouilly's initial. Only then did Ohtavie realize that she was crying. Poor dear Grandmere. She'd wanted to be an entirely different woman, but had never managed to summon the resources— of understanding, of virtue, of will, of whatever it was she would have needed—to actually *be* that woman.

Ohtavie no longer regretted her own forgiveness. Grandmere's plea for it was very late, but nonetheless sincere. And . . . Ohtavie felt lighter.

I want to be a different woman, she realized.

But wanting alone . . . wasn't enough. Her wanting would have to be matched by doing. And more doing than she had managed so far. Breaking bad habits wasn't enough. She would have to move altogether outside of the cramped world she'd created for herself. In fact, she would *go* outside, into the bright out of doors. She would go right *now.*

Closing Jovie's last book of letters—somehow 'Jovie' seemed more right a name now than 'Grandmere'—Ohtavie placed it gently on the window sill and gathered herself to stand up. As she did so, she heard Lealle's voice calling faintly from inside the house.

"Ohtavie? Ohtavie? Are you there? Are you awake? I wish I could knock and you could let me in, but I can't! Hello! Are you there?"

∞

Ohtavie had just managed to rise to her feet, crutches under her arms, when Lealle tumbled through the library door with a jumble of words spilling from her lips.

"Ohtavie, I'm so sorry! I must have startled you so much yesterday! You never know when to expect me, and I come and go with no warning. Will you forgive me? Please? I think I'm an idiot!"

The girl fetched up before Ohtavie, a pleading expression on her face. "Oh, do say you forgive me!" she appealed.

Ohtavie clasped Lealle's reaching hands in her own, holding them gently, but giving them a little shake. "Lealle, stop," she said. "You owe me no apology."

"But, I do," Lealle insisted.

"No. *I* owe *you* one," said Ohtavie.

"But . . ." Lealle looked puzzled.

"Lealle, I made you free of my home. And the reason you cannot knock and wait on the doorstep for me to let you in is because of *my* insistence on secrecy."

Lealle's lips formed a silent oh.

"There is nothing about this . . . rather tense situation, that is your fault," continued Ohtavie. "In fact, it's all my fault. The troll-disease is mine. The choice to handle my disease through secrecy is mine. My unreasonable request at the beginning of our acquaintance—that you leave and forget you ever saw me—mine. And while I did not like you descending to the cellars, I never forbade you to."

Lealle was beginning to smile. "Are they really dangerous? The cellars?"

Ohtavie sighed. "No. Or . . . I suppose I might have found the only dangerous thing in them. There could be other hazards, but not known ones. I roamed all through their darkness as a girl, and the only true peril I found was this." She pulled her pendant out from beneath her blouse. The silver of its delicate chain and the graceful cage of prongs holding the black stone gleamed in the daylight filtering in through the windows. "And this danger . . . was a late addition." She sighed again. "My own grandmere—great grandmere," she corrected herself, "hid it there for safekeeping. And I foolishly dug it out from behind its screen of bricks."

"I saw those bricks," gasped Lealle. "I used two of them to stand on."

"What?" Now it was Ohtavie's turn to be puzzled.

"When I needed to be sure I'd made your crutches the right length. I'm too short for them," Lealle explained.

"Oh!" Ohtavie stifled the chuckle that Lealle's 'too short' assessment provoked. It wasn't as though Ohtavie were especially tall.

Lealle pointed a finger at Ohtavie's pendant, carefully not touching it. "What is it?" she asked.

"An artifact from ancient times, but a broken one," answered Ohtavie.

"How is it dangerous? Why do you still wear it, when it's dangerous?" Lealle frowned slightly.

Ohtavie tucked the pendant back under her blouse. "I . . . suppose I wear it because . . ." she trailed off. Why *did* she wear it? Why did it give her a feeling of security even amidst the memory of the onset of her troll-disease? "I wear it because it reminds me that if I try hard enough, if I practice enough, if I persist enough, I can accomplish even things that are very hard, that seem impossible." She'd certainly exerted enough effort, practiced often enough, and persisted long enough with her enigmology when she was a girl. "And it also reminds me of who I am—what I am—and that I need to . . ." She trailed off again, and then resumed, her voice firm. "That I need to hide. But I'm done with hiding. I'm not going to hide any longer."

"Oh!" Lealle's cheeks flushed prettily. "Will you come to the retreat center? Let the healers treat you? Will you come with me now?"

Ohtavie rocked back on her crutches, disconcerted by how swiftly Lealle had seized on her words and how much further the girl had taken them.

"I thought of stepping outside, on the back terrace," she temporized.

"Oh! Yes, yes!" Lealle exclaimed.

"I'm . . . a bit anxious about it," Ohtavie confessed.

Lealle's eyes widened, but she didn't say anything.

"Will you help me?" Ohtavie asked.

Lealle's shoulders straightened, and she seemed to settle herself. "I'd love to help you," she said staunchly.

"Thank you." Ohtavie reached for Lealle's hands again, and the girl let her take them, but with a questioning look on her face. Ohtavie smiled faintly. "Before we get caught up in my first venture out of doors in . . ." she did a quick reckoning ". . . twenty-some years or so, you must let me make a more thorough apology to you than the brief statement that I owe you one."

"But I'm not sure you do," protested Lealle.

"No, listen," said Ohtavie, reseating herself in the leather armchair that they were still standing next to, and motioning for Lealle to sit on the windowsill. It was deep enough to serve.

"Lealle, I gave you an impossible choice when we first met. Requiring that you leave an injured woman, myself, utterly alone and without help was unreasonable. But so was insisting that you lie to your parents and the other adults responsible for your wellbeing. For that was what my insistence on you keeping my secrecy amounted to." Ohtavie nodded. "It was wrong of me," she concluded.

"But what else could you do, when I'd invaded your house?" Lealle burst out. "*That* was wrong of me!"

"I don't think it was," Ohtavie replied gently.

"Of course, it was," said Lealle.

"No. Think it through," Ohtavie said. "If you'd been prying, then it would have been wrong. If you'd been just exploring, for the fun of it, then it would have been wrong. If you'd been looking for mischief, intent on vandalizing the property or stealing perhaps, then it would have been wrong. But you were a child in trouble, seeking help."

Lealle swallowed, looking a little uneasy at Ohtavie's list of potential wrongs, perhaps.

"In the normal course of events," Ohtavie continued, "a servant or the mistress of the house would have come immediately and given you the help you needed. And your flight inside would not have been trespassing at all."

Lealle sighed. "But it wasn't normal. And things didn't go that way. And . . . and, here we are."

"Yes," agreed Ohtavie. "Here we are. But do you understand that I was in the wrong, not you? And that I am very sorry for it."

Lealle's smile flashed. "Of course, but there wasn't any way you could know that troll-disease has a cure. Well, a treatment," she corrected herself. "So it seems pretty reasonable that you would act to preserve your life."

"But you told me there was a treatment."

"Why would you believe a complete stranger?" countered Lealle.

"I think we can agree that there was every excuse for me," answered Ohtavie, "but I was still in the wrong. I was the adult present, and it was my responsibility to decide well for both of us."

"What do you want to do now?" asked Lealle, a gleam in her eyes.

Ohtavie swallowed. "Shall we step out onto the terrace?"

Lealle jumped to her feet and gestured with a hand. "Let's go!" she urged.

Ohtavie grimaced, trying to conceal the prickle of nerves fluttering in her stomach, and hoisted herself up onto her crutches.

∽

Ohtavie felt her heart begin to pound as Lealle turned the thumb lock on the middle pair of windowed doors between the loggia and the back terrace.

The day outside looked very bright and beautiful, the sky a soft blue adorned with a few scarves of wispy cloud, the sunshine clear and inviting as it shone down. The lilac blossoms had faded, but the first buds on the roses were starting to unfurl, their petals a rich garnet red. She longed to be out in all that loveliness. But her stomach felt queasy. And she wanted just as much to turn tail, scuttle back into one of the dimmer rooms of the house.

You can do this, she told herself, you can.

The queasiness stirring her stomach increased, and the pounding of her heart grew stronger, heavier.

It was hard not to retreat when Lealle swung the doors open and beckoned Ohtavie forward with an excited smile.

The calling of birds fluted through the doorway along with a rustle of breeze-stirred leaves and the scent of the rose blooms.

Ohtavie straightened her shoulders, refrained from touching the pendant beneath her blouse—that would not help for this—swallowed, and crutched forward.

There was a moment of pure panic as she crossed the threshold, a moment of sheer terror as she moved forward over the white stone of the terrace, and then—when she exited the slip of shadow clinging to the house and entered the sun's domain—she was drowning in light, in warmth, in the caress of the air, and in the vastness of the waiting world.

Oh! It was dizzying, it was magnificent, it was utterly beguiling, it was too much.

Ohtavie shut her eyes and paused.

The roses' exhalation, rich and sweet, filled her nose. Birdsong teased her ears. Brightness pressed upon her closed eyes, and a strangely sustaining warmth lapped her limbs.

She could do this, she could just barely do this, so long as she kept her eyes shut.

The sense of space spreading out around her, the garden and everything beyond the garden's walls, both astonished her and horrified her, but she need not take even one more step right now. Right now she would savor . . . all that was wonderful in this moment, and withstand that which terrified her. She would not flee. She would stand fast.

She heard Lealle draw in a quick breath beside her. She could see the girl in her mind's eye, turned solicitously toward Ohtavie, perhaps sensing Ohtavie's tumble of feeling, perhaps merely noting the thrill that must be visible on Ohtavie's face.

Ohtavie turned her attention outward again, tasting the vastness before her.

Was that voices she heard in the distance?

She shivered in the warmth. Not so many days ago she'd mistaken voices for gull cries. And those voices had presaged . . . disaster. No, not disaster. They'd heralded change, which could be as terrifying as disaster, but the two were not one and the same. Of course she would hear voices, now that she stood out of doors.

The sound of running footsteps on scritching gravel interrupted her idyll of birdsong and breeze and distant murmurs.

Then came a boy's high, alarmed voice. "Lélé! *Run!* She's a troll! An *untreated* troll! She's dangerous! Lélé, run!"

Ohtavie's eyes flew open.

A boy—about nine years?—with a neat crop of chestnut curls pounded up the terrace steps from the garden, an older boy puffing at his heels.

The nine-year-old's face was clenched with fury as he reached the top of the steps and charged forward, yelling, "Don't you dare hurt my sister, you witch! Don't you dare! I'm summoning the armigers! So there!"

Ohtavie's heart constricted within her.

She'd known this was coming. From the moment when, as a child, she first understood her troll-disease, she'd known it. Again when she'd forsaken the outdoor world, she'd known it. Later when she'd dismissed her servants, she'd known it. And later still when she'd stopped looking out the windows, she'd known they were coming for her.

The mob armed with flaring torches and anger.

The armigers, ready to slay a witch any way they could.

The Troll Watch, with their more sophisticated array for enigmatic defenses and weapons.

They'd been coming for decades, and now at last they were here, led on by one small, furious boy.

Oh, why had she come out of doors? Why had she been so certain she must expand, not contract? Why, oh, why! She'd been a fool. And now look what it had brought her. Look at what she herself had come forward to meet. This scared boy would bring the armigers. The armigers would bring the Troll Watch. And the Troll Watch would escort her executioner.

Her heart froze within her breast.

Desperate—despairing—she reached deep inside her being for something, anything—anything at all—that might save her.

A surge of internal heat, scalding like overly hot tea, answered her panic.

Dear saints.

Truly that had to be the wrong help to grab for, even in this moment of personal disaster.

Chapter Twelve

FOR AN INSTANT, Lealle stood shocked.

Oh, son of the mother, what should she do? What *should* she do!

One moment all had been peaceful, the sunny garden spreading before them, Ohtavie gathering herself in the first aftermath of her courageous venture out, and Lealle smiling proudly at her protegée, smiling proudly at herself for *having* a protegée.

And now—oh, Thiyaude, no!

Ohtavie was lunging forward, and this Ohtavie was nothing like the Ohtavie Lealle had come to know and like. The troll-woman's neck hunched down in her shoulders, and the features of her face clenched in a demented mask.

Lealle seemed to see her all afresh, as though she'd never seen her friend before. The curving, elongated nose seemed longer and more curving than ever before. The corners of the eyes sagged more direly. Even the mouth curved down.

Ohtavie was a *troll*—how had Lealle ceased to see this?—and trolls were dangerous.

Worse than Ohtavie's trollish features were her hands with their crooked thumbs.

Her hands—oh, saints—acrid orange sparks wreathed those outstretched hands, the bitter glitter seeming almost to sear the air. This was troll-magic. The safe blues and greens of antiphony were invisible to the outer eyes, but troll-magic, oh, perilous troll-magic flared all too visible.

Lealle's eyes burned with the searing light. How had she ever thought Ohtavie to be safe?

"No!" Lealle screamed.

She lunged herself, determined to come between her brother and hazard. One leaping step, then another, and she was there, facing the troll-witch down.

"Never!" she yelled, trying to catch her balance and stand firm.

A small, wiry arm wrapped itself around her waist and hauled, turning her wobble into an outright dive. She was falling.

Down and down she went. It felt like the plunge went on forever, while those lethal orange sparks glittered in a nimbus around Ohtavie's outstretched hands, aimed at Remy.

It felt like years, but it was over in an instant, her teetering surge transformed into the jarring crunch of the terrace stone beneath her hip and side.

There was just time enough to think that she'd done everything wrong. At the very least she should have told her papere.

But it wasn't her sins that mattered now! It was *Remy* who mattered. She could be as sinful as sinful could be, if only her sins hadn't led to right here and right now, with her baby brother about to be scorched by troll-magic.

Lealle struggled to get her feet under her, desperate to scramble up and *save him*.

∽

The orange, sparking radiance rushing from Ohtavie's core to her outstretched hands hurt, the way a grazed knee burned, or a sip of broth just off the simmer. What was she doing? What *was* this?

She'd imagined she might cast a tiny enigmological charm, perhaps one of forgetting. But this scorching flow bore no resemblance to any enigmology she'd ever learned. Surely it was wrong, whatever it was.

For along with the alarming heat came a sense of vigor and grace, the feeling that Ohtavie could do . . . anything.

Was this power troll-magic? Was this why most troll-witches went too far, plunging toward madness and death rather than refraining—as Ohtavie had—from the use of their magic?

It was shocking to feel so powerful, she who had sought shadows and seclusion in her vulnerability.

Would she feel more powerful still, if she released this gathered magic to smite her enemy down?

But she couldn't, mustn't, didn't *want* to—he was a *child*!

She stared a moment at the boy confronting her. His chestnut curls were lighter than Lealle's, and his eyes were hazel, not luminous blue, but his face—even scrunched with fear and fury—held the same shape as hers. What had he said? Yelled? *Don't you dare hurt my sister!*

Dear Thiyaude! He was Lealle's little brother. And—with her almost accidental grab within herself—Ohtavie stood poised to annihilate him with a blast of uncontrolled magery. No, worse than that. Call it what it was: *incantatio,* the proper name for the perilous magic of trolls.

Dear saints, she must not strike, but could she call this fiery energy back from her reaching hands and fingers, stuff it back down, stopper it within herself? Or was it even now too late, unrecallable?

It didn't matter, she realized abruptly. Or rather, it mattered too much for her to fail in such a recall.

If she loosed her terrible magic upon this innocent boy child, she would *be* the troll-witch everyone feared. She would become the terrible beast in the labyrinth, the one she'd imagined lurked in the cellars of her own home.

Never! she vowed, and hauled on the fierce orange sparks wreathing her hands and forearms, pulling them back instead of flinging that lethal fountain out, determined to cram it down instead of letting it go, to slam some inner lid shut instead of blasting it open.

The reversal rocked her on her feet. And then the mild burning of all that sparking magic *seared* as it burgeoned forward, still anchored by her will to contain it, but just barely.

Were her bones become molten lead? Did her very flesh smoke with the heat of it? Would she burst into flames on the spot? Maybe she would, but she held on, despite the agony. She. Would. Not. Let. Go.

And then the fire within ebbed, as swiftly as it had intensified a moment ago. Like a cooling stream, it rushed back inside her, down and down, cold and icy and gone.

Ohtavie burst into tears, covering her face with her hands and balancing on her good foot as her crutches clattered to the terrace stones.

✐

Ohtavie sobbed.

She'd not cried in . . . twenty years? more?—and now she'd cried three times in less than twenty-four hours. Were tears always a part of change? Perhaps so. Because change was a kind of breaking, the destruction of one way of being, the sudden advent of another way. Perhaps the tears eased the transformation, as well as stemming from it. It would not hurt her to cry.

And so she sobbed.

Then Lealle's slim, young arm slipped around Ohtavie's waist, and Lealle's slender, young fingers tucked a handkerchief into Ohtavie's hands.

"Shh," whispered Lealle. "Shh, it's all right. You're all right."

I *am* all right, Ohtavie realized. She was not hurt. She had not hurt anyone. Or . . . suddenly anxious, she dropped her hands. Was the little boy all right? Had she recalled her dangerous troll-magic in time?

And there he was, crouched at her feet, quick eyes glancing from her face to his sister's. What must he think?

His mouth stretched in a sudden grin—taking in Lealle's comforting embrace and soothing words?

"Wow!" he exclaimed, his voice sounding very like his sister's. "Wow! You really are a troll-witch, aren't you?"

His hazel eyes were bright with excitement, as though the danger he'd so barely escaped had been a gallop on his pony or jumping from his swing at the apogee of its arc—not death or horrific injury. But he was whole. He was unharmed. Ohtavie had been strong enough, fast enough, just barely, to preserve him.

She nodded gravely. "I am a troll," she answered him.

"Wow!" he repeated. "I never thought I'd meet a troll, not a real one, an untreated one!" he exclaimed.

"Oh, Remy!" Lealle interrupted him. "How can you? It's not like you're visiting the zoological gardens."

Ohtavie couldn't help chuckling—she'd never had a sibling herself, but she could remember some of the brother-sister interchanges between her friends well enough. Her laughter unbalanced her, and she teetered.

The older boy who'd accompanied Lealle's little brother bent to retrieve her crutches and fitted them under her arms when she nodded her permission, steadying her as he did so. "You okay, ma'am?" he murmured—to which Ohtavie nodded again—while Lealle continued her elder-sister scold.

"Remy, Ohtavie is a *person*, not a sideshow, and you startled her! I think you owe her an apology!" Lealle insisted.

Ohtavie shook her head. "No," she said. "No more apologies, not now. Remy—it's Remy, is it?"

The boy nodded.

"Remy didn't hurt me. And I, for a miracle, didn't hurt him. Perhaps you'll introduce us properly, Lealle," Ohtavie requested.

Lealle swallowed. Clearly she wanted to go on scolding, and her manners had to fight her inclination for a moment. Then she settled her shoulders.

"Ohtavie, this is my younger brother, Remy Meridar, and, and—" Lealle lifted her chin "—a new friend of his and of mine, Gaetan Laurent."

A brief expression of surprise crossed the face of the older boy. Then he gave a slight bow.

Lealle continued, "Gaetan, Remy, this is my good friend Ohtavie de Bellay. Lady de Bellay," she corrected herself.

Ohtavie intervened quickly. "No, no. Please call me Ohtavie." Her mamere had been 'Lady de Bellay.' Even after Mamere had died, the servants had persisted in calling Ohtavie 'Miss Ohtavie,' and she had preferred it that way.

Remy echoed Gaetan's bow and said, "Pleased to meet you, Ohtavie." His gaze was clear and straight, and his little boy smile, sunny and uncomplicated.

"I am pleased to meet you, as well," returned Ohtavie, "both of you." She nodded at Gaetan, who blushed, and then rushed into speech.

"I shouldn't think you'd be pleased at all, ma'am, the way we're intruding on you, but . . . but . . ." his formal stiffness suddenly evaporated. "Lealle! You have to help! That's why we're here at all. I bumped into Remy, and he was looking for you, and couldn't find you, but I said I thought I knew where you might be, and you're here, but we have to do something! Fast!"

Lealle looked bewildered by his spate of words, but Ohtavie was following it well enough. There was some emergency that had the boy considerably upset.

"Will you explain?" Ohtavie said gently.

"Oh, yes, ma'am!" gasped the boy. "But I think you should sit down."

That galvanized Lealle. She searched the terrace hurriedly, turning her head this way and that, but not—of course—finding the cast iron tables and chairs that had once been present.

"Maybe we should go indoors?" the girl suggested uncertainly.

Ohtavie could feel a strong pull to go inside, but she was sure it would be better if she didn't. The longer she could stay outside, stay away from the cage she'd made for herself inside, the stronger she would become in the change she was making.

"The steps," she said.

They settled themselves there, Lealle next to Ohtavie, both boys two stairs below and looking up. Composedly, Ohtavie dried her damp eyes on the handkerchief Lealle had lent her. The sun felt warm on her face, and the slight breeze welcome. But the garden, even enclosed by the fading lilacs, felt too large. The sky, especially, was so big.

Well, she would just have to grow accustomed to it all.

"Now, Gaetan," said Ohtavie, "Gaetan, right?"

Gaetan nodded.

"Tell us about your trouble."

⁓

The stone step under Lealle's sit bones felt very firm, very steady, very welcome. It wasn't that she was trembling exactly. At least, she wasn't trembling outside, where everyone could see. But it felt like she was trembling inside, where no one could see, but where she could feel it even more strongly than if it had been in her lips and fingers and limbs.

The confrontation between Ohtavie and her brother had been *so scary*. And so . . . *confounding*.

She'd been regarding Ohtavie as her good friend. Ohtavie *was* her good friend. But then Ohtavie had threatened her brother, and suddenly everything was upside down. Instead of the nuisance that she was always trying to make into . . . not a nuisance, her brother was the most precious little boy she'd ever known, and Ohtavie was her resolved enemy.

And then, a moment later, Ohtavie was her friend again—a friend Lealle respected more than ever. She suspected that what Ohtavie had done, reining in incipient *incantatio*, was a more spectacular feat of antiphony than anything Lealle had ever seen before or would ever see again. But Remy was still the most precious little boy ever.

It was confusing enough that Lealle felt dizzy. She wished she could talk about it with . . . Mamere. And that was another disorienting thing. Mamere? Mamere, who spent most of her time with Lealle telling Lealle what to do and what not to do? Mamere, from whom Lealle spent much of her own effort trying to escape? Yes. Lealle sensed that Mamere could help with Lealle's current confusion.

But Mamere was not here. And Gaetan was speaking. And Lealle suspected that she'd better listen. Gaetan had not sought her out when he was in danger of losing his arm. So if he was seeking her now—Lealle shivered—it had to be something . . . truly awful.

Lealle hugged her arms around her ribs and tried to focus.

"My da wasn't a bad man, not at th' start," Gaetan was saying. "But, but, as things got settled and his business fell off 'cause of his bein' a Loyalist, he got . . . stubborn. And angry. And then he started listenin' to my uncle, and so . . ."

Ohtavie, at Lealle's side, nodded sympathetically. "I do understand, Gaetan," she said. "Your father fell on hard times. And hard times . . . sometimes that warps even good people in ways they would not expect."

Was Ohtavie thinking about her own troll-disease? And how it had warped her? Lealle's trembling insides seemed to quiet a little at the thought.

"What is it that your father has done?" asked Ohtavie quietly.

"Not him!" Gaetan burst out. "It's *l'oncle.* Da and L'Oncle Bardot already did something bad. They stole from the tax collector." Gaetan looked shocked. "They were tricky about it, not, not violent, and I thought maybe they had a right, 'cause of how the Empire made them poor. And they hadn't hurt anyone. Not really."

Lealle could see that Gaetan didn't really believe his excuses for his da, but she couldn't blame him for clinging to his vision of his da as a good man. She knew she'd do the same.

"But now?" questioned Ohtavie.

"L'Oncle is going to blow up the Fortin de Garde! And my da is *in* the Fortin de Garde. And even if he wasn't, people will get *hurt*! But I *saw* him! I *saw* him packing gunpowder into the foundation stones near the ground of that round bulge of the fortress where they store the weapons. It *had* to be black powder. I smelled it! And I tried to warn the guards at the portcullis"—his words were tumbling as they had earlier—"but they wouldn't listen and told me to scram, and I didn't know what to do, or who to tell, and then I thought of Lealle, and I was sure she could make someone listen, and I figured she would listen to me, and then L'Oncle could be stopped, if only someone could stop him running the fuse, except it's already too late, but if he hasn't *lit* the fuse—"

Ohtavie reached out a gentle hand and touched Gaetan's shoulder.

"Gaetan," she said. "It's not too late."

The boy gulped and fell silent.

"Your uncle has placed gunpowder and probably a fuse, so as to destroy the arsenal of the Fortin de Garde, correct?" said Ohtavie.

Lealle's inner trembling, the last residue of it, transformed into an icy chill. The Fortin de Garde was just down the road from her home. Her papere walked back and forth between home and the Fortin all the time, questioning prisoners, receiving reports from the guards, coordinating with General Roche. If the Fortin was due to explode at any moment . . . *Thiyaude,* she prayed, keep my papere and my mamere safe.

She thought she'd been scared when Ohtavie threatened Remy. But somewhere underneath, she'd known that Ohtavie was *Ohtavie,* that Ohtavie would never hurt someone Lealle loved. This . . . Gaetan's L'Oncle Bardot was truly an enemy. "Oh, Thiyaude," she whispered.

Lealle hardly knew what else to do, or say, except pray.

But Ohtavie seemed not to be so flummoxed as was Lealle.

"Remy," said Ohtavie, after a quick glance at Lealle, "do you run as fast as your sister?"

Remy perked up, apparently unfazed by Gaetan's revelation.

"Hah!" he boasted, "I'm way faster than Lealle!"

"Good," answered Ohtavie. "Can you get to where your father would be without going past the Fortin de Garde? I suspect Gaetan's Oncle Bardot will not light his fuse until later. He must have some kind of uprising planned. But . . . I don't want you to take any chances you need not."

"I'll run and fetch Papere here!" exclaimed Remy, understanding Ohtavie's plan instantly.

"Ye-e-s," Ohtavie answered. "Except—how well do you know your father's armigers? Could you convince one of them to run for your papere? Fast? Because while I think we have a little time, I also think we don't have much."

Remy's brow wrinkled. "If I got Armiger Folliere, he'd go right away. But if I got Armiger Bichon, he'd argue. And . . . and, I dunno about some of the others." Remy looked up, desperate for the first time since he'd arrived here in Ohtavie's garden. "He didn't tell me what it was. Gaetan," Remy explained, glancing aside at his friend and back. "He just said he needed Lealle really bad. But now he's said, I believe him. Do *you* believe him, ma'am?"

"Oh, yes," Ohtavie breathed. "That's why I'm working out how to get your father here as fast as may be, Remy. But I don't want to put you in danger. I believe we would have heard something if the Fortin de Garde had exploded. It's . . . not that far away. And the size of the explosion, with all that gunpowder inside the arsenal, would be immense."

Remy's disquiet subsided immediately. And Lealle noticed that even Gaetan was looking calmer. Both boys clearly trusted this adult to solve their problem. Lealle . . . was not so sure. Ohtavie had been shut up in her home from her girlhood. Lealle doubted she had the experience solving adult problems that, say, Mamere displayed. And yet . . . Ohtavie had survived her troll-disease, a lethal dilemma, for decades. Maybe that disaster would make her adept at solving this one?

A flicker of motion at the corner of Lealle's vision teased her attention. She looked up.

And there in a gap between a pair of raggedy lilac bushes stood a brown-haired, hazel-eyed man, with two armigers at his back.

Oh, thank the saints!

Chapter Thirteen

OHTAVIE FOLLOWED the line of Lealle's gaze.

Framed by the untidy foliage stood a neatly made man wearing an elegant uniform: dark and severe wedge cap; plain epaulettes at his shoulders, fastened by ornate gold buttons; a badge in the form of a gilded wreath on his left breast—*the Ordre de Victoire, dear Thiyaude*; white doeskin belt; trimly dark frock coat to the knee; dark trousers ornamented by a wide green side-stripe.

Abruptly she knew who he was. Justice to Claireau's Court of Audire. Of course a pair of armigers would stand at his back. Her breath caught.

So. Her confrontation with Remy had been but practice for the real conflict.

Well, she had learned from it, at least.

It might have been easier to perceive the innocence within a little boy, but these men were equally innocent of evil; they were merely fulfilling their appointed responsibilities. The fact that their responsibilities must include Ohtavie's death . . . did not make them evil.

She could fight her capture. But she wouldn't. It was time to surrender.

Still seated alongside Ohtavie, Lealle gasped, then sprang to her feet with a smile of relief. "Papere!" she shrilled, dashing forward.

All the tense resolution drained out of Ohtavie's stiff posture.

Of course.

She'd been seeing the *Justice*, the man she'd feared most all these years. Lealle, naturally enough, saw her papere, not the legal authority.

Lealle's dash across the ragged lawn was swift, but still it gave Ohtavie time enough to register every response in the girl's parent as he awaited his daughter's arrival.

His eyes, quite calmly, noted both boys on the step below Ohtavie, noted Ohtavie herself, catalogued her troll's ears, troll's nose, and troll's hunch. Just before Lealle threw herself into his arms, his gaze met Ohtavie's and he nodded—as though to say, *fear not*—and then his arms wrapped his child in a surprisingly fervent embrace.

Ohtavie released a small sigh. So. This high judge—Lealle's father—was inclined to help, was he?

She started to lever herself to her feet, but then paused as Lealle began spilling an account of the present emergency, a jumble of words: Gaetan, who he was, his father, his uncle, the imminent explosion of the arsenal.

It was almost frightening how quickly the man took in what his daughter was saying, parsed it, and determined his course of action. Or it would have been, if they'd not needed him to be exactly that capable. He set Lealle a little away from him, turned to give terse orders to the armigers behind him—one of whom departed forthwith—gave another small nod to Ohtavie, and then checked his daughter's continued tumble of speech.

Lealle stopped, a tremulous smile on her lips, and led her father toward the group on the terrace steps, the remaining armiger trailing them. A soft movement of the air carried the warm scent of the grass over which they walked to Ohtavie's in-breath.

She resumed her struggle to stand, impeded by how broad were the stair's treads and how shallow the risers. She couldn't get her feet under her. But then it didn't matter, because Lealle's papere knelt down when he reached her, stretching out his hand so compellingly that Ohtavie placed hers within it almost without thinking.

His clasp was firm and gentle. He brushed his lips respectfully to her twisted knuckles, murmuring, "Lady de Bellay?"

"Yes," she gasped in astonishment. Lealle hadn't mentioned Ohtavie at all in her concentration on the danger posed to the arsenal. How did he know who she was? She didn't feel quite up to correcting his address the way she had the boys.

"I must thank you for your care of my daughter and her friends," he continued. "I'm Bello Meridar, Lealle's father," he explained. "I think you know this is no good time for anyone, let alone children, to be on the streets of Claireau."

Ohtavie labored to choose which of her competing thoughts to utter—*how do you know I'm safe? why are you trusting me? what do you intend to do?*—and settled upon: "Will your armigers be in time?"

"I trust so," he answered, "if Gaetan here"—he glanced aside at Gaetan, who was sitting with his mouth gaping open—"will give me the one piece of information I'm lacking."

"S-sir?" stuttered Gaetan.

Lealle, standing beside her father, shifted uneasily on her feet.

"Tell me your uncle's street address, please," instructed Meridar firmly.

Gaetan gulped. "Th-thirty-eight Rue Longeurs," he answered.

Meridar spoke over his shoulder to the armiger waiting there. "You have that, Poinchette?"

"Yes, sir."

"You know what to do?" Meridar's voice was assured.

"Yes, sir." The man saluted, turned *volte-face*, and strode briskly away.

"W-what *is* he going to d-do?" quavered Gaetan.

Meridar smiled reassuringly. "The Capitaine of my armigers has known for quite some time that a group of dissidents was planning to engage in an uprising. What we'd not been able to pin down was exactly when it would take place and the true identity of their leader, 'Le Chevalier Résolu.'

"Now we know." Meridar's tone was firm, but his face kind.

"How?" burst out Remy, scrunched little boy-like on the lower step.

"They would not be packing the arsenal foundations with gunpowder unless they meant to fire it very shortly, this evening, in fact. And we had already narrowed down the domicile of 'Résolu' to either Rue Fauquier or Rue Longeurs."

Remy's lips formed a silent 'oh.'

"Will you hurt L'Oncle?" asked Gaetan, that question perhaps standing in for his real concern: *have I betrayed my kin?*

"Bardot Laurent will receive a fair trial," answered Meridar. "I myself will ensure that one of our best advocates represents him." The justice paused, seeming to gather Gaetan in with the sheer quiet force of his personality. "You would not condemn innocent men, women, and children to the death that your silence would have brought."

Gaetan's quivering mouth steadied, and he sat straighter. "No, sir. Thank you, sir."

"Well done." A muscle in Meridar's chin jumped.

Lealle, an expression of beaming satisfaction on her face, nodded across to her friend.

Meridar returned his gaze to Ohtavie. "I must trespass upon your presence and your property yet awhile longer, milady. My armigers will be reporting back to me here, you see."

Ohtavie hardly knew how to answer him. She felt he should be hurling accusations at her, not mouthing politenesses.

"My Lord Justice," she managed, "I suspect you may not understand the situation here. I doubt I deserve your courtesy."

His eyes crinkled ever so slightly at their corners. "And I am rather certain you deserve every courtesy, milady. But you may explain it all to me as you wish. I am at your service."

Lealle was staring at her father in astonishment. Perhaps she, too, had expected scolding, directed at herself once the immediate crisis had been addressed.

Ohtavie swallowed, her mouth suddenly dry. "I'm a renegade troll, you see. I eluded capture . . . long ago. And lately . . . Lealle tells me I've eluded my required treatment as well. I'd . . . not known such existed until . . . just a few days ago."

Meridar dipped his head in a respectful bow. "Indeed, milady, I do urge you to seek your proper treatment. I shall be happy to provide you an escort of armigers later this afternoon—when I am certain the streets will host no uprising—so as to see you unmolested to the retreat center."

"My Lord Justice, surely there are consequences visited upon trolls who avoid treatment!"

"From the unarrested progress of the disease, yes," he stated. "Most painful, I'm told."

"Legal consequences," Ohtavie insisted. "Imprisonment. Flogging. Execution," she elaborated.

"You've not harmed anyone as a result of your troll-disease?" Meridar queried.

She'd nearly killed the man's son. "Not . . . yet," she faltered.

"Well then." He glanced over his shoulder, and an armiger pushing a velocipede emerged from the lilacs. "Excuse me, milady," he converted whatever he'd been about to say into an apology, and rose from his knee, going to meet the newcomer.

Lealle bounced on her toes. "You see! I told you!" she proclaimed proudly.

"You did," admitted Ohtavie. Was her head spinning? It seemed to be spinning.

Remy whispered something in Gaetan's ear, and Gaetan whispered back. Were they as impressed by Bello Meridar as was Ohtavie? Well, Remy was surely used to his papere's concentrated presence, but Gaetan?

Ohtavie lowered her voice, speaking to Lealle. "I feel as though the ground has lurched beneath me and tipped me over," she confessed.

"Me, too," agreed Lealle. "Papere does that sometimes. You're all set for remonstrance or resistance or punishment . . . *something,* and then he turns everything upside down. Which is confusing, but also . . . the way Papere does it, it's better. He makes everything better."

While Lealle beamed anew at her papere, he dismissed the armiger and his velocipede to some further task, and then stepped quickly back toward the terrace stairs.

"All is well," he informed them. "Bardot Laurent has been detained. Peaceably," he added, with a nod to Gaetan. "General Roche's Brigade Rouge is guarding all approaches to the arsenal until the ordnance experts form their plan for examining and cleansing the building's foundations. And I expect to hear shortly that all danger of any uprising has been forestalled."

Ohtavie's breath blew out with the relief of this news. She'd not realized how tense she'd remained, even in the face of the Lord Justice's obvious competence.

Meridar sketched an abbreviated bow. "Milady, I wish most strongly to resume our interrupted conversation, but I must have some private words with this young man first. Will you await me?"

"Of course." What next would the man do? It seemed he continued to be at least three steps ahead of . . . just about everyone else. Ohtavie couldn't help but notice that even Lealle looked bemused, while Gaetan was decidedly nervous.

The Lord Justice nodded at the boy reassuringly.

∞

Lealle heaved a large sigh of relief and then blushed. Mamere would say sighing loudly like that was vulgar. A lady's sighs should be imperceptible . . . or absent altogether. But Lealle was so relieved. And a little embarrassed. She'd spent so much effort ensuring that Papere knew nothing of her doings with Ohtavie. And, now, within very little time after his arrival, Papere had solved the immediate emergency and was rapidly sorting out all the smaller problems still remaining.

Ohtavie and her troll-disease had not seemed like a smaller problem when Lealle was wrestling with it alone. That had shrunk only in contrast to the arsenal scare. But still . . .

The next time she encountered real difficulty—not silly stuff, like one of her friends badgering Lealle for gratis tickets to the annual Armigers' Velocipede Exhibition, but something serious like Ohtavie's troll-disease—Lealle would seek Papere's advice right from the start.

She looked up to see him smiling at her. Did he know what she was thinking? He might, he was so—intelligent wasn't the word for him. He was just *knowing*. He knew people. And he knew her.

He transferred his smile from Lealle to Gaetan.

"Come," he said, indicating that Gaetan should walk with him.

Gaetan's eyes clung to Lealle's in a silent, frightened message.

"Of course I'll come with you," she answered.

"I believe Gaetan might prefer your absence," said Papere. "I must ask him some rather personal questions."

Gaetan looked even more alarmed at this. "Please, sir, I'd ruther Lealle heard. I—" He couldn't seem to find words for whatever he wanted to convey.

"Very well," Papere assented. "But you must let me know if you change your mind."

Gaetan nodded earnestly.

Papere led them through a gap in the lilacs on the far side of the garden from the one through which he and the armigers had entered. That gap was the one through which Lealle had run five days ago, come to think of it. This one opened onto a tiny, graveled square, weedgrown as were all the other outdoor spaces here, and enclosed by overgrown hedges. The center of the courtyard featured a large, shallow stone bowl raised upon the backs of miniature stone gryphons. A froth of leafy greenness filled the bowl, and four curving stone benches surrounded it. A warm, herbal scent rose from the greenery.

The gravel scritched under their footsteps.

Papere gestured for Lealle and Gaetan to sit, while he perched on the edge of the bowl, comfortably low, so that they need not crane their necks to look at him. He focused his attention on Gaetan.

"You've just saved the lives of all the people living in the townhomes crowded around the Fortin de Garde," he said, "as well as everyone in the fortress itself, including your father. Do you realize that?"

Gaetan bit his lip. "I—that's why I had to tell," he said. Something that looked like pain crossed his face. "Do you think my da knew?" he burst out. "Knew what L'Oncle was planning? I don't—" He stopped and shook his head.

"I don't know, Gaetan," Papere answered him."That will be something that will come out in his trial. But—" Papere hesitated, then went on "—knowing about a conspiracy to do bodily harm to a multitude is not the same as actually doing such harm. And your da is innocent of such action by virtue of being locked in one of the Fortin's prison cells, even if he did have knowledge of your uncle's plans.

"Your uncle did take active steps, and he will have to answer for that. But my questions are not about your da and your uncle. Lealle could tell you"—he smiled at her, his eyes warm—"that it would be improper for me to question you on these matters without your parent's or your guardian's permission and presence. Indeed, even the questions that I am about to ask you, you need not answer, if you choose not to."

Gaetan's brow wrinkled. Lealle suspected he'd likely never encountered someone so measured and so fair as Papere. Lealle herself didn't even know anyone who was quite like Papere.

"You really can stay silent," she assured Gaetan. "But I bet he wants to help you." She tamped down her own smile, and turned back to face Papere, eager to hear what he would say next.

"The reason I asked if you understood how many lives you saved was because I want you also to understand that you are owed more than just praise. Any help I offer you, you have earned."

Gaetan hunched his shoulders uncomfortably. "I don't want no reward for turnin' in my kin," he muttered.

"Of course not," said Papere. "But do you have a home to go to, now that both your da and your uncle are in prison? Is there an adult who will provide you with food, clothing, shelter, and guidance? My understanding is that your mother no longer lives."

Gaetan's feet twisted in the weedy gravel. "Tante Racelle don't like me much, but she gives me bite and sup. And a bedroll." He shrugged.

"She is your uncle's wife?" Papere queried.

"Yeah." Gaetan studied his twisting feet, then he looked up. "M'sieur, you don't have to do anything for me. Just—just let me go. Let me get on."

Lealle thought Papere's face looked a little sad. "If you insist upon that, I shall, of course," he said. "But, Gaetan, you have done something extraordinary, and I believe you can do more extraordinary things, if you simply have access to the resources that will allow you to grow strong and wise. I'd like to see that you have those resources. And I am in a position to do so, if you'll permit me."

"Like what Lealle did for me, you mean?" Gaetan asked.

Oh, no!

Lealle ducked her head down. She'd known she would eventually have to confess to turning Gaetan's arm to wood, but she really, really had hoped it could be later. Much later.

Haltingly, she explained what had happened on the steps of the retreat house: Gaetan tormenting her, her own fear and anger, the accidental use of antiphony. She felt like her face must be beet red.

Papere pursed his lips, when she finished. And then he ignored the matter entirely. Lealle felt utterly let down. Although . . . she supposed it made sense that he wouldn't head off down such a tangent until he finished settling Gaetan. Which meant . . . Lealle would be confronting the issue again with Papere . . . later. There was an uncomfortable thought.

"No, that's not what I meant," said Papere, answering Gaetan. "I envisioned you attending a good school, one with room and board for those of its students whose families live at a distance. But, you need decide nothing right now. In fact, you shouldn't. Your future deserves more careful thought than can be achieved in a few minutes of an afternoon." Papere rose to his feet. "You have shelter for tonight, which is the first thing. And I'll come visit you at your aunt's on the morrow."

Gaetan scrambled to his feet. "Oh, you needn't," he said hastily.

Papere's left eyebrow rose. "I *shall* find you there, Gaetan," he stated, not asking, but instructing.

"Yeah," mumbled Gaetan.

The corner of Papere's mouth turned up. "I'll search you out elsewhere, if need be," he said easily. "You know I must find you, don't you?"

Gaetan's own mouth found a reluctant smile. "Yeah," he agreed. "But—I'd ruther Lealle came." He ducked his head. Was he blushing?

"I suspect that could be arranged," said Papere. "Lealle?"

"Of course I'll come, Gaetan," she answered. "I'd like to."

Gaetan's cheeks turned pink. He *was* blushing. "Thanks," he muttered. Then he turned a worried face up to Papere. "My aunt—she, she won't think you should do anything at all for me. She'll say—" He shook his head.

"We'll meet you at your aunt's and then take a walk by the river, with a stop at Celeste's for scones or tea cakes or something. Will that do?"

"Oh, yes, sir! Thank you, sir. And"—he turned to Lealle—"thank you, too. You don't have to come," he added. "I wouldn't want to make you."

"But you aren't," she said. "I really do want to."

He nodded, evidently believing her. "Can I go now, sir?" he asked her Papere.

"I'd like you to keep Lady de Bellay company," said Papere. "Would you?"

Gaetan nodded. "I'll just go to her now, shall I?"

"Yes."

Papere watched him through the gap in the lilacs before turning to Lealle. She swallowed.

So, this was the reckoning—the later—she'd been dreading, she supposed. She knew better than to assume Papere would scold. Papere never scolded. But he did admonish, and his admonishments . . . were worse than any of Mamere's scoldings, because Lealle always ended up *agreeing* with him and wishing she'd done better.

"That went rather well," Papere commented, "better than I would have forecast." He started moving toward the gap between the lilacs.

"Gaetan?" she queried. Maybe that later she was dreading for herself wasn't now after all. Or maybe she could delay it.

"Yes," answered Papere. "But never mind that now. Lélé, we must speak."

So. She couldn't delay the reckoning for Gaetan's wooden arm, her own disobedience, the dangers she'd courted. Lealle stifled a sigh. Mamere would have been proud.

"Yes, Papere," she said, submissively.

"Lélé, I'm not angry. And we aren't going to talk now. I've got a string of armigers who will be lining up for my further direction within minutes." His hand came under her chin, urging her to meet his gaze. His face was tender.

"Oh, Papere, I've made such a mess of things," she whispered.

"No, you haven't," he said. "You've done quite well, and that is what we must discuss. You, like Gaetan, need more resources. And I'll need your input in order to discern what those resources should be."

"But, but, Gaetan's arm. My sneaking. My *lying*!" she burst out.

"Yes, your tactics were a trifle lacking. Which we will also discuss. But, Lélé, I'm *proud* of you."

"Oh!" She felt a little blank, getting praise when she was expecting censure.

His hand turned to brush its back against her cheek in a caress.

"Come," he said. "Let's finish up your first good deed, shall we?"

Maybe everything was going to be all right after all.

"Thank you, Papere," she answered.

His smile turned into a loving grin.

∽

Ohtavie could just see Bello Meridar (facing her), and Lealle and Gaetan (their backs to her), through the gap between the lilacs. Which meant that Meridar could likely see her as well. Had the man positioned himself just so for his words with Gaetan? So that he could monitor what happened near the terrace even while preserving the privacy he believed Gaetan deserved? No doubt he had. The justice seemed accustomed to thinking in a dozen directions at once.

Somehow his foresight made Ohtavie feel safe rather than endangered. His words and his demeanor had put him firmly on Ohtavie's side. She suspected he was a good ally to have.

What did she make of his suggestion that she allow his armigers to escort her to the retreat house this very afternoon?

It felt too soon.

She'd imagined herself stepping out onto the terrace for a few short moments, then returning inside to question Lealle about the treatment offered to trolls. Supposedly offered to trolls. Did she still have doubts about that? Could it all be an elaborate ruse? A less violent way of handling the troll menace?

Surely it would be much easier to escort a troll who believed she walked to kindly healers than to escort one who believed that the executioner and his axe awaited her. That had a horrible plausibility.

But . . . no. Such a deception was utterly at odds with Lealle's nature. And she was her father's daughter. Bello Meridar had the will and the wit to create and follow such a scheme, she judged, but not to both trick trolls to their doom *and* rear such a caring and honest daughter as Lealle.

Ohtavie shifted a little where she sat, glancing at Remy sitting quietly—uncharacteristically so?—nearby. The stone step under her was growing harder the longer she stayed put. But the vastness of the outdoors was becoming less uncomfortable than it had felt when she first emerged from the house. And the sunshine was lovely in its warmth, a faint breeze moderating that warmth and rustling the leaves of the trees pleasantly.

So. Was Ohtavie ready to undergo treatment for her troll-disease?

She could think of no good reason for delay, much as she wanted to. Was it just that this would be the final breaking of the constricted ambit she'd constructed for herself? Breaking it wide open to set her free in the world?

She suspected that was it, but still longed to drag her heels.

She needed to think about this, but she wasn't going to be able to, because Remy was emerging from the quietude—unaccustomed, Ohtavie suspected—that events and his father's magisterial handling of them had thrust upon the boy. Remy . . . chattered, apparently fully confident that he deserved and could secure Ohtavie's attention. Perhaps he was justified in that belief, given that her attention was, in truth, shifting to him.

"Papere never yells at Lélé as much as she deserves," he remarked, his tone matter-of-fact rather than whiny, despite the content of his words. "It's not fair, really, especially this time, you know." He gazed confidingly into Ohtavie's eyes.

"Why is it not fair?" she asked, obligingly.

"'Cause there was really danger. Papere *said*. And Lealle promised to always take a hansom or our carriage or the baillie. And she *didn't*.

She broke a promise." Remy sounded shocked. "That's why I was prowling all over Claireau myself. Which meant Lealle breaking *her* promise made *me* break *mine!*"

"Surely you are responsible for your own promises?" she suggested.

Remy gave a small grin. "That's what Papere would say," he admitted. "But if I hadn't found Gaetan, and if *he* hadn't known where to find *her,* then she would *still* be in danger. In fact, *everybody* would be!"

"So that's how you two ended up here!" She'd wondered. Except . . . "How did *Gaetan* know to find Lealle here? She's been most careful of . . . my privacy."

Remy stared at her, astonished. "But o' course he knew she might be here. He's the one who chased her in here in the first place."

Ohtavie frowned. "Wait, *he's* the bully, the leader of those dreadful schoolboys?" Lealle had named him as her friend, a new friend. And the boy had clearly looked to her for support. But Ohtavie had not suspected the origin of that friendship to be in enmity. How very . . . strange.

"Well, yeah," answered Remy. "O' course he didn't know she'd be here for sure. And he hadn't even thought to check, because why would he? But then when I said I was looking for her, too, and I bet she was sneaking somewhere secret, because I couldn't find her the day before *either,* then *he* said that it was worth trying this place he knew. And he was right. Because she *was* here." Remy nodded decidedly and grinned.

"I . . . see," she said. And she did see, even though it all seemed rather unexpected—but fortunate, when one considered the matter of the arsenal and the gunpowder. It also confirmed her belief that once one person discovered her secret presence . . . her secrecy was destined for exposure. Lealle really had been the beginning of the end.

Except . . . the end looked to be considerably brighter than anything Ohtavie had been taught to expect.

She looked up from Remy to see Gaetan crossing the overgrown lawn, heading back to the terrace stairs. He looked . . . steadier. Older, somehow, in a good way. Had Meridar been able to restore some of the boy's confidence?

Meridar had lingered a moment with his daughter in the courtyard beyond the lilacs, but as Gaetan reached the terrace steps, the judge and Lealle started to follow in the boy's wake.

"Ma'am? Lady de—I mean, Ohtavie?" Gaetan addressed her.

"What is it?" she asked him.

"The—the Lord Justice said I was t' wait on you, and I'm wonderin' if there's anything you want especial. Can I get you anything from the house? Or, or run a message, or something?"

"That's kind of you, but no. I suspect the Lord Justice will sort out all the remaining details rather swiftly, and then we'll know where we stand."

Another two armigers, both pushing velocipedes, entered the garden before Meridar reached the terrace steps, and the justice broke off from his intended destination to attend to them.

Lealle walked over to join her brother on the lower step.

"Lealle!" Remy accused her with his tone. "Ohtavie didn't know Gaetan was the one who'd chased you in here!"

"Oh!" Lealle's gaze flew to Ohtavie's face. "I . . ." the girl shook her head ". . . rather a lot has happened since—a lot happened yesterday. And the day before. I—" She looked down, looked up again. "I'm sorry," she said simply. "Are you—do you mind terribly?"

Ohtavie took Lealle's hand in a reassuring clasp. "I don't mind at all. I was merely . . . a little confused. It's a good thing, truly, that Gaetan did know where to find you."

Lealle's eyes widened at this. "Oh, yes!" she agreed, rather fervently.

Indeed. No doubt they could all imagine what might have happened if Gaetan had *not* found Lealle.

Lealle's papere had finished with his two armigers, Ohtavie noticed, and was coming briskly to join the group on the steps.

228 ∝ J.M. Ney-Grimm

"The streets are secure now," he announced, "for ordinary citizens, at least. Gaetan, I do want a pair of armigers seeing you safely to your aunt's. I think you can understand that you might still be an unfortunate focus for your uncle's followers, can you not?"

Gaetan nodded. "Yes, sir. But—" He bit his lower lip. "Will my aunt still house me, when I'm the reason L'Oncle is in jail?"

Meridar gave him a shrewd glance. "She does not know that, as yet. And I recommend that you not tell her immediately. But my men checked that she would indeed shelter you tonight, and that she understood the importance of doing so. It's not a permanent solution, of course, but you and I will talk about that tomorrow."

"Papere," Lealle interrupted, "could not Gaetan come home with us?"

"Oooh! Yes!" exclaimed Remy.

"He could," Meridar replied. "But I suspect he'd prefer to go to his aunt. Is that not so?" he asked Gaetan.

Gaetan looked a little appalled at Lealle's suggestion. "Yes, my aunt. Please," he gulped.

"Good." Meridar nodded crisply. "Lealle, you and your brother shall come with me, and we shall have our own escort of armigers."

"But, Ohtavie," protested Lealle. "What about her?"

Her papere tamped down a smile. "Indeed," he said, turning to Ohtavie. "What is your wish, Lady de Bellay? I am at your command."

She didn't suppose he was, not truly, but this was it. What would she choose for herself.

She could go back inside. She could spend the approaching evening in her old home. She could recapture . . . as many of her old routines as she wanted to, she supposed.

But she did not want to recapture . . . any.

Oh, her old home, her old routines, still pulled. She could feel that longing to go back, to return, to nestle into . . . limitations, familiarity, solitude. But it wasn't what she truly desired, deep in her heart.

"If you'll provide me with safe escort also, I'd like to walk to the retreat house right now," she stated.

Meridar's eyes warmed, and it looked almost as though he repressed a salute in her direction.

"My armigers will be here directly to accompany you," he said with a bow.

✆

Gaetan was dispatched with his own escort of armigers, but Papere decided that he, Lealle, Remy, and their larger contingent of armigers would accompany Ohtavie to the retreat house. It took them out of their way, but Lealle suspected her father wanted to see for himself that the streets were indeed quiet.

Lealle worried at first that the walk would be too much for Ohtavie. Should they have summoned a hansom?

But Ohtavie moved easily on her crutches, seeming to enjoy the excursion. Her face remained eager and interested throughout, her gaze darting here and there, and her pace never flagged. What must it be like for her, to be ranging through Claireau after a close confinement of decades? Lealle couldn't really imagine it.

Lealle herself found the walk through the late afternoon streets to be particularly lovely. The flagways of Boulevarde Châtelaine especially soothed her senses, its double passage arched and shaded by well-grown elms, the extensive front gardens of the estates there vivid with flower beds and tidy with smooth lawns. Its verdant peace seemed the perfect anodyne to the violent chaos she—they all—had feared would erupt.

On Rue Chatoyer, a narrow, twisting street, one of the townhouse dwellers leaned from his casement with a massive copper urn to water the flowers in the windowbox. The scent of the fresh water and moist earth seemed almost a taste of Thiyaude's heaven. A small songbird hopped around under the box in the wet spot on the pavement, cheeping.

"How did you find us?" she asked Papere, walking beside her. "How did you know we were in Ohtavie's garden?"

Papere's mouth quirked in a not-quite laugh. "One of the bailies—the one I'd assigned to *you*, in fact—spotted Remy at a distance, running across the Valendras Bridge. Etienne was well aware that neither you nor your brother should be on the loose, today of all days. He informed me of the problem after calling out the armigers to quarter the town. One of them recognized Remy's voice on the other side of the garden wall and summoned me."

Lealle felt a little sheepish. "Do you always know everything?" she murmured.

Papere did laugh at this. "A lord justice needs to feel the pulse of events within his jurisdiction," he answered easily.

Lealle reached for his hand, and Papere took hers in a reassuring clasp.

Papere handled everything at the retreat house—explanations, arrangements, courtesies—and then aimed himself and his children home via the southern Pont du Ciel, instead of the more direct route over the Valendras Bridge. How long would it take to be sure the arsenal was safe, Lealle wondered.

Once home, Papere and the armigers plunged into the cluster of offices on the ground floor connected with the Court of Audire, while Nurse swept Remy off to a bath, and Lealle climbed the stair tower to her bedchamber. She half wanted to follow her papere, to participate in the winding up of the emergency. It felt . . . unfinished to leave off before everything was complete. But completion was Papere's job, and it wasn't hers. He'd sent her and Remy off quite firmly, with a reminder that he himself would talk with Lealle later.

"I'll ring for you," he'd said. "And if I do not, come to me in my chancery."

She didn't know what to expect from the upcoming meeting with her papere. Clearly he had something in mind far beyond admonishment.

And yet . . . surely there would be admonishment. Lealle had made far too many mistakes for there not to be.

Her bedchamber was very bright, with the afternoon light flooding in through its windows, gleaming on the pale yellow of her lacquered wardrobe, dressing table, bureau and four-poster.

She crossed to the window seat and plumped down on its cushions, staring out upriver. The mirror finish on the water, the golden light on the stone embankment walls and town homes, the arching drape of a tree here and there, and the vast sea of the sky—warm turquoise with a hint of gold at the horizon—was just as peaceful as had been the walk home.

Perhaps she could finally let the last feather of anxiety troubling her go. She need not do anything, solve anything, prevent anything, or conceal anything any longer. All the stresses of the past few days were over. Even with the upcoming discourse with her papere looming—but really she was looking forward to that, not dreading it.

Perhaps she would just sit for a little while, sit and let peace seep into her soul.

The quietude and the light and the stillness lulled her into sleep.

She awoke at sunset, the sky a glory of gold, and the long amber rays of the sun stretching all the way across her room to illuminate the carved panels of the door.

A maid came bustling through it with a laden tea cart, rattling and clinking.

"Your mamere's staying late at a board meeting for Alet-les-Bain, and your papere is still busy with Capitaine Duval," the maid announced. "So Cook thought you might like to eat in your bedchamber, rather than all alone in the dining room."

Saints, yes, thought Lealle. Sitting at that long table without company, and *with* all the footmen serving, would be too tedious. "Remy?" she asked.

The maid laughed. "Sound asleep," she answered. "Nurse plans to let him dream all the way through to morning."

Lealle rubbed the drowsiness out of her eyes, trying to wake up all the way. If Remy were napping, too, maybe there was some excuse for her own slide into slumber.

The supper Cook had sent up was perfect in Lealle's opinion: baked eggs, dumplings of minced chicken accompanied by roasted courgettes and pickled cucumbers, and a plum compote to finish it off. A chilled mint infusion provided her beverage, cool and soothing. She wished she could dine so simply every day.

Once the maid had taken the remains of her meal away, Lealle took thought.

She could simply wait until Papere sent for her. And if he continued busy with the armigers, baillies, and clerks of the court, that might be the way things fell out.

But wouldn't it be better if she could control some of the timing?

She wasn't afraid precisely. Or at all, really. That wasn't it. It was that she sensed the upcoming discussion was important, really important. And she wanted to arrive at it with more authority than she usually possessed. If only she weren't so small for her age. If only she had something to wear like Papere's uniform or his judge's robes.

Although . . . that gave her an idea.

She went to her wardrobe. All her frocks were so pretty and so girly. Ordinarily she liked their prettiness, but right now . . . ah! There it was! All the way in the back left corner hung a plain white ensemble given to her by her Great Aunt Caroline.

Mamere had deemed it too old for Lealle. The dress had a square neck, trim elbow sleeves, and a narrowly flaring skirt that fell to the ankles. A panel of sewn tucks across the front placket added a bit of elegance, and a single tuck above the skirt's hem gave definition there. The matching jacket was fitted, also with short sleeves, and sported a low band collar.

Lealle tumbled out of her wrinkled frock in a hurry, but donned Great Aunt Caroline's gift with care. Buttoning up the buttons in back was a trifle awkward, but she managed. Once the jacket was on, she surveyed herself in the freestanding mirror beside the wardrobe. Maybe Mamere was right after all. She looked . . . almost grown up. Which was perfect for right now.

Seized with a further idea, she sat down in front of her dressing table. She was too young to put her hair up, but if she braided it as close to the hair ends as possible and then tucked the plait inside her jacket collar, it would present a similar effect.

Her hair was tangled from her nap anyway, and needed tidying.

Getting her comb through the snarls took some time. What if Papere sent for her before she were ready?

Then you'll just finish and go to him when you've finished, she told herself. It wouldn't take that long.

But no summons came.

She checked herself once more in the freestanding mirror. She looked tall and slim and elegant, she thought. Her face even looked slightly older, the cheekbones more evident. A rush of delight filled her, but then ebbed into doubt. Maybe this wasn't such a good idea after all. What if Papere merely thought she looked like a little girl playing dress up and laughed at her?

If he did . . . that would be mortifying. But if he did . . . she would try gazing at him blankly, the way Mamere had once looked at a fellow charity-supporter who had insulted her. That gentleman had blushed red as a cherry and backed down fast.

Lealle couldn't imagine Papere backing down for anyone, but . . . if he laughed at her, she would try Mamere's look.

Raising her chin, Lealle turned to leave her room.

❧

The closed door of Papere's chancery—thick oaken boards bound by iron straps—was quite as usual. Papere always kept the door shut when he was working. And he locked it at day's end when he was done—which was sometimes quite late. Lealle refused to be daunted by this ordinary state of affairs.

She lifted her hand and knocked.

"Enter," came Papere's voice from within.

There were three stone steps just on the other side of the door. Lealle took them briskly, her half-boots tapping, and then she stood in the round, vaulted chamber where her papere spent so much of his time.

She'd run in and out of it as a child, of course. But this was the first time she'd come to the chancery at her papere's behest. It felt different.

Oh, the glass-fronted cabinets encircling the chamber, housing shelf upon shelf of legal books and case records, were the same, as were the tall desks for Papere's clerks, the oil lamps—all lit now at sundown—and the richly patterned red carpet underfoot.

But Lealle herself was different.

Papere sat at his own massive desk, more a table with a few drawers than a writing desk.

His eyes widened ever so slightly as Lealle gained the top of the steps and came into the well-lit circle of the room. If she'd not known him very well, as a daughter knows her father, she would have missed the change in his gaze. It was the only indication he gave of noticing her grown-up dress.

Good. No laughing.

Coming out from behind his desk, he stepped forward, took both her hands, and smiled.

"Let's sit comfortably, shall we?" he suggested, leading the way to a clump of leather armchairs grouped around a low round table. She was relieved that she need not perch on one of the spindly chairs before his desk, while he sat in state behind it. The armchairs were much more comfortable, but she held herself very straight as Papere sank into the one next to hers. He clearly felt no qualms about relaxing.

"You did very well with Gaetan," he began. "Do you realize that I would have had no chance with the boy today, if you'd not prepared my way?"

Lealle swallowed. She wasn't convinced that she had done well with Gaetan. Not convinced at all. "But, Papere, I turned his arm to wood!" she protested.

"So you said," he answered. "A training accident," he dismissed it. "That is why you have had lessons and will continue to have more." He glanced sidelong at her, a glimmer in his eyes. "You need not worry that your mamere will prevail in this, Lealle. She and I disagree, but it is precisely because of accidents such as Gaetan's wooden arm that I must insist you continue your antiphonic education to its fullest extent."

That was very good to hear, but . . . "Maitresse Aubry will be angry and disappointed in me," said Lealle. "And . . . I think she will be right to be."

Papere crossed one ankle over his other knee. "That may well be. *She* has the teaching of you. And you . . . must answer to your conscience. It's as well your conscience be well-developed. But I am not worried by your error." He straightened in his chair. "You owned your mistake. You made good upon it. You befriended a prior enemy, successfully, let me note. And you intend to take steps to ensure you do not repeat your mistake, do you not?"

She nodded. She would tell her teacher and seek her guidance. And she would practice as hard as she needed to.

"Then I call that excellent work," said Papere.

Lealle felt a smile creep onto her lips. If Papere approved of her dealings with Gaetan, then maybe, just maybe, she could find some ease in the aftermath of her error, too. But . . . what would Papere think of . . . everything else?

"Papere . . . I made more mistakes than the one with Gaetan," she confessed. "There's also Ohtavie."

"Yes, Lady de Bellay," he said. "Tell me about her."

Lealle drew in a deep breath. Where to begin? At the beginning?

She told it all, from seeking refuge in the Maison de Bellay through making friends with Ohtavie, and on to Ohtavie's determination to step out of doors.

Lealle wanted to stop there, but she knew she couldn't. It was the risk she'd brought down on Remy that had shown her so suddenly and clearly that she'd been wrong in how willfully she'd pursued helping Ohtavie. Remy might have *died,* because of the way Lealle had gone about offering aid. Gaetan's wooden arm, as bad as it was—and it *was* bad—was nothing compared to what might have happened to Remy, had not chance intervened.

She gulped and told the rest.

Papere's eyes narrowed as Lealle narrated the worst of it, but he didn't say anything until she'd finished. Then he took her hand, very gently.

"Lealle, my dearest, your sense of responsibility is admirable, but you must remember to allow others their share in it," he said.

Lealle's brows knit. "What do you mean?" she asked.

"First off, chance had nothing to do with Remy's preservation. Your friend, Lady de Bellay—in spite of her understandable alarm and surprise—took action to preserve him. Secondly, your little brother has a whole list of his own wrongs that contributed to his exposure to such peril."

Papere started ticking them off on his fingers. "One, he was out on Claireau's streets in direct defiance of my rules for this time of hazard. Two, he was spying on *you* and intruding upon your business without either your knowledge or your permission. And, three, he was trespassing upon Lady de Bellay's property, partially to help Gaetan, but partially out of sheer nosiness, if I know my son."

"But, but I was wrong, too," protested Lealle.

Papere smiled easily. "So tell me about your wrongs. But don't inflate them. Tell me with accuracy and justice," he said.

His composure steadied her. She *would* tell him her wrongs, as specifically and correctly as she could do it.

"I, too, trespassed when I first entered Ohtavie's home, but she instructed me to disregard it when I apologized for trespassing, and I . . ." Lealle sighed—a very small sigh ". . . think her instruction was right."

Papere nodded. "Good," he said. "I agree."

Lealle continued. "When she bade me leave her, right there at the very beginning, to leave her and forget that I ever saw her, I did not."

"And what do you now think of your decision?" Papere asked.

"I think it was wrong of me to take away her freedom for herself, but I also think it was right of me to insist on helping someone who was injured and, and . . . who might be disoriented because of her injury and not thinking clearly."

"Would you do it the same, if you had it to do over again?" Papere queried.

Lealle's forefinger tapped her middle finger. "I think . . . that if I'd known everything—well, everything not including Gaetan's situation—I would have gone to the retreat center for help right away."

"Because?" Papere's brows were raised.

"Because it really was more than I could handle, and because I trust the antiphoners at the center. I know they would both mean well and *do* well. They are going to help Ohtavie now, and they would have helped her sooner, if they'd known to."

"But since there was no way you could have known everything, and you won't know everything the next time—whatever next time brings—how would you decide?" asked Papere.

"I think I'd still ask for help, because I have good people to ask. You and Maitresse Aubry. Even Mamere." She felt herself blushing and ventured a peek at Papere's face to see if he disapproved of that 'even,' but he was smiling, and she added, "Sometimes," because Mamere was great in some situations, but awful in others. That was just the way Mamere was.

"If I am ever in a situation where I don't have good people there, I might choose differently," she ventured.

"What of Lady de Bellay's option to choose for herself?" Papere probed.

Lealle nodded. *That* was important. She *knew* that was important, and would continue to be important in . . . in everything.

"Because she was injured and might even have hit her head, I think I was right to decide for her. At first. But later, when she still insisted that I go . . . that was more complicated."

Papere tilted his head to one side, listening. The lamp light shone warmly upon him. It was solely lamp light now. The windows, their drapes still open, showed no vestiges of evening sun. The sky looked dark through the glass.

"Because Ohtavie is a troll, and because her troll-disease will continue to get worse, if she is untreated, she puts others at risk by continuing as she was," said Lealle slowly, thinking as she spoke. "The law requires trolls to accept treatment for that reason, and"—the memory of orange sparks wreathing Ohtavie's arms and Remy standing in the way of them flashed from Lealle's memory—"I think the law is right in this. But if Ohtavie had suffered from some other complaint, something that would not endanger others . . ." Lealle paused. This was hard to think about, and hard to decide about.

She drew in a deep breath.

"If Ohtavie had been thinking clearly, and she'd not been a danger to others, then I think she deserved to decide for herself," Lealle concluded.

"Bravo!" said her papere, clapping softly. "That one is hard. Very hard. Every time."

Lealle felt a blush overtake her cheeks. Papere's praise felt very,

very good, but when he opened his mouth to say more, she lifted her hand to stop him.

"There's more," she said.

He nodded and settled back in his chair.

"Ohtavie also asked me to keep her presence a secret, from everyone, and I agreed to do so. And I now know I was wrong to agree to that."

Papere's brows lifted again. "Ah?" he said.

"If Ohtavie had been threatening me, or if I thought she might hurt me if I refused, then it might have been right to simply say nothing, one way or the other, and depart. And *then* break her secrecy," explained Lealle. "But I never did feel scared of her. I wasn't in danger from her. So I should have refused to keep her secret and told her to her face."

"Ah!" Papere breathed, repeating himself, but with his tone utterly different.

"Because," Lealle continued, "I'm only fifteen, and, and . . ." she blushed again, but from embarrassment, not happiness ". . . I trust my parents and I want to deserve their trust also."

Papere stifled a smile.

Lealle ignored it, and carried on with what she wanted to say. "And even if I were older, even if I were a grown-up, if I were in a situation that I knew I might need to involve others in, I would want to decide for *my*self!" she finished. "It wasn't right for Ohtavie to decide that for me."

Papere's smile escaped his efforts to contain it. "Well done, again!" he pronounced.

A brief silence fell.

Papere broke it first.

"So," he said, "you were not as careful of Ohtavie's freedom to decide for herself as you would have liked, and you acquiesced to her request for secrecy when you should not have. Is that all?"

Lealle swallowed. Those two elements were the heart of the matter, yes. But they'd led to three other wrongs. She sat up very straight and looked Papere directly in the eye.

"I disobeyed you by sneaking visits to Ohtavie, because I went unaccompanied through the streets of Claireau," she stated firmly. "And I now know you were right to insist on my protection. There *was* danger."

Papere nodded, very slightly, acknowledging her.

"I lied by omission to you about what I was doing, because I wanted to keep helping Ohtavie, and I couldn't do that unless I either broke her secrecy or else lied."

Lealle swallowed again. It felt rather horrible to be stating her dishonesty so baldly, but there was no help for that. She *had* lied, and she wanted to be absolutely honest now.

Papere nodded again.

"And I encouraged Remy, by my poor example, to do the same: to disobey and lie by omission."

And that really was everything. What would Papere say about it all?

He was smiling again, very kindly.

"You're a clear thinker, sweetheart," he said.

"Papere! Why are you praising me? You, you should be admonishing me! Punishing me, even!" she exclaimed.

His smile broadened. "But a parent punishes—or admonishes—so as to shape his child's thinking and behavior," he said. "And I believe that this discussion will serve to do that admirably. So why should I admonish or punish, when those choices would only impede the result I desire?"

She wanted to growl at his reasonable tone—this was so typical of Papere—but found herself laughing instead.

Papere laughed with her.

∾

As Lealle's laughter ran down, she relaxed back into the leather armchair, feeling really good and clear for the first time since she'd discovered Ohtavie hiding out in the deserted mansion. It was almost like Papere had taken a broom to her inner self—her soul, she supposed—and swept out the dirt and dust that had accumulated there.

There had been admonishment, just as she'd expected. But it hadn't been administered by Papere. She herself had devised and delivered the admonishing. And it had been uncomfortable, very. And yet, it had also felt . . . good. This is what grown-ups do, she realized. They assess their decisions and actions and then apply correction to themselves, as necessary. Huh. So that was what being grown up felt like on the inside. She rather suspected that what her outside looked like—in Great Aunt Caroline's white dress—wasn't nearly as important as what went on inside.

Although it was easier, probably, if your insides and outsides matched. Because, right now, she still looked a lot like a little kid, and the people she encountered would have no way of knowing that she could do adult thinking . . . sometimes, anyway. She suspected it might take more practice before she did it most of the time.

She looked up from her cogitations to see Papere watching her, a small proud smile on his lips.

She smiled back at him. "How do you do that?" she asked.

"Do what?" he replied.

"Straighten out my thoughts like you did," she answered.

"You did the straightening," he said. "I merely asked questions."

"Well . . . they were good questions," she said, leaning forward. "Is it because you're a justice?"

"That might be a contributing factor. Although, I suspect my forté for questions might be why I'm a justice, rather than the reverse."

She could see that.

"Are you tired, Lealle? You've had a long day," he stated.

"I feel . . . ready for anything, right this moment now," she said. "Like I could tackle anything. I had a nap when we got home," she added.

"Good," said Papere, "because I'd like to take some thought for your future."

Lealle settled back again in her chair, but her papere got up and went to the nearest window to draw its crimson drapes across the glass panes.

"I really should have done this sooner, when dusk arrived," he said over his shoulder.

Lealle thought about hopping up to help him with the other windows, but the embrasures were very tall and Lealle was still short, even if she had grown inside. So she merely watched him, wondering what else he would discuss with her. Whatever it was, he would build her up, never tear her down. She was sure of that.

The chancery, although large and occupying the entire base of a tower, seemed a bright nest with the drapes drawn, a sanctuary of light and comfort. But it probably wasn't the warm carpet and leather-cushioned armchairs that produced that effect nearly so much as it was Papere.

"Back in the days of the old principality," said Papere, as he returned to his chair, "before the civil war, Pavelle's prince maintained a special group of . . . not advisors, really, but troubleshooters. They were called the Prince's Djinn, and he sent them out both to resolve known trouble and to seek unknown trouble, with an eye to resolving it before it grew big enough to notice."

"Were they"—they wouldn't have been called antiphoners back then—"enigmologists?" asked Lealle, her brow wrinkling in puzzlement.

"Some of them were, but it wasn't a requirement of the office," he explained. "You're wondering about the term 'djinn,' aren't you?"

Lealle nodded. The djinn featured in old fables were magical beings with powers far greater than those of antiphoners. Or enigmologists.

"The history of Pavelle goes back a full millennium," continued Papere, "and the origins of the Djinn are nearly that old. They were the

Cuniculariorum Princeps—the Prince's Engineers—when the old Ennesh tongue was common, but became L'Ingénieurs du Prince when Florish swept Ennesh away on the tides of the trade ships. Time wore it down to Génie du Prince, and you can see where it went from there." One corner of Papere's mouth turned up.

"Génie du Prince, Gêne du Prince, Djinn du Prince," she murmured, stifling a giggle at the middle version. *'Malaise of the Prince'* was its translation. Some of those old troubleshooters probably *were* a discomfort to have around. Especially if you were the trouble in hand.

"The Djinn were all killed in the civil war." Papere's lips tightened. "And when the dust had settled after the Empire's annexation, their office was not reinstituted, understandably given the changed political structure. But I've had some ideas about reconstituting the old Djinn under the wings of the Court of Audire. I think that could work very well, and . . ." the strain in his face lightened ". . . the Pivot Office agrees with me."

Lealle wasn't sure where Papere was going with all this, but his mention of the Pivot impressed her. The Pivot was the seat of governance for the entirety of the Giralliyan Empire, of which Pavelle was one small canton. The Emperador himself ruled from the Pivot. And if the Emperador—or at least his staff—approved of Papere's ideas . . . well, then those ideas stood a good chance of being acted on.

"Lélé," said Papere, reverting to her baby name, and then pausing. "I've been pondering what direction for you might be most fruitful, most satisfying for you, where your gifts could be well used, and where you would feel satisfied."

Lealle could feel both her eyebrows rising at this. It was almost intimidating to envision Papere giving her such concerted thought. She felt rather . . . exposed.

"Of course, it is each individual's responsibility to figure this out for him or herself, but a parent likes to help where he can." The corner of Papere's mouth twitched up. "And I think being one of these new Djinn—a Djinni of Justice—might suit you very well."

Lealle had only thought her eyes were wide a moment ago. Now she wondered if they might drop right out of her head. Saints!

"I—I don't know what to say," she stammered.

"Naturally not," said Papere. "This is something to think over, to ask questions of both me and yourself, and to let yourself grow up some more. But . . ." Papere paused again ". . . I've sensed you've been thinking about your future yourself, and maybe been a little frustrated in discerning what you want for yourself."

Yes, that was true. She couldn't see herself adopting Mamere's life for herself, but neither had she felt like Papere's suggestions that she consider being an advocate or judge were right. And she hadn't been able to hit on anything else either. It had been, as Papere said, frustrating. But Papere's new suggestion rather took her breath away.

"Your activities of the past few days fit the duties of a Djinni to a tee, you know," said Papere, his smile a bit sly. "You found trouble in the making, trouble no one else knew existed, and by your actions ensured that it was resolved."

Lealle sat back in her chair again, thinking. "Because if Ohtavie had continued as she was for too much longer, her troll-disease would have overtaken her, wouldn't it," she mused.

Papere nodded. "And trolls far gone in their disease do vast damage in the convulsions of their end," he agreed. "You prevented that," he said. "And you prevented the explosion of the arsenal that would have set off rioting this very evening."

"No, I didn't," she protested. "You did that."

"My part was critical, of course," said Papere. "But think about it, Lealle. I would never have learned of the danger to the arsenal in time, had it not been for you. *You* earned Gaetan's trust, and he trusted you enough that he told you in time. And *you* then told me. You were the pivotal element in all this." Papere smiled. "I did say 'well done,' did I not ?"

Lealle felt a smile of her own growing to match his. "You did, Papere," she assured him.

He let a silence fall and lengthen.

Lealle thought about what he had said. She had stumbled upon Ohtavie and Gaetan just like an old Djinni might have. Helping both of them had felt . . . really satisfying. She would like to do more things like that, she realized. Huh. Maybe Papere's new Djinn really would be the right place for her. She wasn't feeling any of the resistance she'd felt toward all the previous occupations she'd imagined for herself. This felt . . . exciting!

She knit her brows as a following question occurred to her.

"Papere, how do you know when it's right to help someone? Ohtavie didn't want my help, but I think I was right to help her. And . . . Gaetan didn't want my help at first either. I was right to help them, but it won't always be right to help."

She nibbled at her lower lip. "You're going to help Gaetan now. How did you know that you should?"

He sat forward, almost as though he'd been waiting for her to make this specific inquiry.

"I have two rules for myself," he said. "One, has life thrown this individual or individuals in my way? And, two, is this person available to my help? If the answer to both those questions is 'yes,' then I help."

Lealle frowned. "How do you know whether life threw them in your way?" she asked.

"If I am pursuing my clear responsibilities, and there they are, then life has granted me an opportunity."

"But—but—" Lealle still felt confused.

"Whereas," her papere continued, "if I am avoiding something hard in my own life, and I go poking my nose into other people's business to avoid it, then most of what and who I encounter has *not* been given me as mine."

"Huh." Lealle sat up straight. "So, so . . . if I'd been worried because . . . because a project for school wasn't going well, because the two other girls were each insisting that the other one had to be assigned to a different group, and they weren't either of them doing any work at all"—that had actually happened this past year—"and if I then went off in a huff and . . . and started bugging Remy to do *his* homework, instead of getting Alice and Babette to talk to each other"—oops, she hadn't meant to name names—"that would be how *not* to help someone," she concluded. "Am I right?"

Papere was actually grinning. "Precisely right," he concurred.

"Whereas, when I encountered Gaetan and Ohtavie"—her brow smoothed out—"when I encountered Gaetan and Ohtavie," she repeated, "I was just walking home as usual from my antiphony lesson."

"There you have it," said Papere.

"It's not usually that easy, is it?" she said.

"Was it easy this time?" Papere asked.

"Noo . . ." she admitted.

"Things are always clearer in hindsight," said Papere.

"Mamere doesn't follow your rules," Lealle observed.

"No, she doesn't," Papere agreed.

"Is she wrong not to?" That felt like a daring question. Would he answer it?

"Your mamere's way would not work for me, but it seems to work for her. She *is* happy, you know."

Yes, that was true. Mamere was happy in a fussy sort of way, but she *was* happy, just as Papere said. And Lealle suspected that after today, she herself would be better at deflecting Mamere's fussiness from her own concerns.

Lealle frowned again. "Won't helping Gaetan take a lot of your time? How will you fit him in? You can't help everyone, can you?" Papere was not a Djinn. He had plenty of his own responsibilities already. Really, Papere never seemed to stop working. Although he never shirked family engagements either. But he didn't seem to have much time to himself, time when he just did nothing. Maybe he liked it that way?

"Gaetan is worth helping." Papere's mouth firmed. "Really the boy is extraordinary. Most kids in his position would be saying, 'My da, right or wrong.' Gaetan saw the larger perspective. And acted on it." Papere straightened. "And, yes, it will take time. But I've always found it possible to make the time for the really important things. And Gaetan is important."

Lealle nodded. She agreed with that, somehow. Maybe Gaetan would become one of Papere's Djinn, too. And maybe he would go on to solve a trouble so huge that everyone would regret it if he did not. Maybe she would, too.

The future suddenly seemed full of marvelous possibilities.

The Seventh Day

LUNDY—LUNA'S DAY

Last Secrets

Epilogue

OHTAVIE SAT on a comfortable bench in the colonnade surrounding the retreat house garden and pondered all that had happened in the past few days: the advent of Lealle, breaking out of her old routines, reading Grandmere's letters, participating in foiling a dissident plot, and finally leaving her home.

So much had changed. Everything had changed.

It was late morning, and the sun shone clear of the roof line of the townhouse next door, its bright warmth lapping her limbs and torso, while the colonnade itself yet shaded her face. This spot, out of doors, but partially sheltered was perfect. She could enjoy the free air; the buzz of bees in the vivid blooms scattered amongst the gray-greens, yellow-greens, and blue-greens of the healing plants filling the courtyard; the intricate knot patterns into which the edging foliage was trained; and the heady mix of herbal and floral scents. She could enjoy all that—was enjoying all that—without having to withstand the hugeness of the open sky.

She didn't know when she would grow accustomed to just how large the outdoor world was. It might take a while.

She'd received her first antiphonic treatment for troll-disease this very morning. It had not been in the least bit painful, just as she had been told. But it had felt peculiar. Lying on a padded examining table, she'd not been allowed to watch with either her eyes or the inner sight of antiphony.

And now, in the aftermath, she had a funny stretched feeling in her body.

The healers had warned her that while the treatment process itself did not hurt, the days in between each treatment would be uncomfortable. She would experience muscle aches and clumsiness.

"It is much like when a teenage boy grows eight inches in a year. His limbs ache with it, sometimes he feels short of breath, because his diaphragm must move his enlarged ribcage, and he never seems to know where his hands and feet are," they'd explained.

The antiphonic foundation of Ohtavie's body would be lengthened as her radices were moved toward their proper locations, the root radix lowest of all, her crown radix highest. Her flesh and her bones would labor for a time, growing to match the new and healthier energetic pattern established by the change.

Apparently the earliest treatments, devised more than seven years ago by Lord Gabris in Bazinthiad, had moved the radices quickly, over a matter of a few weeks, and that had been very uncomfortable indeed for the troll patients.

Ohtavie wondered about that word 'uncomfortable.' She suspected it might really have meant 'agonizingly painful.'

But these days, the treatments were spaced over the course of several months. Ohtavie would be living in the retreat house for the first six weeks, so that the healers could keep an eye on her for any complications and address them without delay. Ohtavie was glad of that.

The healers were understandably concerned about Ohtavie's physical health. Well, Ohtavie was concerned about it, too. She intended to follow all of their instructions—there would be special exercises for her later—to the letter. Troll-disease had claimed her for too long. She wanted to be utterly free of its chains. And it was her understanding that she could be, so long as she let the healers do their work fully and then kept up with her schedule of maintenance treatments.

But her troll-disease had eaten more than her body. It had swallowed down all the life she would have led in the absence of disease and warped her way of being in the world.

It was not only her torso and limbs that would need to grow. Her thoughts, her approach to living, her ways of relating to the world and the people in it must change almost more than would her body. She would be as stretched in mind as anything else. And the retreat house . . . would be a better place for all the mental expansion than would be her old home with all its pull toward old habits.

What a waste her treatment would be, if she used it only to bunker down in solitude.

She refused to let that happen, and her chances of winning out to the larger freedom she desired for herself were much better here, exactly here, where she would also have support from the healers in the mental changes she must make. Evidently there had been other sequestered trolls who needed such support. The healers had grown skilled at treating agoraphobia—as they called it—alongside troll-disease.

Feeling strangely happy and hopeful, she drew in a large breath of the floral and herbal aromas permeating the courtyard garden. It was glorious here, absolutely glorious, and life was a miracle of wonder.

A flicker of motion at the far corner of the colonnade caught her eye, and then Lealle scampered through the open archway leading from the interior there.

The girl wore more fitted raiment than the swinging frocks Ohtavie had seen her in before: no fichu, but an elegant peach-colored jacket with short, fitted sleeves; matching gown beneath, with a narrower skirt; and neat kid half-boots, also peach, but fastened with decorative ribbons rather than schoolgirl laces. Her hair was more severely confined as well, but her face held the same young eagerness that Ohtavie had come to love. And her pace—that scamper—possessed nothing of a grown lady's dignity. Thank the saints!

✧

Ohtavie smiled in greeting as Lealle called out, her voice excited and happy.

"I have so much to tell you! I talked with Papere last night, and Mamere over breakfast, and they've *both* forgiven me, and they even both *agree* about what I should do next, and I'm *so* lucky!"

She arrived at the bench at the end of her rush of words and plumped down next to Ohtavie, seizing the nearest of Ohtavie's hands.

"How are you?" Lealle demanded. "Did it go well? Are you pleased? Are they taking good care of you here? Tell me everything!"

Ohtavie couldn't help chuckling softly at all this unrestrained enthusiasm.

"I'm very well," she answered, "and nearly as excited about the changes to my life as you sound about the changes in yours. I hope you'll do some telling of your own."

"Oh, I will," Lealle promised. "But, Ohtavie, you know how you asked me to fetch a few more things from the Maison de Bellay this morning?"

Ohtavie nodded. She'd thrown a fresh blouse and some undergarments into a valise yesterday afternoon to bring with her to the retreat house, but she'd been too flustered to pack with any coherency.

"Well," said Lealle, "I did, and I sent the valise up to your room here with one of the footmen. So you'll have more clothes to wear and your own brush and comb, too. But! I brought a few more books from your papere's library, because the books here are all about herbs and medicine and antiphony and stuff like that. No stories! The healers and antiphoners will give you things to do, besides exercises, if you ask them, but *I* think you'll want to read, especially in the early days of your treatment, before they let you leave the retreat house on visits and such."

"How thoughtful of you, sweetheart. Thank you!"

"But!" Lealle brushed Ohtavie's thanks aside. "But! When I was looking at that bottom shelf, I found this!" Lealle's hand dove into a pocket on the inside of her jacket and emerged flourishing a scrap of faded, folded note paper. "I read it, to see what it was, and it looked like an old family letter. I think . . . I think it might be important, so I brought it!" Lealle thrust the scrap toward Ohtavie.

Ohtavie accepted it, but held the paper a moment, making no move to unfold it. She felt a curious reluctance to learn its contents. Her thoughts had been ranging ahead to her future, and she felt an aversion to returning to her past, especially the part of her past that involved Grandmere. She suspected this was one of Grandmere's letters, one that had somehow escaped being bound into a book with all the others.

Lealle, observing her hesitation, must have drawn a wrong impression, because she blushed and hurried into renewed speech. "I'm so sorry for reading private family correspondence. I didn't quite realize what it was right away. And then . . ." the girl hunched slightly "I should have stopped when I did realize, of course. But—"

Ohtavie pressed Lealle's hand.

"Please!" she urged the girl. "No need to apologize. I perfectly understand that you were well caught by then. If this is from my Grandmere, well, her style is a compelling one. I doubt anyone would be able to stop reading in mid-flow."

"Thank you!" Lealle blurted. "But Papere would still say that I was in the wrong, and . . ." she straightened her shoulders ". . . I agree with him."

"In principle, yes," Ohtavie admitted.

"But you should read it!" insisted Lealle.

"Right now?" murmured Ohtavie.

Lealle nodded emphatically.

Ohtavie reached for her pendant—no longer hanging about her neck—and unfolded the letter.

It proved to be two pieces of paper, not one, and neither held Grandmere's handwriting, which Ohtavie had come to know very well indeed.

The first note was written in a delicate, flowing hand.

Callesonne, 5th Falnary 1820

My dearest Joviane,

I am so very glad to have received your letter after all these years. Please know that I never thought ill of you, and I never blamed you. Dear friend, you confided enough in your earlier letters to make clear that the hand life dealt you was a difficult one. I suspect you were overmatched, my dear. And while I missed you, I could not be angry with you. I could only weep for you and pray for you and love you.

Indeed, I believe I have some apologizing of my own to do. It is true that traveling to come to you would have posed considerable difficulty when the children were babies. But dear Joviane, by the time your letters to me ceased altogether, even my youngest was away at university. How I wish that I'd made my own dear Francis bring me to Claireau, with your invitation or without it. I wanted to respect your autonomy, but now I wish I'd respected my love and friendship for you instead.

I am old and confined to bed these days—although happy and well-attended upon by my loved ones—but unable to travel. Otherwise, I would come to you even now. Because I cannot, please banish all your worries and regrets for the fate of our friendship. I declare that you are still my dear friend, and that I will love you and pray for you through all the rest of my days and then on into heaven, when I reach it.

With all good thoughts from,

your loving, Berdine

Ohtavie let her hands sink down into her lap.

She wanted to weep once more for her poor Grandmere, and yet she also didn't. Something about this letter healed the grief inside her. Perhaps it was just knowing that Grandmere—Jovie—had had such a faithful friend.

Ohtavie swallowed, letting the warmth and light of the retreat house garden fill her awareness again, further soothing her sadness away. She looked over at Lealle, sitting quietly beside her and gazing back at Ohtavie, but unspeaking.

"It was important?" Lealle questioned.

Ohtavie nodded. "Yes," she answered. "I'll tell you all the story sometime," she said, "when you're a little older."

"Isn't it too private for someone who isn't a family member?" Lealle suggested.

"It would be," Ohtavie agreed, "if it weren't also an important part of my own story, a part I'd like you to know some day."

"All right," said Lealle. "Then I'd like that."

Ohtavie reached again for the pendant that no longer adorned her neck. She was not accustomed to its absence. "There's a second letter," she said. "Did you realize it?" she asked.

Lealle shook her head. "I thought it was just a protective wrapping, and, anyways . . . once I'd read Berdine's letter, I remembered what I was about and that I shouldn't be reading these family papers at all." Lealle looked down, and then back up. "I feel embarrassed about that."

Ohtavie patted the girl's hand. "You'll do better next time," she said.

Lealle's face took on an arrested look. "So I will," she agreed. "Do you want to read the other letter?"

Ohtavie smiled. "Yes, I do." Oddly, she didn't feel any of the resistance she'd felt a moment ago.

She bent to the next missive, written in a very irregular and erratic, but bold, hand. Perhaps written by someone very ill?

Claireau, 26th Jubiante 1804

My darling,

You have wept your regret and your sorrow in my presence and refused — in your own wish for my forgiveness—to heed all my pleading for your forgiveness of me. My own, you owe me no apologies. My fault was far greater than any of yours. I allowed my passion for the past to overrule my passion for the present, for you, for our beautiful daughter who left us much too soon.

I would beg you afresh for your forgiveness, but this may be the last chance I have to convey anything at all to you and I would not waste it on my own selfishness.

Instead, I will beg you to believe that if you did owe me any apology, which I cannot ascribe to, that I forgive you wholly and unreservedly and in steadfast love. And please believe also that you are entirely beautiful, inside and out, in your perfections and in your imperfections.

Your ever loving,

Hugh

Ohtavie found herself smiling as she lifted her gaze from the wilted paper and blotched, fading ink. She could guess that those blotches stemmed from Grandmere's tears, but Ohtavie herself no longer felt like crying. Grandmere's life had been unhappy, but there had been healing in it, too. Ohtavie could imagine the tenderness that must have followed Grandpere's acknowledgement of his wrongs—his neglect of his wife and daughter—and his avowal of his continuing love.

She glanced over at Lealle. "More of the same, really, and equally beautiful: the heartfelt reconciliation between two people with profound hurts from one another." She nodded. "Thanks to you, I have the chance to do better than did my forebears," she said. "And I intend to."

"What will you do?" asked Lealle.

Ohtavie gave a soft laugh. "I hardly know. It's all so different. In the short term, I suppose I'll do exactly what the healers tell me to. After that . . . I'll have to work it out."

"Papere would say that you'll build your future day by day," said Lealle.

"And he'd be correct," said Ohtavie. "But you may be sure I will not waste this gift of health and time that you've given me."

Lealle blushed, her cheeks rosy.

"But what will you do?" queried Ohtavie. "You said something about wonderful plans made with your papere and mamere."

"Oh, yes!" Lealle's flush of embarrassment softened to one of pleasurable enthusiasm. "I can't wait!" She gave a little seated hop, and then poured out a jumble about Pavelle's ancient history and the old prince and djinn. It would have made little sense, except that Ohtavie retained some memory of her old governess' lessons, and she'd actually once written an essay about the Prince's Djinn. She grasped what Bello Meridar might be intending for his daughter.

"You'll be able to say that I was your first attempt and your first success," she told Lealle.

Lealle, who'd been leaning eagerly forward, sat back at this. "Huh," she said. "I guess you're right."

"Your mamere doesn't object?" Ohtavie probed.

Lealle giggled. "Papere brought her around, and he'll probably have to persuade her again. But . . . I think that if I worry about *pleasing* Mamere a little less, she'll actually worry about me less, too. And we'll both be more comfortable."

Ohtavie felt the corners of her mouth turn up. "That's . . . very wise. I suspect I could stand to worry less about what others think of me as well."

"Do you worry about what people will think about your troll-disease?" asked Lealle.

"The treatment merely keeps my symptoms at bay, you know" said Ohtavie. "I'll need treatment for the rest of my life. It doesn't re-anchor my radices in their proper locations; it doesn't truly *cure* me."

"I know," said Lealle.

"Which means," Ohtavie continued, "that I'll remain a troll in my essence. I suspect people will always be a little . . . unnerved by that. But . . . I spent decades worrying about how people would respond to my troll-disease, and . . . I don't want to waste any more time and energy upon such a worry going forward. So I shall work to banish that concern. Some people will remain wary of me. Others—like you—will become my friends!"

Lealle grinned. "Good!"

Ohtavie grinned back at her.

Lealle sat forward again and barely restrained herself from pointing. "What happened to the chain you always wore? With the pendant hidden under your blouse?"

So Lealle remembered that, did she? Despite how briefly she'd seen it before? And despite the chaos that had erupted right after?

Ohtavie lifted her chin. "I gave it away," she announced.

Lealle frowned. "What?" she asked, her voice puzzled.

"That pendant was an old *energea*-stone from ancient Navarys," Ohtavie explained. "Or, more accurately, a lodestone. But it was damaged, and dangerous." She nodded. "When I showed it to the antiphoners here, we worked out what should be done with it to preserve others from harm."

Lealle's brows lifted. "It's what made you a troll?" she asked.

"Indeed," Ohtavie answered. "And now it is going to Lord Gabris himself in Bazinthiad, to be studied in his ongoing research into troll-disease, troll-magic, and antiphony."

Lealle's eyes widened. "That sounds important," she said.

"I believe it will be." Ohtavie nodded again.

Lealle turned her gaze back to the garden filling the courtyard before them, sitting quietly for a moment. Thinking, perhaps?

Ohtavie settled back herself to do a little thinking of her own. It was companionable, sitting together like this. She would never have imagined anything like it a sennight ago, before Lealle had intruded so fortuitously upon Ohtavie's long solitude.

Ohtavie had once imagined the cellars of the Maison de Bellay as a labyrinth housing a monstrous beast. She'd been a child then. She'd never imagined *herself* as the monster, although her neighbors—if they'd ever learned of her presence, a troll—surely would have. But perhaps her *home* truly had been a labyrinth, a tangled maze from which she'd had to struggle mightily to escape, from which she never would have escaped on her own.

Except it was not her home, per se, that had formed the maze that had so bewildered and enervated her. It had been her troll-disease and her own response to her troll-disease.

Or . . . maybe there was another way of looking at it.

A maze was a puzzle with many dead ends and false paths obscuring the true way, the way that led out and to freedom. But a labyrinth, while it might look like a maze, and seem just as confusing, possessed no false routes at all. There was only one way through, and it was the right way, the way that led onward to a stillpoint of contemplation at the center, and then out again to the larger life awaiting there.

Ohtavie had surely lingered overly long on the tangled loops of her own path, but now she had emerged, guided by Lealle, and she intended to claim the larger life that could be hers.

Perhaps all of life itself was a labyrinth, with many twists and turns, but always a way forward, if one only dared take the next step.

"I can't wait," Ohtavie murmured.

THE END

Glossary

antiphoner—a mage who manipulates antiphony

antiphonically—having to do with antiphony

antiphony—term used by citizens of the Empire to describe the study and use of magic

armiger—police

audire—to hear

baillie—guard of the court

bazin-berk—an insult meaning: jerk from Bazinthiad, the capital of the Giralliyan Empire

bon-papy—grandpapa

bonne-mémé—grandmama

chanson de geste—an epic poem narrating the marvelous adventures of heroes

chevalier—knight

connard—turdhead

demi-radix—a smaller, less important node of *energea* in a living being

energea—the energy of life and existence; can be manipulated by rare, gifted individuals to create magical effects

energea-stone—a pebble-sized talisman, made of meteoric iron and forged by an engineer of ancient Navarys, used to focus the magical force wielded by a mage

enigmological—having to do with enigmology

enigmologist—a mage who manipulates enigmology

enigmology—term used in Pavelle, before the principality was annexed by the Empire, to describe the study and use of magic

epergne—an elaborate centerpiece intended to hold flowers, fruit, or candles

fichu—a triangular scarf or shawl, worn around the shoulders and neck, sometimes fastened in front with a brooch, sometimes crossed with the ends tucked into the sash

fortin—fort

fricassée—pieces of stewed or fried meat served in a thick white sauce

garde—guard

gêne—indisposition or malaise

génie—genius

haricot (of beans and lettuces)—a salad (of green beans and lettuce sliced or torn into bite-sized morsels)

incantatio—the dangerous magic wielded by trolls

incantor—a troll-mage

l'ingénieurs—the engineers

lodestone—an *energea*-stone transformed into a magical focus that is more powerful and more dangerous

maison—house

maman—mommy

mamere—mama

merde—crap

papere—papa

Parc Monceau—Park of the Mound

pivot-pute—an insult meaning: bitch from the Pivot, the office of the emperador who rules Giralliya

Pont du Ciel—Bridge of Heaven

radices—plural of radix

radix—one of the significant energetic nodes, sources of *energea,* in a
   living being

résolu—resolute

Rue Allongé—Long Street

Rue Chatoyer—Shimmer Street

Rue Étroit—Narrow Street

Rue Longeurs—Street of Lengths

Rue Tulipe—Tulip Street

Rue Verte—Green Street

sennight—a seven-night or a week

Timeline of the North-lands

ANCIENT TIMES

Skies of Navarys

3000 years before *Troll-magic*

THE BRONZE AGE

The Tally Master

~10 years before *Resonant Bronze*

Resonant Bronze

2000 years before *Troll-magic*

THE MIDDLE AGES

Hunting Wild

800 years before *Troll-magic*

BEFORE THE STEAM AGE

Rainbow's Lodestone

~100 years before *Troll-magic*

Star-drake

immediately after *Rainbow's Lodestone*

THE STEAM AGE

Sarvet's Wanderyar

52 years before *Troll-magic*

Crossing the Naiad
concurrent with *Sarvet's Wanderyar*

Livli's Gift
38 years after *Sarvet's Wanderyar*
(14 years before *Troll-magic*)

Troll-magic
the "now" of this timeline

The Troll's Belt
contemporaneous with *Troll-magic*

Perilous Chance
contemporaneous with *Troll-magic*

Winter Glory
3 years after Troll-magic

A Talisman Arcane
7 years after *Troll-magic*

The North-lands

J.M. Ney-Grimm lives with her husband and children in Virginia, just east of the Blue Ridge Mountains. She's learning about permaculture gardening and debunking popular myths about food. The rest of the time she reads Robin McKinley, Diana Wynne Jones, and Lois McMaster Bujold, plays boardgames like Settlers of Catan, rears her twins, and writes stories set in her troll-infested North-lands.

Look for her novels and novellas at your favorite bookstore—online or on Main Street.

J.M. Ney-Grimm maintains a blog featuring flash fiction from her North-lands and other tidbits unearthed by her ever-active curiosity.

Visit her at http://jmney-grimm.com.

Made in the USA
Middletown, DE
18 April 2019